PRAIRIE DOG
BLUES

PRAIRIE DOG BLUES

A Novel

MARK CONKLING

SUNSTONE
PRESS

SANTA FE

Sunstone books may be purchased for educational, business, or sales promotional use. For information please write: Special Markets Department, Sunstone Press, P.O. Box 2321, Santa Fe, New Mexico 87504-2321.

Book and Cover design ❦ Vicki Ahl
Body typeface ❦ Constantia
Printed on acid free paper

Library of Congress Cataloging-in-Publication Data

Conkling, Mark, 1941-
  Prairie dog blues : a novel / by Mark Conkling.
     p. cm.
  ISBN 978-0-86534-801-1 (softcover : alk. paper)
  1. Prairie dogs--Fiction. 2. Domestic fiction. I. Title.
PS3603.O535P73 2011
813'.6--dc22

                        2011000184

Published in

WWW.SUNSTONEPRESS.COM
SUNSTONE PRESS / POST OFFICE BOX 2321 / SANTA FE, NM 87504-2321 /USA
(505) 988-4418 / ORDERS ONLY (800) 243-5644 / FAX (505) 988-1025

Acknowledgements

I want to thank my friends, Patricia, Bert, Pete, Randy, Rochelle, and Roland who read early versions of my manuscript and offered comments. I am especially grateful to Kirt Hickman for his critique, and to Brooke Foster, editor with Iowa Wordwrights.

Dedication

I dedicate *Prairie Dog Blues* to Dr. Kim Hamel, my best critic and favorite daughter.

One does not meet oneself until one catches the reflection from an eye other than human.
—Loren Eiseley

Some stories are true that never happened.
—Elie Wiesel

1

Most people thought the Corleys would give up and scatter to the four winds after what happened. It came at them suddenly on the morning of January 18, 2002, in Albuquerque, New Mexico: the land of enchantment. Today they expected a cool 3 million dollars. The title officer and the Corleys' lawyer sat at the head of the gleaming mahogany table, and the buyer sat on the side with his attorney. Above them, warm air whispered from the heating vent, somehow ominous.

"You kids sit over there," Mom said as she settled in next to Pop. She put her hand on his leg, covering the denim knee patch. Their grown children arranged themselves in their birth order: Jeff, Ida, then Junior. Jeff sported a new gold chain. Ida smelled slightly sweaty, like early-morning sex, and Junior reeked of alcohol. Pop twisted his neck and pulled at his wrinkled collar, frowning. Mom's thin face creased with a bright smile, her eyes sparkling.

Just one month ago, the children had lined up in the same order at the dining table for Mom's Christmas dinner, one of the four annual family dinners they could not miss. Junior had jabbed his finger at Ida and called her a slut. Mom had raised both hands to stop Pop from coming over the table at Junior. "It's the liquor talking," she said. "Just ignore him."

Jeff had quickly changed the subject, and Junior had muttered an apology and had left the house. She hadn't seen him until today.

Their lawyer, Robert Epstein, shuffled papers, walked over to Mom, and slid the deed in front of her.

"It's ready for your and Roy's signatures," he said. "I've written the legal description exactly as you instructed. Pop squinted at him. You're selling

15.12 acres and keeping 4.18 acres, the house, barn, machine sheds, and all related improvements."

Mom put on her reading glasses and beamed. Her smile was infectious, her face impish and sunny. She read the document carefully, as though it were an old biblical parchment. Fifteen acres in Albuquerque is valuable, but in the northeast heights near the Sandia Mountains, it's like gold. Pop's eyes grew wide as he looked at "Three million dollars ($3,000,000)" printed on the closing statement. It took Mom a moment to translate "Roy John and Janice Pauline Corley, husband and wife." She had been known as "Mom" ever since the evening 36 years ago, when she said to Roy, "Well, Pop, it's time we went to the hospital to have this baby."

Roy jumped up. "Okay, Mom, let's go." Jeff was born later that night.

Mom wanted her family to get along, like a real family, and she wanted each one to be happy. She would do anything to make that happen. She worried about the fact that all three of her children were single. Jeff pursued his dental practice, worked all the time, and was normally broke. She suspected Jeff spent time at the casino, although she didn't want to anger him by asking. Thirty-four-year-old Ida was an intensive care nurse, and seemed unable to settle down with just one man. Thirty-two-year-old Roy, Jr.—whom the family just called "Junior"—loved mechanics and carpentry, but lived with some sort of darkness that was a mystery to Mom. Sometimes she wondered where she had failed as a mother. Her worrying often made her stomach ache; for her, the pain in her abdomen was inseparable from the pain she felt for her still-immature children. Mom and Pop had talked about this sale over the past four months, and Mom had convinced Pop to give each of the children $500,000 now instead of making them wait for their inheritance. If life could be easier for them, Mom thought, maybe they could find a way to be a real family. Maybe some of the damage could be undone. Maybe, for heaven's sake, they could grow up.

The title officer said, "I appreciate you all being willing to be here together for the closing. Normally, we would have the buyer and sellers come in separately, but this is a large sale, and all parties can watch the transaction and be clear about details."

"Mr. Whitman," she said to the buyer, "I need your check for one-million fourteen thousand. That covers your down payment. Your bank will wire the balance."

Henry Whitman raised his eyebrows, and his attorney nodded his head, saying, "Everything is in order. Go ahead and write the check. The bank has agreed to honor the funds today."

The door opened.

"Hello everyone, I'm David Holden, attorney for Land America Title Company. I'm sorry to interrupt, but we have a problem."

Mom glanced at Pop. Three attorneys in the same room spelled trouble and was certainly a waste of money.

"I know this is a surprise," Holden said, "but let me explain. Today our inspector went to the property to check the survey flags and the survey inspection report, and he said there are hundreds of prairie dogs on the fifteen acres. He said there are prairie dog holes everywhere."

"So what?" asked Pop. "Those prairie dogs have been there for years. My dad used to poison them. They're a menace. What's the big deal?" The bright fluorescent lights made deep shadows on Pop's wizened face. He had become expressionless from years of setting his jaw and focusing while operating heavy equipment for the family's business, We Move Dirt, Inc. His eyes were clear blue under furrowed bushy eyebrows, and his permanent frown gave the impression that he was easily angered. Everything about Pop seemed weathered and humorless.

"Here's the problem," Holden continued. "The City Council is on their third reading of a new Prairie Dog Ordinance that restricts development and creates a number of requirements for property owners. The ordinance is due to become law next month. That is a material fact that affects the sale. I've checked with our underwriters, and Land America will not insure the title against endangered species or city animal ordinances."

"Would the ordinance stop development?" Whitman asked.

"It could," Holden replied. "I talked with the attorney at your bank, and he said they can't fund the loan unless the title insurance covered the endangered species and city ordinance risk. Our company can't take the chance. I'm sorry to be the messenger. I know this is bad news."

"You mean we can't sell our own property?" Mom put her hands on the table, touching the papers, and glanced at her three children. They wouldn't be together again until Easter dinner.

"You can sell your property just like it is. However, the buyer runs the risk of being unable to develop it until they solve the prairie dog issue.

Technically, an environmental issue clouds your property title. I'm sorry."

Whitman's attorney handed him a note. He read it quickly.

"I'm sorry, but I don't have the resources to go ahead without the loan," Whitman said. "My development money is from partners, and I can't in good conscience take the risk. I mean, if I can't develop the property, my partners could lose millions."

Pop slammed his gnarled fist on the papers and stood up. "We've been waiting four months for the money, and now this."

Junior wiped his mouth with his hand. "Well, shit, we should have known. Nothing goes right in this family."

Ida crossed her arms and began to tremble. Jeff stared at the wall and his eyes welled up with tears. Jeff had a fine-featured face, well scrubbed and with blond peach fuzz standing in for whiskers. For a moment, his perfect smile faded. The florescent lights hummed. Mom felt the room turn cold.

Whitman stood up. "Believe me, I know how you must feel. We may have to wait for a while, but I still want the property—it's prime for development. I won't give up." He reached over the table and gave Pop his card. "Keep this, and don't worry. We'll stay in touch and get this done."

"What do we have to do?" asked Pop. "We're talking about three million dollars here."

Jeff spoke up. "There might be a way around this. If we can get the city's zoning office to go along with Whitman's plans, the bank should be okay with this, right?"

"That's a reach, and it will take a while," Whitman said. He turned to his attorney. "Francisco, maybe you and Mr. Epstein can check things out with the city manager and see what this ordinance really means. Maybe we can comply with the requirements."

"Don't count on it," Holden said. "The ordinance is modeled after the Santa Fe ordinance. No one can develop a prairie-dog habitat. Many owners just give up and donate their land to a land preservation trust in exchange for the tax deductions."

Robert Epstein looked at Jeff and then at Pop.

Jeff nodded his head. "Robert, please see what you can find out. We're prepared to pay."

"Someone tell me what this all means," Mom said.

"It means we don't get the money and you have to kill all those prairie dogs," Junior replied coldly. "You should have killed those varmints years ago. Way to go, Pop." Junior's eyelids appeared heavy. He had a drawn, hollowed-cheeked face that was often haggard and impassive. His dark brown eyes darted around, rarely making contact with anyone else's. He cursed under his breath and clenched his teeth.

Mom folded her hands and composed herself.

As they left the room, Mom found herself dwelling on the private thoughts she knew haunted each of them. Pop's thirty-two-foot Winnebago disappeared, along with his bass boat, and her remodeled kitchen and new dining room table evaporated into the clouds. Jeff's office addition, lab, and two new dental chairs faded away, as did his new Mercedes, and his bills continued to pile up. Ida's condominium on Juan Tabo Boulevard, along with all new furniture that would fill it, dropped out of sight as her dingy one-bedroom apartment in Mountain Run reappeared. Her Master's degree in nursing faded away. Junior's new Dodge diesel pickup reclaimed its place in the dealer's showroom, and his new Harley Sportster had the "sold" sign removed. Pop would be deeply embarrassed because he had promised to sell his heavy equipment to friends around Albuquerque. Some of Pop's old competitors had spoken for his loaders, scrapers, backhoes, dozers, and trucks. He had announced that he was going to hang up the earthmoving and excavation business. We Move Dirt, Inc. had been in the family for 50 years, and Pop had installed several hundred miles of water line, sanitary sewer, and storm drainage all over Northern New Mexico. He would have to call all of them, back out of his promises, begin overhauling the hydraulic pump on the loader, and find a used transmission for the motor grader. He just wanted to retire and travel, but today, without warning, fate hurled him back into yesterday's life. Mom knew Jeff would bury himself in work at his dentist office, Ida would take on extra shifts in the intensive care unit at University Hospital with all her doctors, and Junior would take the day off from the framing company and get drunk.

Junior climbed into his truck. "Just like the rest of our life," Junior said. "Whenever this family does anything, it all falls apart. We really suck." He glowered at her.

"I'm sure it will work out, " Jeff said. "It will just take some time and effort."

Ida waved at Mom showing the hint of a smile. Ida had a delicately sculptured pink doll face and often sported a come-hither smile, like what you'd see on a lingerie model ten years past her prime. Mom hated that smile. She even preferred Ida's condescending smirk to it. As if she could read her mother's thoughts, Ida made her face unreadable as she chewed her lip and drove away.

Mom and Pop got into the Suburban.

"Prairie dogs," Pop said. "I could have poisoned them years ago. Junior was right."

"It's not your fault," Mom reassured him. "There's no way you could've known. Let's go home and see what tomorrow brings. God will provide."

"I'm going to kill them. Kill them all. I'll run the dozer over the whole field if I have to."

Mom took a breath, folded her hands, and closed her eyes. "Lord help us," she whispered.

She sometimes thought of herself as a spiritual magnet that drew the family together. As they had done at the title company, they gathered like obedient little iron filings on a piece of paper, with Mom hovering underneath. On some occasions, like Thanksgiving, her magnetism was bright and light. She had hoped things would be different, somehow. Her children often criticized her for arguing with Pop about how to improve their lives. Mom's strong spirit, holiday meals, birthday cards, phone calls, and the promise of substantial wealth lured her kids into minimal contact. Mom worried that if anything happened to her, the tenuous thread that held these people together would snap. Then, any sense of a family would disappear into a spray of isolated lives, a fear that chilled Mom more deeply than her death.

In her heart, Mom didn't really want to sell the land, because it helped bring balance to her life. Yet the sale was a way to create happiness for her children and peace of mind for Pop. It was worth the sacrifice if her family could heal, even a little. They'd still have the house, the machine shops, the construction yard, Junior's trailer, and a little space to the east that would serve as a buffer against the new neighbors. After taxes, the sale would provide 1 million for Mom and Pop's retirement. Pop was sixty-three, so the earnings on the money, his coming social security and Medicare, and a home with no mortgage would create a comfortable life.

Before dawn each morning, she curled up in an easy chair with her coffee. She faced the Sandia Mountains and watched the light flicker across the gray rocky crevices and dark-green cedars. Whenever she opened the window, the cedar smell was pungent, almost refreshing. March, the coming of allergy season, brought wheezing and sneezing, a time when she couldn't smell anything at all.

The sunrise splashed over the mountain in a different place every morning, and the emerging light gave her a focus for her prayers and her emotional balance. Sometimes she wrapped her mind around the soft folds of the mountains, much like God probably does.

This was her home, a safe place, predictable in the midst of change. The county built Bernardino Avenue. The Flood Control authority built a huge pond directly to the east, which held back the water that used to rush down the Domingo Baca Arroyo during rainstorms. The arroyo was dry now, scattered with leftovers from the fall—purple asters, yellow daisies, sunflowers, and brown native grasses, leaving a soft cover over what used to be sharp cuts through the earth.

To the north, the Presbyterians built Sandia Presbyterian church on the old Armando Garcia property. After the city widened and paved Paseo del Norte, it built the Sibrana Northeast Police Substation, another huge flood control pond, and the Griener Soccer Field, which often filled with happy people. To the northwest was Saint Peter's Anglican Catholic church and the Altamont Little League Field. At night, she could hear children playing and parents cheering. Across Eubank Boulevard to the west were several new million-dollar houses and a view that was endless.

The sunsets spread out across the horizon like warm fire in the winter and a cheerful carnival of pastels in the summer. To the southwest, on the corner of San Francisco Road, a new Latter-Day Saints Temple appeared among the throngs of grateful people, and across Eubank, south of the Corleys' property, the Grace church welcomed hundreds of folks during the week. Grace was Mom's church, her spiritual home. No one else in her family attended. Pop went once a year, on Christmas Eve. They both knew why Pop didn't go to church, but they didn't talk about it, because it made Pop have nightmares. Pop became a bear when he didn't have enough sleep. For years, Mom had run the church hospitality programs as a volunteer; her pastor saw her as an anchor for church gatherings.

Mom rested easily here. While she often said that she'd done the best she could raising her children, she believed she'd overlooked something important. During her morning prayers, she often felt a deep quivering behind her stomach, just before the daily pain started. There might be something alive in there, she thought. It haunted her, pulling at her innards like a tight shoelace. Over the years, the discomfort became reassuring, as though it might be a companion provided by God Himself. Although she believed she deserved the pain, she thought perhaps God had given it a friendly face to remind her of His power to lessen suffering. She knew she was a good wife to Pop, even when she did not feel like it. That gave her some satisfaction because Pop was fond of saying that good wives are hard to come by. Besides, Mom believed that being good was not about feeling good.

This place held her like a blanket, surrounded by mountains, churches, police, and children: a combination that she believed was impregnable by the forces of darkness that plagued other people and tugged at the heart of her family. Often Mom imagined a filmy roof, a light silver and white veil of comfort, billowing up in the gentle breezes and tied by tethers like a tent. They were tied to Grace church, to the Sandia Mountains, to the Presbyterian church, to the police substation, to Saint Peter's Anglican Catholic church, to the roof of a million-dollar house, and to the top of the steeple on the Mormon Temple. Embedded in the Grace church wall, the bronze Jesus and his outstretched hand blessed the traffic that whizzed by on Eubank. On top of the Temple steeple, high above it all, Maroni, the Latter-day Saint prophet who spoke to Joseph Smith, stood with his trumpet, like a sentry prepared to warn everyone of a common enemy, or like the herald of a coming truth. Behind him, a huge American flag rippled gently in the breeze. Mom felt loved and protected—yet her family was miserable, and all the blessings of safety seemed somehow wasted.

2

Junior jumped out of the truck, called his dog, Popeye, from under the trailer, and went inside. A sense of calm washed over him as he put a couple Bud Light twelve-packs in the refrigerator and four pints of tequila in the cupboard. Mom had left him a casserole in the freezer. He grabbed it and put it in the microwave. He chugged half a beer, opened a pint, sat down, and slipped off his motorcycle boots. After swallowing two gulps of tequila, he took a deep breath, and shuddered. Over the past year, like a new shadow growing behind him, alcohol had become his best friend; craving had become his steady companion. It took more lately to quiet his restlessness and to get a lift. He couldn't sleep without it. The nightmares haunted him. Although he wouldn't admit it, he no longer drank to feel good. Instead, he drank to feel normal.

Tough day, glad I'm alone. Those people in the title company are too weird. He glanced at his list of chores on a clipboard on the wall, which covered a couple of holes he'd punched in the sheetrock. *Pop's so critical. His harping is endless. If he could just be decent occasionally, I wouldn't need to get drunk. They could have poisoned all those prairie dogs years ago. Why am I stuck here? I really need that money.*

It was time to change the oil in most of the equipment, and the loaders needed new transmission fluid. Junior didn't mind that part of his work. When he was just a toddler, he rode with Pop on the heavy equipment. He could sit for hours, and Pop let him tinker with all the controls. Over the years that he grew up with We Move Dirt, Inc., he learned well, and he could operate all the equipment better than Pop. Junior had long believed that if he were good enough at running the equipment, Pop would admire him. Instead, all he got was Pop's irritation and criticism. Even though he was a more adept operator, he knew down deep he would never be skilled enough to earn Pop's praise.

In exchange for taking care of the equipment, he got free rent in a two-bedroom trailer Pop had traded for a small TD-340 dozer. Pop pulled the trailer home one day with a dump truck, backed it into place, and later installed a septic tank. With water, electricity, and cable TV from the main house, the trailer became livable. This all happened the year Junior turned eighteen and was due to move to his own place, fourteen years ago. Junior worked full time as the lead framer for a construction company on the Westside. His boss always counted on Junior to do the initial layout. Junior could picture the finished framing before the work even began, making the layout an easy activity. He was good at his work but often missed a day here or there, because he felt so tired.

Junior smiled as his gaze fell on a photo of Julie, which he kept on the table by the TV. He had comforted her when her father died, and they had some wonderful nights at Gino's where they drank and played pool until closing. Julie liked to wait for last call, then order beer with a shot, and start a new game of nine-ball. She came home with Junior a few times, and he thought he was in love, although he always felt out of place with her. It was though he was thirteen years old. His mind searched for clues about what to say next, and he didn't know what to do with his hands. When she moved away to California, she told Junior that when you love someone, you don't own her. He was still confused about that. He hung out at Gino's for a while after she left. Soon it became easier to come home and drink alone in front of the TV. He didn't want to risk a DUI. No sense being stupid. One of these days, he thought, I'll get a new truck, drive out to California, find Julie, and take her on a vacation to South America. She'd like that.

Junior put some milk in a bowl for Minerva, opened another beer, and started surfing channels. Popeye jumped up into his lap.

"Hey, little buddy," he said to Popeye. "Hard times today. Pop screwed up again, and Mom's useless." He scratched Popeye behind the ears, and the dog happily licked his face. Popeye smelled as if he had eaten a rat. "Wow, doggy breath. What have you been into?"

"I remember how you smelled when I found you." He kissed Popeye's nose. "You were a mess."

Junior would never forget the smell of dead puppies. One Saturday morning four years ago, he had just finished changing the transmission fluid on the 510 International articulated loader. He put the pump away, checked the level again, and headed down the back road. The sun had just come over the mountain and was melting the light frost on the grass. The shadows backed away quickly to the west, as if they knew the time. He'd wanted to run the loader until the fluid was hot, and then come back and check it again. Junior put brandy in his coffee, drank half a cup, and thought how much he loved taking care of equipment. He smiled and imagined that the loader, which he and Pop knew as "five-ten," appreciated having a transmission full of clean fluid. Five-ten slid though its shifting routine and moved along at fifteen miles per hour into the sunlight.

"What the hell is that?" Junior said. He brought the loader to a stop, jumped down, and went back to a burlap bag someone had thrown into the ditch. He looked in the bag. The acrid smell of decomposition made him gag. He held his breath as he grabbed the bottom and began dumping out the carcasses of a dozen puppies. Maggots covered their closed eyes and slit throats. Junior figured there were two litters, unwanted puppies from a nearby neighbor. His knees nearly gave out beneath him, so he sat down on the bank for a moment and just stared, moist eyed, at the pile. "What a waste."

Then something moved—a puppy turned his head.

"Hey, who are you?" Junior took the puppy in his hand and felt its throat—not cut. The puppy's eyes were barely open, and it was nearly dead. Junior kicked dirt over the bag and the bodies and carefully carried the puppy to the loader and back to his trailer.

"Time for a bath." In the kitchen sink, Junior ran some warm water in a green plastic salad bowl and carefully washed the puppy with dish soap. The pup was dusty white with liver spots and had a tail that seemed too long for its body. He looked like a terrier and a beagle cross, and Junior noticed that he had a lazy left eye. He made some soupy apple cinnamon oatmeal with milk and fed it to the pup with a turkey baster.

Junior wiped his eyes with his sleeve and fetched an old toolbox from the barn. He lined it with a bath towel to make it into a puppy bed. On Sunday, he braved calling Ida about the right kind of formula to feed a sickly animal, and within a week the puppy was lapping by himself and eating some soft dog food.

After two weeks of carrying the puppy to work in the toolbox and feeding him at lunch, one of the other framers asked Junior if the dog had a name. Junior held the puppy up to his face, rubbed noses with him, and said, "Yup, his name is Popeye." From that day forward, Popeye never left Junior's side, except upon command. "Mutts like us belong together," Junior liked to say.

Two months later, Junior was sitting on his porch, whittling a whistle with his scout knife, a trick he had learned as a church scout at Mom's church. Popeye was chewing on a piece of rawhide. He stopped, cocked his head, and looked toward the barn.

"What do you see?" Junior asked. Suddenly, a calico cat walked right up to them, as if she were in charge, and rubbed on Junior's leg. "Easy does it," Junior told Popeye. The puppy whined, but stayed put. "Stay," he said, and slowly went into the house. He poured some milk in a bowl and then set it down on the step.

The calico cat looked at him, meowed, and lapped at the milk until it was gone. Then she went to the door and meowed again.

"You want in?" He opened the screen and the calico cat went in, investigated the trailer from the living room to the back bedroom, jumped up on Junior's bed, and curled up and went to sleep.

"Well," Junior said, "I guess you're home."

A few days later, Junior bought a cat carrier and took both Popeye and the cat to the vet, who checked them over, gave them their shots, and pronounced them both healthy. Popeye's left eye injury was permanent. As Junior was digging in his pocket for money, the receptionist asked him for his pets' names and dates of birth.

"Why does that matter to you?" Junior asked.

"We need the information for their shot records," she said quietly.

"Well, the dog is Popeye," he said. "I think he's about ten weeks old."

"How about the cat?" she asked.

"I don't know how old she is, but her name is, ah…Minerva."

Junior opened the door to his truck and put the cat carrier by the window. Popeye jumped in the driver's side and assumed his place in the middle. Junior grabbed a pint of brandy from under the seat and took two long swallows. Life would be a lot easier without so many people. Somehow, he always missed the mark when he was around them. People usually shied away from him. Pop often called him a loner. Maybe that was his destiny. He put his hand on Popeye, and just for a moment, he felt a wave of pride. He ruffled Popeye's neck, and stroked Minerva. "You guys are good buddies."

"Yup, today was a bad one." He spooned some of Mom's casserole into the dog's dish. Junior ate some himself, and opened another beer.

"Our money went bye-bye. That's no bueno. It's time we killed ourselves some varmints."

Popeye followed Junior, who put a twelve-pack and a pint of tequila in a wheelbarrow. Then he found his .22 rifle and four boxes of high-velocity hollow-points, which he liked because even if you missed a kill shot, you still tore up a lot of flesh, and the wounds were likely fatal. A good head shot would spray red all over the place. The prairie dog sport shooters in Wyoming and Colorado used Remington .22 long-rifle hollow-points as their official ammo. Junior searched until he found an old tarp, and then rolled the wheelbarrow out to a mound of earth next to the road ditch on the north side of the property. He put the folded tarp down by the wheelbarrow between some scrub cedar and two mounds of tall grass, tied his hair back with a bandana, and turned his blue Marvin Windows cap around so the brim was in back. This was just like shooting rats in the barn: the elimination of an outright menace. He watched, waited, drank, and thought about his new truck, moving to California, and finding Julie. Late in the day, Popeye's ears perked up from under the wheelbarrow, as prairie dogs began to peek out of their holes and look around. Junior hushed Popeye and, imagining he was a sniper, shot nearly 50 rounds, missing every shot. The prairie dogs scurried into their holes, peeked out as if to taunt him, and then disappeared again. His rifle sights blurred in the dusk, and shadows fell on the barrel. "Die, you little sonsabitches," he said, over and over. Junior stayed in his prone shooting position, waited, and drank more. He had put his head down to rest just when the sheriff parked his car, red lights blinking, climbed the fence, and walked over to Junior. Popeye growled softly. The sheriff put his hand on his holstered pistol. He wore a hat that made him look like Smokey the Bear coming out of a campsite, intent on putting out a fire.

"What the hell do you think you're doing?" asked the sheriff.

"I'm killing rodents, getting rid of these fucking varmints," Junior replied. "What's it to you?"

"You're going to have to stop," the sheriff said.

"This is my property, and I can shoot them if I want."

"You can't discharge a firearm in the city limits. You have the neighbors all upset. If you don't stop, I can confiscate your firearm, run you in, and you can do ninety days in jail. I don't want to do that."

"You don't get it," shouted Junior. "I have to kill them. They're ruining my life."

"You've got two choices: Stop, or stand up and get in the car." The sheriff jingled the handcuffs on his belt.

A half-dozen neighbors pointed and walked toward the sheriff's car. He looked up at the sheriff. Then he rolled over on his back, threw his box of .22 bullets out toward the prairie dog hills, and screamed, "I hope you little rats choke on these!"

Junior tossed his rifle into the empty wheelbarrow, and stumbled along as he weaved back to the maintenance shed. He stopped a couple of times, raised his hand, and gave the neighbors a one-finger salute.

Once he arrived home, Junior had another drink, calmed down, and went to bed. He patted the pillow and called Popeye up beside him. Popeye licked his face and pushed his nose under the pillow. Minerva jumped up on his stomach, kneaded him for a while with her paws, and then curled up at his feet.

"You guys are something else," Junior said. "Check it out. Tomorrow we're going to kill some varmints. Junior Corley doesn't give up."

3

Mom awoke to waves of nausea. Pop was already out in the machine shed, working on a hydraulic pump or something. He hadn't spoken at all the previous evening, and Mom knew that he'd been blaming himself for the land sale falling through. She should encourage Pop and be supportive, but she didn't feel like it. She had missed the sunrise and her prayer time, and she noticed a gray pall creeping through her normally sunny bedroom window. She tended to her bathroom rituals, dressed, ate some toast, and drove to the parking lot behind the church.

Mom unlocked the back door to the kitchen and went in quietly, turning on the lights. They shone on the bright array of stainless-sinks and food-preparation areas. She placed her hands on the island. It felt cool and smooth, almost like satin, and smelled of vinegar and Windex. She lifted her hands, saw her palm prints, and instantly began to feel better. This was her domain. The church's pastor, June Forrester, had said once, "When God created you, Mom, He put hospitality in the center of your spirit. Hospitality is truly your spiritual gift." She also had the spiritual gift of administration, a big help for her bookkeeping and scheduling work for We Move Dirt, Inc. She looked up as her best friend, LeAnn, burst through the main double doors. LeAnn had the air of a woman who sought to be light on her feet and cheerful in her attitude, but was constrained by her weight and a dark pull from within. She was short waisted, round-shouldered, and often tugged at her dress or smoothed the back of her skirts. She gave the impression of a woman who simply could not get comfortable. Her dark brown eyes seemed simultaneously distressed and critical, and her mouth often crumpled into a wary frown. Her tightly curled permanent could withstand a strong wind.

"How did the sale go? Are you rich now?" LeAnn asked.

Mom grabbed her friend's hand. "I don't know what's going to happen. The whole thing fell apart, and my family is a mess." Her eyes filled with tears. "Roy won't even talk."

"What happened?"

"They can't buy the land because it's covered with prairie dogs." Mom wiped her eyes.

"I've never heard of such a thing."

Mom ran her fingers through her graying hair, and they both sat down as Mom explained about the new city ordinance and the bank loan.

"What are you going to do?" LeAnn asked.

"Roy is out working on equipment, and I guess we'll just keep running the business. My faith feels like it's gone. I mean, why us? After all we've been through."

"Maybe you were a little too eager for the money."

"But it's for my family," Mom's chin began to tremble. She was verging on hysteria; it seemed as though her voice wandered through a full octave as she added, "I don't care about the money. I just care about their lives."

"Can you get rid of the prairie dogs? Move them or something?"

"Roy wants to poison them. He said we should've done it years ago."

"You can't let him do that!" LeAnn exclaimed. "They're alive, part of God's plan."

"Roy says they're just rodents, and rodents are varmints. I mean, we set traps to kill rats in the barn. What's the difference? For Heaven's sake, God doesn't have a plan for rats."

"You can't just kill them," LeAnn insisted. "You'd be killing them for the money. How could you live with that?"

Mom felt a little dizzy and began wiping the sink. *Be careful, just get along and don't make an argument.* She sprayed the counter, wiped it off, and took a fresh apron out of the drawer and put it on. It had red-checkered pockets and a red sash for around her waist. She was in the habit of wearing overly large shirts, jackets, blouses, and aprons to cover the slight bulge from her colostomy bag. She and LeAnn had attended the same cancer survivor group for the past six years, so LeAnn knew about the bag. That meant she had probably told her daughter Laura, which meant Laura's fiancé Fred knew. And Mom had told Pastor June, but as far as she knew, others in the congregation were unaware. She was worried that people might be alarmed if they knew she prepared church dinners while wearing a colostomy bag. Roy was still squeamish about it—after six years—even though she had a supply of small discreet cloth bags and a cover for their rare intimate moments.

"How's Laura doing with her wedding plans?" She began taking dishes out of the cabinets and washing the shelves.

"This wedding has really stirred things up." She and Fred are about finished with their wedding preparation counseling. They've got some issues."

"Are they serious?" asked Mom.

"Well, there's the age difference of nearly twenty years, and I don't think Fred is over his wife's death. It's only been a year, and he's still angry about the medication error. He's hired an attorney to sue the drug company and the doctor. Fred is no bright light, but he seems like a loyal companion. He doesn't talk much. He's quiet, like Roy."

"Fred seems like a decent man," Mom said. "He just joined Pastor June's Bible class, and he contributes."

"Oh, he's decent all right, but he doesn't have much energy. You're older than he is and you have five times more energy. You never sit still."

"They seem happy enough." Mom forced herself to smile. "She holds his hand in worship and they sing together. He seems to admire her, so I don't think her weight bothers him."

"She's joined Weight Watchers, and she's going to meetings," LeAnn said. "I think she's lost five pounds or so. She's trying to get me to go. I'm just grateful that she seems to sleep through the night. Anyway, she wants to have both the rehearsal dinner and the reception here at the church."

Mom began musing. Chicken cordon bleu, asparagus spears, small new potatoes, and a fluffy lemon dessert for the rehearsal dinner...fresh-flower table centerpieces with blue-and-white table runners and light blue candles. She could have a festive Mexican buffet for the reception, with bright red-and-orange balloons and little Mexican hats for centerpieces, and bright red, yellow, and orange peppers in the fajitas. Maybe she would prepare a flan. She pulled down a couple of cookbooks from the shelf.

"How many people?"

"Probably about twenty-five or thirty for the rehearsal dinner, and two hundred for the reception. He's inviting most of his family from Farmington. They're Mormon and love to eat."

"Is he Mormon, too?" Mom asked.

"He told Laura he'll be whatever she is, so I guess he'll soon be a Lutheran. Laura is proud of their shared spiritual life."

"I'll get the menus together for Laura to see," Mom said.

"Relax. We've got five months, for Heaven's sake."

LeAnn had been by Mom's side in the hospital when Mom had her colon cancer surgery six years ago, and supported her with continued prayer. Their friendship had deepened when Mom supported LeAnn through the breakup of her marriage three years ago. LeAnn's poor excuse for a husband had betrayed her with another woman for more than two years, and he wouldn't stop drinking. Both LeAnn and Laura gained forty-five pounds in the three years following the divorce. Mom figured that they just ate their way through their sadness.

LeAnn followed the lives of Jeff, Ida, and Junior, and shared Mom's hope that someday they would all be a real family. LeAnn, Pastor June, and Mom's prayers were always for "health and family," and they had a special understanding of what that meant. They had developed a deep compassion for each other, and they agreed about most things.

Still, Mom thought LeAnn was a bit nosey and patronizing.

"How's Junior?" was LeAnn's way of inviting Mom to talk about his drinking or about Ida's sleeping around or about Jeff's spending, or any of her other worries. Mom asking, "How's Laura?" allowed LeAnn to talk about Laura's weight or her bossiness or unemployment or LeAnn's own loneliness. And LeAnn asking, "How are you?" meant "How is your soul and what should we pray for?"

"How's Junior?" LeAnn asked.

"Oh, he's about the same. Lately he's been angry and his drinking has picked up. I'm afraid this episode with the land sale will really set him back. He can get mean."

"I so wish we could get him to church," LeAnn said. "And for that matter, Ida and Jeff too. It would be great if they could hear Pastor June's preaching."

"I've given up on that. I can get Roy to come on Christmas, but that's all. Did I hear that Laura is working?" Mom started a fresh coffee pot.

"She has a part-time job as a graphic artist, helping some nonprofits with slogans, logos, and other stuff. Art was her favorite subject in high school."

"Have you seen any of her work? I'll bet she's pleased."

"I think she's waiting to show me something that is really good."

"I don't doubt she'll come up with something. Laura has a lot of creativity. Is she still painting?"

"She started up again. I think she's eager to show Fred her work."

Pastor June came through the double doors. "Is there coffee on?"

"It should be ready in just a minute," Mom replied. "I'll get you a cup."

"I'm sorry about yesterday," June said.

Mom's head snapped around. "You know?"

"I probably shouldn't know, but Joyce, one of the nursery workers, has a sister who works at the title company. Sometimes she gossips. Are you doing okay?"

Oh God, now the whole church knows.

Pastor June held Mom's hand with both of hers. June had likely just come from Defined Fitness. Her short gray hair was still damp above her ears. Her high forehead and cheekbones glowed with health. She was taller than Mom and a trim one hundred thirty pounds. At first glance, she could have been Mom's younger sister by about ten or twelve years.

LeAnn interrupted. "Pop wants to poison all the prairie dogs. I told Mom I don't think you can just kill God's creatures for money."

"We do slaughter beef cattle and chickens every day for money." She released Mom's hand.

Mom poured coffee for everyone and avoided meeting LeAnn's gaze.

"It seems there is always conflict when cities grow," June said. "Prosperity always brings conflict. It's a difficult balance. I'm worried about you and your family. This is quite a blow."

Mom dabbed her eyes with a tissue and took a deep breath. "I've told Roy that God will provide, but I'm not very confident. Mostly I'm worried about Junior." Mom took a breath and clasped her hands.

"Is the marriage counseling with Laura going okay?" LeAnn asked.

"Laura and Fred will make a lovely couple," June replied. "Fred will be joining the church this Sunday, and Laura will stand up with him."

"Oh, she didn't say anything about that. I'm happy for them, but I worry about his age."

June turned to Mom. "Can we have some private time together?"

In June's office, Mom asked for prayers for health and family, and then settled back into an easy chair. She took a deep breath. Mom felt as though this was her first rest since she left the title company the day before.

"I'm truly sorry about this setback," said June. "I know you were counting on the land sale and all that would mean for your children. Is there anything I can do for you?"

"Your prayers have already helped," Mom said. "You know, like I told LeAnn, I'm afraid of what might happen to Junior. Any little thing sets him off, and this isn't little." Mom stood up, and then sat down, folding her hands. "It's as though God is testing us. I just don't know what to think. Roy is quiet as a rock. I think he blames himself. I don't know why Ida won't settle down. She's a nurse and all, but what if she turns up pregnant? And, God forbid, what happens if she has an abortion? The money was going to pay off Jeff's bills and give him a fresh start. Now he'll just spend more money and charge up his credit cards. What's going to happen? Oh, I'm so confused." Mom held her face in her hands.

"Wow, there is a lot going on in there. Slow down. Let's see if we can sort some things out. First of all, you really don't have any control over Junior and his life style."

"I know that, but still, I am his mother and I should be able to help somehow."

"Have you tried that Al-Anon group I told you about? As I said, they meet at the Methodist church, so people won't know you."

"I went by there once, but they just complain about their husbands. They're not my kind of people."

"You might have gone on a bad night. I think you should try it again. Or, try a different group." June handed Mom a printed schedule of meetings.

"Well, I'll think about it."

"This is a complex world, and given the laws of nature and people's free will, things just happen. Our test is to see how our faith deals with the problems we encounter. I like to say that problems happen and we react, but it's how we respond that's the test. In a sense, God is testing all of us all the time so we can grow closer to Him. We're all in this together. You're not singled out."

"I feel like my family just fell apart. How would you react?" Mom squirmed in her chair.

"I understand how you feel. This is a tough setback. It might be a chance for your family to grow. Here you are facing adversity together as a family. Have you thought about that? Could there be a spiritual leading somewhere in this problem?"

"I don't know. It sure doesn't feel like it. It does kind of put us in the same place, but everyone is miserable. Junior is convinced we've screwed up." She looked up at the ceiling. "Fate at work, Roy would say. He thinks this setback was inevitable. Oh, I don't know."

"Give Roy some time. You've been by his side for over thirty years. Maybe you should use your gift. Make him his favorite dinner. That ought to get things moving."

Mom's discomfort lifted as she pondered dinner. Sirloin steak, baked potatoes, creamed green beans with mushrooms...maybe a cherry pie.

"Let's meet again on Tuesday," June said. She and Mom stood up and hugged. "Stay in prayer. I know God won't let you down."

"Thank you. I always feel better when we talk."

Mom went to the grocery store, then to the craft store. She got a basket and walked up and down the aisles, gathering brown and orange paper flowers, little bamboo baskets, beige and orange votive candles, a bamboo table runner, and other odds and ends. She would make a centerpiece for Ida's table when the land sold and Ida moved into her new condominium.

4

Jeff worked the rest of the day, changed clothes, and went to the Santa Ana Star Casino. He got a $1,000 advance on his Visa card, bought chips, and sat down at the blackjack table. His mind raced as the dealer won six straight times. A woman sat down beside him, sloshed her drink, and knocked over his stack of chips. "Whoa, sorry."

Jeff restacked his chips and nodded with a lukewarm smile.

"My name's Betty, but you can call me Betty." She tipped her head back with a throaty laugh.

Jeff glanced into her mouth. He saw four crowns on her molars, and her two upper front teeth revealed a yellow-white shade of porcelain that didn't match the rest of her teeth. Her brown complexion highlighted the defect. *Color selection is easy. This dental work is downright sloppy.* She had recently freshened up her lipstick, and the color ran up above her lip on the right side, giving her an uneven and clownish smile. She ran her fingers though her short brown hair.

"I'm Jeff." The dealer tossed him an ace to his $200 bet. He peeked at his hole card, an ace. Betty saw it too. "Go for it. Double down."

Jeff turned up the ace and put his last $200 down. The dealer flipped out two face cards: double blackjack, $800. Jeff grinned at Betty.

"All right," Betty said. "I guess I bring you good luck."

Betty kept drinking, and Jeff kept winning. *It's about time.* Although he wasn't counting, he figured he was down about $2,000 for the month. Tonight put him ahead $8,000.

"Shall I keep knocking over your chips?" Betty asked.

"Why not," Jeff replied. "What brings you out tonight?"

"I'm going through a divorce."

"Sorry, I didn't mean to pry."

"Oh, no, it's a good thing. I left the house at noon and left him a note. Eight years down the drain."

"Bad memories, huh?"

"We never did click. Like a patchwork quilt that never would fit together. Our patches never matches." She put her hand over her mouth and laughed through her fingers.

Jeff stood up. "I guess I'll cash in. Nice to meet you, Betty."

"Hey, you can't let go of your good luck charm that easy. Buy me some coffee." She grabbed Jeff's arm. "I shouldn't be driving. Come on, buy me some coffee and a donut."

Jeff didn't have the heart to turn a drunken woman loose on the streets. "Okay. We'll go to Starlight Cafe and then I'll bring you back to your car." As Betty grasped his arm, Jeff could smell her sour breath and a hint of gardenia perfume. She was shorter than he was and seemed unaware that he could look down her scoop-neck top and see her smallish, jiggling breasts squeezed into a push-up bra. Her bra color matched her pink lip-gloss. *Odd. Careful with her colors, but unaware of her crappy teeth.*

They took a booth at the café and Jeff ordered two breakfast plates. "You should eat something. How far do you have to drive?"

"Not far. I live in Rio Rancho."

"Where do you work?"

"At Intel. I'm an efficiency coordinator." She dug a business card out of her purse and handed it to him. "And you?"

"I'm a dentist, a prosthodontist. I do restorative dentistry." He smiled at her and showed his nearly perfect teeth.

"Oh really? That's a coincidence. My husband's a dentist, too. He did my crowns. That's how we met." She smiled and then opened her mouth and pointed with her finger. "He fixed my front teeth too. I fell off a bicycle. We moved here from California a couple of years ago. He works in Santa Fe and drives every day. We don't see each other much. I told you, right? We're getting a divorce. I left him a note."

Jeff felt a curious mix of attraction and disgust. Maybe she did bring good luck. *Who knows? Luck is part of life. Today was a bad-luck-good-*

luck day, that's for sure. Losing a half-million dollars is about as bad as luck gets. At least I have a chance at fixing it. Mom's counting on that. Maybe winning $8,000 was good luck. Who knows? Did this drunken woman bring it? Hell, who cares? Maybe in an hour she'll be able to drive, but if a cop stops her, her blood alcohol is way beyond the legal limit. Why do I have to take care of people? Why am I always the one? Mom's hopeful look as they left the title company had tugged at his soul. And now Betty, looking to him for God knows what.

"You're awfully quiet. What are you thinking about?" she asked.

Jeff chewed on his toast and wiped his mouth with a napkin. "We've got to get you home."

"I can't go home."

"I'll tell you what," Jeff said. "Let's get you a room at the Super 8 and then you can get a cab to your car in the morning. You're in no shape to drive."

"Okay, whatever. I can't go home. I don't live there anymore."

Jeff drove them across the street and used his Visa to get a room. He led her up the stairs, found her room, and opened the door. "There you go, Betty. Have a good night."

Betty flopped down on the bed on her back. Her skirt flared up and showed her white panties. She pushed her dress down over her knees and opened her arms.

"Stay for a while?"

"Goodnight." He turned and walked to his car. He figured he'd put $6,000 away in the freezer and use $2,000 as a stake for Saturday night.

That night, Jeff slept fitfully. His mind wandered into woolgathering, purposeless fantasies of winning at blackjack, scurrying prairie dogs, Betty's teeth, her jiggling breasts, her clownish smile. He would drift off, and then the excitement of winning would wake him. Finally, at 4 am, he got up, made coffee, and tried to read his dental journals, but his duty to Mom distracted him. He knew he could talk with a city councilman, and if the final reading of the ordinance could be delayed, there was a good chance the property could be exempt or grandfathered in before the law took effect. He started to call Epstein, but noticed it was too early. As he paced around his apartment, Betty's smile interrupted his thoughts, and he remembered her saying, "You can't let go of your good luck charm." There, deep in his scientific mind, adrenaline rushed into the crevices around his fickle belief in luck. He grinned and counted out eighty $100 bills in eight stacks of ten on the kitchen table. Maybe Betty *was* good luck; more likely, though, his skill with cards made the difference. Maybe he could win again and pay off some bills, at least one of his credit cards. He put the money into the freezer, got ready for work, and drove to his office for his 8 a.m. appointment.

At noon, he called Betty's work number. She had taken a couple of days off and would be back on Thursday. Jeff left a message.

Betty returned Jeff's call on Thursday afternoon, and they decided to meet for dinner at the casino's buffet on Friday evening. He thought briefly about Betty's husband. She hadn't said much, but Jeff was able to piece together that he was fifteen years older, drank a lot, and had to leave Los Angeles because of a malpractice suit from a movie actor.

On Friday, Jeff arrived at the casino at 6 p.m.—a half-hour before he and Betty planned to meet—and bought $2,000 worth of chips. He stuffed them into his blazer pockets, walked around among the blackjack tables, and then sat down in the waiting area by the buffet. When Betty came in, Jeff felt relieved upon seeing her. She appeared sober, poised, and professional in a black suit jacket, skirt, and a white blouse. Her brown skin glowed, and her black wavy hair covered her high cheekbones. He looked away when he saw her front teeth. They walked into the dining room.

"It's nice to see you," Jeff said. "You seem to be feeling better."

"Yes, I don't get drunk very often, but when I do, I'm a mess. I'm sorry if I embarrassed you."

"No problem."

"I'm surprised you called," she said. "Especially after my, you know."

"Like you said, I can't let go of my good luck charm that easy."

"Did I say that?"

"I won a lot of money. You said you were good luck."

"Oh my, well maybe I am."

After a dinner of lobster, scalloped potatoes, and Waldorf salad, they split a piece of cherry pie and went to a blackjack table. Jeff won five times in a row, and they moved to another table. He won again, playing two hands and counting cards.

"Wow, maybe I *am* good luck," Betty said. She was holding his arm and leaning her head on his shoulder. Occasionally, Jeff put his arm around her and dropped a handful of chips into her jacket pocket. "Let's hide these away. I'm liable to lose them."

"Oh, so now I'm your banker?"

"At least my safety net," Jeff said.

Jeff's betting became bold. He won $1,000 on one hand. His eyes sparkled and he turned and kissed Betty full on the lips.

She grinned. "I didn't know I could make you that happy."

"You're pretty exciting," he said.

She leaned her head on his shoulder and spoke softly into his ear. "Okay, Jeff, we are way ahead, and it's time to stop. Anyway, I've got to go into work tomorrow for a new-hire training session."

Jeff nodded, gathered his chips, and they walked to the cashier. Altogether, he'd won $18,700. He floated into the parking lot, stood by Betty's car, and grinned at the three-quarter moon as she took her keys from her purse. Then he hugged her to him. She faced him, and they lingered with a full, gentle kiss. Jeff became aroused.

Betty pulled away quickly and opened the car door. "I'm uncomfortable about getting too close," she said. "I haven't even had time to get all my clothes out of the house."

"I understand. I hope you realize you're attractive."

"Well, thank you for that. Call me in a couple of days, okay?"

"Sure, no problem." Jeff stood with his hands on his hips as she drove away.

Betty stopped her car and lowered the window. Jeff jogged up beside the door.

"You know, my life is really changing. I've got to be more than good luck. That wouldn't be enough."

"Sure, I know that." He waved as she drove away.

When Jeff got back to his apartment, he took a large bag from the freezer and added $15,000 to the $8,000. He kept $3,700 out, and tucked the bag away under the mixed vegetables and the organic blueberries.

On Monday morning, Jeff walked into his office reception area. Betty looked up from a Cosmopolitan magazine and smiled. "I was hoping you could work me in."

Jeff nodded to his receptionist. "You've got an hour after Mrs. Johnson," she said.

"Well, then, I'll see you shortly," Jeff told Betty.

Soon, Betty settled into the dental chair and Jeff put on fresh gloves.

"What can I do for you?" Jeff asked.

Betty hunched over, crossed her arms, and with one finger pointed to her front teeth. "Can you fix these? My husband chose the wrong colors. I think he was drunk. I see him in the mirror every time I brush my teeth."

"I'm sure I can," Jeff said. "It'll be a rather involved process, though. You'll be sore for a while."

"How about now?" she asked.

Jeff checked his watch. "Sure. I'll have to numb you up." He worked quickly—injections, crown removal, prep work, and new impressions. He found some temporary crowns from the dental lab next door. His assistant confirmed the color choice for new crowns. Betty looked at the color choices.

"I think that's it," Jeff said as he held up a mirror.

"Hummm, yes," she said.

"We can have these ready for you in a week or so," Jeff said.

Betty cupped her lips in her hands and mumbled. "Okay, see you tonight?"

Jeff helped her sit back down in the waiting room, and the receptionist handed her a clipboard with financial forms to fill out.

"How about tomorrow night?" he said. "You probably need to rest. Here's some pain pills. Take a couple every six hours." He ran a cup of water from the cooler. "Better start now. Are you okay to drive?"

"Yes. My new apartment is not far away, and then I'm off work for two days."

"Call me tomorrow," he said. "If you're feeling okay, we can meet for dinner."

Betty nodded, smiled though her open fingers, and left the office.

Jeff turned to his receptionist."There's no charge for this patient." He looked at the clipboard, made some notes, and noticed Betty was born October 15, 1966, just two days before his birthday. Her full name was Elizabeth Maria Archuleta, and she had checked "divorced."

He stepped into his office, closed the door, and called Robert Epstein.

"Any progress on the City Council? Can we talk with anyone?"

"Some progress," Epstein said. "I've talked with Councilor Fernando Vigil, and he seems receptive to a meeting."

"What did he say?"

"He thinks this whole thing about the prairie dogs is way out of proportion. Sounds like he's in favor of the tax base that comes from development."

"When can we see him?"

"We're supposed to check back with him next week. I think you should ask Mom to call. She'd be a good one to get the appointment."

"Okay. I'll talk with her, and then we'll both call."

"Don't sound too desperate. Let's stay cool."

"Thanks. Talk with you later."

"Jeff."

"What?"

"Please try to keep Junior under control. An attorney in the neighborhood called. The Sheriff had to stop Junior's shooting. He was drunk. Gave the finger to the neighbors. We don't need that."

"Sure. I'll take care of it."

Jeff met Betty on Saturday night at Santa Ana for the buffet again, and then they moved into the gaming area. Betty played the quarter slots, while Jeff played two hands of blackjack. He lost steadily and was down to his last $400 when Betty sat down beside him. Her upper lip was still swollen, but even the temporary crowns looked better than her old teeth.

"How are you doing?" she asked.

"I'm down quite a bit."

She touched his small stack of chips. "We should probably go. There's still time for a movie at Cottonwood Mall."

"No, I'll play these, win or lose."

He won two hands, doubled his bet, and won two more. Betty put her hand on his as the dealer went bust on 17. Jeff kissed her on the cheek. "That's over $3,000."

"Okay, then, let's go."

"One more," he said. He touched his nose with his finger, put $2,000 aside and bet $1,000. Blackjack. Jeff jumped off the stool and shouted, "Yes,

I knew it." He pumped his fist. Then he grabbed Betty, kissed her, and twirled her around.

She laughed. "Okay, big shot, now we're leaving."

They caught the 9:30 movie, and Jeff drove her back to her car.

"We've got to stop meeting like this," Betty said teasingly.

"No way. We've got to keep meeting *exactly* like this. Would you like to come by for a drink?"

"I'm still moving stuff," she said. "Tomorrow I pick up my bicycle and they move my treadmill. Besides, it's too soon."

He kissed her through the open car window. "Okay, I'll call you."

Jeff walked into his apartment, added $2,000 to his stash in the freezer, and kept about $3,000 in his pockets. As he fell asleep, he felt sad about his family's plight, yet his thoughts of Betty and the sheaves of hundred dollar bills made him quiver with excitement. His desperate financial life was about to change, despite the debacle at the title company. Besides, he, Mom, and Epstein would likely find a way through this mess. It was just a temporary setback.

Over the weekend, Jeff practiced his card counting, studied his blackjack books, and spread out all his money on the dining room table. Shuffling through his $100 bills, feelings of elation strengthened him, convincing him that his winnings came from his years of gambling experience, taking him back to his basic belief that science and probability theory carried the day over a childish belief in luck. How foolish of him to put luck above clever strategy. His skill easily matched that of a professional gambler. To hell with Betty's luck—Jeff had been gambling for years before he met Betty. *Time to use my winning system.*

On Monday, he called Betty and left a message suggesting dinner for Saturday night. He asked his receptionist to work Betty in on Friday for her permanent crowns. He worked all day, took a couple of his little orange diet pills, and went by himself to Route 66 Casino that evening. He lost $3,000. On Tuesday night, angry and focused, he lost $5,000 at the Sandia Casino, and on Wednesday night, he went back to Santa Ana and lost $10,000 after being ahead $6,500. Thursday night he lost the rest of his money, all but $20, at the Sandia Casino. Over $26,000 slipped through his hands in less than four days. When he came to work on Friday, he felt beaten and sore, like a truck had run over him. After an orange pill and a

Pepsi, he worked feverishly most of the day, refusing to feel anything.

Betty came in at 3:00 pm. "Are you okay? You look like you have the flu or something." She sat down in the chair and Jeff tipped her back and put on fresh gloves.

"Might be something I ate," he said. "I just need a good night's sleep."

His hand shook slightly as he placed an injection.

"I don't need to use as much this time. This won't be painful."

He massaged her gums and noticed that her breath smelled like warm cinnamon. It reminded him of Christmas and Mom's hot toddies. He popped off the temporary crowns, cleaned and dried her teeth, and cemented the new crowns in place. Perfect. He raised the chair and handed Betty a hand mirror.

"Wow." She practiced her smile a couple of times. "These are beautiful."

"Can I take a picture?" Jeff asked.

"Sure. Let me freshen up first." Betty got up and stepped into the bathroom. She put on new lip-gloss, ran a comb through her hair, pinched her cheeks, and came out smiling. "Okay, I'm ready for you," she said.

Jeff took several pictures of different smiles.

"I'll get you a nice 8 x 10, and I'll put one up in the office. He motioned to the wall of photos in the hallway. "I've got a spot for you right here in front."

"Who is that?" She pointed to a photo next to her spot.

"That's my mother. Everyone calls her Mom. She has eight crowns."

"She's beautiful." Betty walked to the reception desk.

"How much do I owe?" she asked the receptionist.

"There's no charge," Jeff said. "This is my gift to you. Your husband made a mistake with those other crowns."

Betty tipped her head and wrinkled her nose. "I'm not comfortable with that." Let's talk about it tomorrow night."

Jeff put his hand in his pocket and felt the two ten dollar bills. He swallowed and choked back a wave of shame that filled his throat.

"I'm going to have to take a rain check on tomorrow night," he said. "I have to spend some time with Mom. She needs my help with a family emergency."

"Is everyone all right?" Betty asked.

"I think so. It's a matter about their estate and a land sale. Mom is a cancer survivor and I worry about her stress level. I'll call you next week."

"Okay, we'll put off our discussion about your bill until then." Betty smiled at Jeff and left.

His receptionist held out a stack of mail ready for the post office.

"Shall I mail these checks?" she asked.

"No, I'll take them," he said.

"You need to make a deposit before you mail them. You're short about $2,000."

"Okay, I'll take care of it. Why don't you go home early? I've got to check in on Mom."

Jeff stopped by the house.

Mom was making dinner. "Can you stay for dinner?" She looked like she'd had been crying.

"Not tonight, but I do have some good news."

"Did you hear from our attorney?"

"Yes. Epstein talked with Fernando Vigil, a city councilor, and he's agreed to meet with us. We think you should call for the appointment. I'll follow up and confirm." Jeff handed her a note with the phone number. She hugged him and kissed him on the cheek. "Are you okay? You seem down about something."

"I'm fine. Don't worry, I've got this covered."

"Thank you, Jeff. I know we can get through this. Junior's a mess. The neighbors are upset."

"It'll be all right. I'll talk with him."

"I can always count on you," Mom said.

"Oh, by the way, could you lend me $2,000 for a week or so?" Jeff asked, trying to sound casual. "Some of my patients are behind in paying me."

Mom took her checkbook from the drawer, wrote a check for $2,000, and handed it to him.

"Thanks. I know. We'll get this land sale problem behind us, and then everyone will be just fine. Call Councilor Vigil tomorrow morning, and then we'll go together."

"I'm counting on you, Jeff."

"Don't worry, I know what to do."

5

Mom came home from church, turned into the driveway, and slammed on her brakes to avoid the welding truck. Pop was fixing the gate hinge that had been broken for years. Mom saw several strange cars parked down by the corner. She lowered the window and yelled at Roy, "What in the world is going on?"

Pop turned his head toward her. "I'm fixing the gate," he said simply, as if it couldn't be more obvious.

"Why now?"

Pop motioned toward the cars. "Seems like a good time." He was glad to see Mom, but still, he felt annoyed. Pop rarely smiled. He remained unmoved by the jokes his friends would tell him over coffee. To Pop, humor wasted valuable time that could be spent on more important things. He lived by a simple rule: Check what's coming at you, adjust your tracks, and then plow ahead. Just like the D6 dozer he loved to drive.

Pop pulled his welding helmet down and struck an arc on the hinge. His hand trembled and he felt agitated. He wanted to hurry and get the gate fixed before dark. As though he had suddenly remembered something, Roy stopped and raised his helmet.

"I'm glad you're home," he told Mom. "I don't like this." He waved his hand once again toward the cars.

Mom looked over her shoulder, and then turned back to Pop. She seemed pleased that he had said something. "I've been to the store and have your favorite dinner."

Pop cocked his head like a curious puppy. "I'll be another hour or so. Could you ask Junior to come and help? Just drive around the truck."

"Sure. I'll see you in a little while."

Mom wore an impish smile, but Pop noticed worry in her eyes. He nodded his head so that the helmet came down. The arc lit up the gatepost. The hot ozone smell of the arc welder reminded him of the burning steel and oil smell coming from Janice's 1955 Chevy thirty-seven years before. She had that same playful smile then. On that morning, Roy had felt that something was about to happen. As he walked up to her stalled car, he felt a pause in time, as though everything was waiting for him. The woman— Janice—was shaking her fist and turning around in a circle. Her skirt flared up, showing her thighs.

"What seems to be the problem?" Roy asked.

"Oh, my stupid car just stopped dead," she said.

Roy opened the hood and steam rose up. He pulled his sleeve down over his hand, then grabbed the oil dipstick and took it out. It was dry and smoking. He inhaled the smell of burning steel and winced.

"You've run out of oil and the engine has seized. You know, it's a good idea to check the oil every morning." He shook his head.

"That's impossible. I just had the oil changed an hour ago." She folded her arms and planted her feet. "They said they put in six quarts of 10W30 Penzoil. I paid extra for premium oil."

Smart. This is not your average woman. He dropped down and slid under the car.

"Here's your problem. The drain plug is loose and the oil all leaked out." He stood up and held out the hot drain plug, bouncing it in his hand so that it wouldn't burn his skin.

"Those idiots." She turned her face to his. "You count on people to be competent, and now look. What a mess."

Roy held the drain plug and stared into her eyes until she blinked.

"Well, can you help me?" A slight smile formed on her full lips.

Roy went into the bank, called a tow truck, and then took Janice to a rental car agency. There was a coffee shop nearby, so she offered to buy him lunch. That's where they discovered a peculiar coincidence: Janice was born on December 21, 1942, the shortest day of the year, while Roy was born on June 21, 1940, the longest day of the year. She joked, "The longest and shortest have finally met."

For Roy, fate had spoken. The longest was destined to take care of the shortest. The life that awaited him included this woman.

Roy asked Janice out to dinner that weekend. They went to Little Anita's for green chile burritos, and within six months, they were married and had moved into the house on the twenty acres that Roy had inherited from his father. Here he was, thirty-seven years later, fixing a gate and seeing that same smile that endured through the years. He clamped on a new welding rod and finished the weld.

Junior drove up in his truck, and he and Popeye clambered out.

"What do you want?" He looked down the road a hundred yards or so, and saw five or six cars with people milling around.

"It's not rocket science. I need help hanging this gate. It's at least 300 pounds."

"It's been ten years since we hit this gate with a trailer. Why fix it now?"

Pop motioned toward the people. "It's time we keep this gate locked, and tomorrow I want us to walk the fence line and put up the posts that are down."

Junior got some cement blocks out of the truck and tossed them on the ground to prop up the gate.

"They're not lined up," Pop said.

"I know. I'm not blind."

"Well, line 'em up. It's getting dark."

Junior kicked the blocks into a line, and then he and Pop propped up the gate so that they could lower it onto the hinge pins. Pop banged dirt out of the hinge holes, put some WD-40 on the pins, and then he and his son lowered the gate into place. Junior adjusted the latch, and they swung the fourteen- foot gate back and forth, checking the latch.

"Ready to go." He took a pint from under the seat of his truck and had a couple of swallows.

Pop put his hands on his hips and admired the welding. Without meeting Junior's eyes, he said, "You're drinking is going to kill you. One of these days it'll catch up with you."

"I'm just fine," Junior muttered. "I've got it under control." He looked over Pop's shoulder. "There's a bunch of people coming. What the hell is going on?"

Pop and Junior stood behind the closed gate and waited as a couple dozen people walked up the road to the driveway. Even in the dusk, the two men could see that some of the interlopers were carrying signs that said "SAVE THE PRAIRIE DOGS," "GOD LOVES PRAIRIE DOGS," and "PRAIRIE DOGS ARE ENDANGERED." A woman was handing out light-green baseball caps with pictures of prairie dogs printed on the front. The people were pointing at the Corleys' land and chattering with each other. There was a man at the front of the crowd who looked like a coach or a leader at a summer camp. He walked up to Pop and put his hand on the gate. "Are you Roy Corley?"

"You're looking at him," Pop said. "What the hell do you want?"

"I'm Donald Pressman, the head of Forest Guardians. Just call me Donald."

Pop looked the man up and down. He was tall and lean with short-cropped light gray hair and a tan complexion. He moved gracefully, like a tennis player. He had a Hollywood smile with bright white teeth, and he was dressed in creased blue jeans and a button down dress shirt. A fat blond woman handed Donald a new hat. He adjusted the band, curled the brim, and put it on. On top of the hat, a smiling prairie dog looked Pop in the face.

"Okay, Donald, what the hell do you want?"

"The Forest Guardians take on projects that help with our environment," Donald said. "We believe that humans have an innate sensitivity and a deep need for other living things. We are interested in endangered species, and the Gunnison prairie dogs on your property are clearly endangered."

"The prairie dogs are rodents," Pop corrected him. "They're a menace."

"Not to us. Mother earth connects all living things, and these are helpless, innocent creatures. They are an endangered species. Don't you see? When we kill living things, it's like we're killing part of ourselves."

Yeah, right.

"This is my property, and I can do what I want," he told Donald. "This is America."

"Well, we have an alternative, and it helps make a better America. The Forest Guardians have created some land trusts in New Mexico. We're here to encourage you to give your land to a trust and to save the prairie dogs. Your gift would be at full appraisal, and your tax deductions can carry forward for five years."

"Fuck you," Junior said. "Get the hell off our property."

The sound of a low growl came from Popeye, and Pop put his hand on Junior's shoulder.

"I don't think we're interested." *This guy sounds like a real wheeler-dealer.*

Junior went to his truck, took his rifle down off the rack, and shuffled back to the gate.

"There's no cause for hostility," Donald said. "We're peaceful folks. Be advised, though, we intend to keep some people around to make sure these prairie dogs are safe. We have a duty to these children of the earth."

"You won't be able to stay on our property," Pop said. "We are not fond of trespassers, and I'll call the sheriff."

"I assure you we have done this before. I'm a professional, and Forest Guardians follow the letter of the law. We have permission to set up on a public easement down the street, and our folks will walk only in the public rights-of-way. Perhaps we can visit again in the morning. There are real financial advantages for a land trust." Donald smiled and extended his hand. "It is good to meet you, Mr. Corley."

Pop ignored the man's outstretched hand, turned his back, and whispered to Junior, telling him to put his rifle back in the truck and lock the gate. Junior dragged a chain and padlock out of the truck bed, slapped the chain around the post, and locked the padlock. Pop drove the welding truck back to the machine shed, and Junior followed in his truck. As Pop put away his tools, Junior walked in.

"Hey Pop, who the hell do they think they are?"

"You need to watch your mouth, dum-dum. You're going to make this worse."

Junior shifted uncomfortably. "Can they do this, you know, protest us?"

"I think they're within the law, but I can't understand all that fuss about a few varmints."

"What are we going to do?"

"I'm going in for dinner. Mom's waiting."

Pop opened the door to the house and watched Junior stumble up the stairs to the door of the trailer, Popeye by his side. Pop washed his hands in the utility room, and walked into a home filled with comforting smells: steak, potatoes, and a cherry pie in the oven.

"Who were all those people?" Mom asked.

"We are being *protested*." He spat out the word as if it tasted bad. "There's a wing-nut named Donald who's boss of some kind of Guardians, a bunch of people with signs, and a fat woman handing out prairie dog hats. Why didn't I wipe out those rodents years ago?"

"Oh, Lord. All we want is to help our children," Mom said. "It's not your fault. You didn't know." She shook her head, put their plates on the table, and they both sat down. Pop took a breath and bowed his head as Mom offered a short blessing.

Mom felt a bittersweet ache in her heart. She quietly lamented her solitary life at church and took a small amount of comfort on Pop's bowed head: a rare yet touching moment of reverence. Ever since the accident, Pop had bowed his head for blessings, but that was it. Watching those children suffer and die all those years ago seized part of his soul. They had survived the aftermath that week together, but it marked a dark time in their spiritual life.

The school bus driver had smiled and waved before the tire blew out. Pop was on his motor grader on a county road just outside the small town of Mora. The bus pitched off the road, bounced, and rolled over three times before it came to rest on its roof deep in an arroyo. The motor ran and the wheels continued to turn.

Pop jumped off the grader and climbed down to the bus. He kicked in the windshield, reached in, and turned off the motor. The driver's head twisted over a broken neck, the remnants of a scream frozen on his face. The force had thrown crying and flailing children everywhere. Some didn't move. Pop retched and ran back to the highway, flagging the first car and telling the driver to find a phone and call the sheriff.

He grabbed his first aid kit from the grader, went back to the bus, and started patching up bleeding children. It was hard to see through his tears as he made places on the overturned roof to lay the children. He pulled cushions from seats and made a little corral in the back, out of sight, where he gently laid four little girls and one boy. They were about seven or eight years old.

Darkness covered the scene as paramedics transported the last of the children to the hospital. Six dead, including the driver. Twenty had serious injuries; four, the ones who had sat in the middle, were bruised but not seriously hurt.

Pop drove home and puttered in his shop for the rest of the week. He couldn't stop the unexpected heaves of sobbing. Mom wanted him to go to the doctor.

"He can give you something so you'll sleep," she said.

"I'll be okay. I just need a little time." Each night that week, he lay down with six-year-old Jeff until he fell asleep. He read Dr. Seuss stories to Ida as she giggled and pointed at the pictures.

On Sunday, Mom said, "Come on, Pop. Let's go to church. It will do us good."

"You go ahead," Pop said. "I can't go. I've seen too much."

That Sunday marked a wide crack in their spiritual life. As they each passed through, they came out on different paths. Since then, Pop went to church only on Christmas, and that was for Mom's sake. Pop wiped his closed eyes with a napkin.

"Thank you, Lord, for the blessings of this food and home. Please help us to understand all this hostility around us and guide us in our days. Give us strength in these times of trial. Amen."

Pop smiled and dove in. He loved Mom's cooking, and she had prepared all his favorites. He began to feel calm, and his irritation began to wane. He remembered his horoscope from earlier that day, which suggested he might enjoy some romantic times at home. Mom's horoscope implied that social encounters were in order. What might be next?

"Did you get a chance to see some friends today?" Pop asked.

"Yes. I talked with LeAnn about her daughter's wedding. You know, Laura is getting married to Fred later in the year. I'm going to organize the rehearsal dinner and the reception dinner." Mom spooned some more potatoes onto Pop's plate. "Do you have a job tomorrow?"

"No, I told Junior we're going to walk the property and make sure the fence is up everywhere. I don't want any of those protesters to wander in here. I'm not going to put up with trespassing."

Later, Mom cleaned up in the kitchen while Pop read the paper and looked through *Machinery Trader* magazine. Mom showered, fashioned a discreet flannel bag for her colostomy, and put on her satin nightgown and robe. She came into the living room, sat down near Pop, and smiled.

"Let's go to bed early," she said.

Yup, a romantic evening at home. It's about time. He followed Mom into their bedroom and they made love on clean sheets. Then they both tossed and turned all night.

Pop got up twice and checked the doors. Out the window, he could see the lanterns of the protesters who were camped in tents down the road.

6

Junior pulled a pillow over his head to quiet the pounding he heard at the door.

"Junior, get up. We've got things to do," Pop yelled.

Junior stumbled to the door and opened it.

"What the hell do you want? It's six in the morning."

"I've got a plan. Meet me in the shop in an hour."

Junior pulled on his jeans, splashed some water on his face, and started coffee in the kitchen. Pain seized his stomach, and he threw up in the sink. *Damn, maybe I'm getting the flu.* He splashed some brandy in his coffee and sat down at the table. *Saturday morning. Don't have to go to work. Pop is all wound up and acting like a crazy man.* He heated up some cold pizza in the microwave, put out some food for Popeye and Minerva, and turned on the news while he ate.

When Junior came into the shop, Pop was sitting at the bench, reading over some pamphlets and making notes.

"I think we have enough for two acres," he said.

"Enough what?"

"Kaput-D Prairie Dog Bait. I've got twelve 50-pound bags from a couple of years ago." He motioned to a pallet covered with a tarp and lumber. "Kaput-D is the best prairie dog poison around. Help me move the lumber."

Junior and Pop worked together, restacking some old 2 x 12s, and Pop pulled away the tarp.

"I used some of this a couple of years ago, but I stopped when I found some dead hawks and a dead owl. I figure they ate the dead prairie dogs and died from the same poison. Collateral damage they say."

"Does the poison work fast?"

"Damn straight. The rodents bleed to death after a couple of days."

"So what's the plan?" *Pop may actually have something here.*

"Let's load these bags on both trucks and work on fence today. When it gets dark we'll put out the poison."

"What about those protesters?"

"They'll think we're just fixing fence, dum-dum. We can work our way around the whole place that way."

Junior felt a stabbing pain deep in his gut. *You know, I'm a grown man, and I've let this old geezer call me dum-dum for years and I don't do anything about it. What the hell is the matter with me? I'm a gutless wonder.*

"I'll get my truck," he said. He walked back to the trailer, put Popeye and Minerva inside, got a couple of pints of tequila out of the cupboard and put them under the passenger's seat. He put his .22 rifle on the rack and backed the truck into the shop. They loaded the 12 bags of Kaput-D into the pick-up bed and covered them with the tarp. Then they loaded some wire, posts, the come-a-long, and other tools. When they were ready to go, Pop said, "I'll meet you back here in an hour. I'm hungry, and I think Mom made breakfast."

Junior watched Pop walk to the house. Pop limped toward his left, and Junior watched Pop's foot flop a little as he took each step, an injury from more than 50 years ago, when Pop's father had run over his foot with a track loader. Junior remembered the story: Pop, or Little Roy, was to carry his father's lunch to him on a road-building job. His mother had handed him a red lunchbox filled with baloney sandwiches, biscuits, a huge piece of chocolate cake, and a fresh thermos of coffee.

Twelve-year-old Little Roy jumped out of the car and ran up to the track loader, waving to his dad. Apparently, from high up in the cab, his dad didn't see him and didn't slow down. He ran over Little Roy's foot and just kept on going. Little Roy watched his dad driving away as he passed out from the pain. His mom ran from the car screaming for his dad to stop. By the time his dad noticed, Little Roy's mom was dragging him to the car. He woke up in the hospital with his foot elevated and in a cast. All his toes were gone, but when his foot healed, he learned to walk on it again. The foot hampered him in his work and hurt all the time. Pop never told anyone, but he felt ashamed as many of his friends became marines and fought in Viet Nam. He tried to volunteer as a mechanic at Kirtland Air Force Base, but he wasn't certified. His brusque nature was often an attempt to cover up the feeling that he was not equal to other men.

Junior gritted his teeth, pushing away any momentary sympathy he had for his father. *I hope that foot hurts him a lot. He's been putting me down for years, and he deserves some pain.* Junior grabbed a pint from under the seat and took a swig, and then decided to change the oil on the backhoe. As he searched for the keys, he heard someone come in and turned around.

"Hey, what's happening?" Ida asked. "Has anybody heard anything?"

"No, nothing." He stood still as the light from the door framed Ida from behind and made her radiant. Even after all these years of being in the same family, he shook his head at her beauty. *Astounding.* She tied her dusty blond hair in a ponytail, and she had only a hint of make up on her face. Her blue-green eyes seemed innocent yet filled with promise, and her smile often reminded him of Mom's. Although it was the end of January, she wore a tight tee shirt with spaghetti straps. Her pink bra straps pulled at her shoulders and raised her breasts almost too high. She smelled fresh, a smell that reminded him of the forest and made him feel proud of her beauty, a feeling that quickly changed to annoyance when he saw other men watching her. *Why the hell does she wear that shirt?*

"Are we doing anything about it? Has Jeff heard anything from the lawyer?"

Junior walked to the bed of his truck and pulled back the tarp.

"Pop's got a plan. We're going to poison those critters."

Ida read one of the bright yellow labels of Kaput-D. She skimmed the warnings. "This is nasty stuff. You have to be careful. Don't get any on your skin, and whatever you do, don't breathe it."

"What does it do?"

"It prevents blood clotting. The prairie dogs bleed to death internally. It takes a couple of days, and you only need a little."

Junior took a long pull from his pint of tequila, and gritted his teeth.

"Jeez, are you drinking in the mornings now?" Ida asked.

"Lay off. Pop has been on my case. He's mean."

"Be sure to wear heavy rubber gloves. The label says to put the bait down in the active holes at least six inches."

"Can't we just spread it around?"

"They want the prairie dogs to die down in their burrows so birds and other animals don't eat them. It says to bury dead prairie dogs at least 18 inches."

"Sounds like vile stuff. Just what the doctor ordered."

"Please be careful."

Junior felt calm listening to Ida share information about his safety. *You can always depend on Ida to know about medical stuff.*

"Is that builder on Eubank having a big open house or something?" Ida asked. "There are all kinds of people down the road. Some of them are even camped out."

"They're protesters. Can you believe it? They're protesting us. They want Mom and Pop to give the land to some kind of trust and preserve those fucking prairie dogs."

"No way." Ida shook her head. "We need that money. I have a half shift this morning, but I'll be back before dark. I'll talk with Mom about the protesters. Maybe she can call our lawyer. I'll see you then."

Ida drove away as Pop came back to the shop.

"What did Ida say?" he asked.

"She said to be careful with the poison. Apparently it works on humans, too."

Pop shrugged as if he already knew, or didn't care. "Come on, dum-dum, let's get busy."

Pop and Junior worked on the fence all day. They took a long break for lunch, and Pop napped for a couple of hours. Later they drove Pop's truck back to Junior's truck and fussed with a couple more fence posts until it started to get dark.

"What the hell is Ida doing here?" Pop asked. He watched his daughter drive her car slowly down the fencerow. She stopped by Junior's truck and motioned to them to come over.

"I want you to put this stuff on," she said. She handed them new tan Carhart long-sleeved shirts, heavy rubber gloves, and surgical masks.

"I brought home a vial of Vitamin K-1. It's the antidote for Kaput-D. We need dead prairie dogs, not dead people, so you guys be careful."

"Wow, thanks," Junior said.

"You sure we need this stuff?" Pop asked.

"I'm sure. Don't argue with me, just do it."

Pop and Junior put on the shirts, and tossed the gloves and masks into the back for later.

Ida smiled, got back in her car, and drove back down the fencerow, past the house, and out onto the road. She waved and smiled at Donald Pressman and the rest of the protesters as she went by.

As the dusk and shadows swept over the prairie dog mounds, Pop and Junior drove Pop's truck back to the shop. They made coffee, waited for an hour in the silence and their new shirts, and then made their way across the field to Junior's truck. They put on their rubber gloves, opened a bag of Kaput-D, pulled their masks over their faces, and started working. They each had a bucket of poison and a coffee can filled with lime. They spoke in whispers, and Junior worked to the left of the truck while Pop stayed on the right. They sprinkled Kaput-D deep into each hole, marked the hole with a splash of lime powder, and then moved on to the next one. Junior leaned against a fencepost every so often to have a drink from the pint in his back pocket. After an hour, they sat quietly behind the truck and checked their work. They had spread a full bag of Kaput-D into holes on the perimeter.

"I think we're using too much poison," Junior whispered.

"Hell no, the more the better," Pop said.

"The label said..."

"I don't care about the label. I want these rodents dead. If we put plenty into these old burrows on the outside, we'll surround the active holes and keep them from escaping."

They filled their buckets and went to work again. Junior heard a truck engine, and then two. He saw two sets of lights pull up to the north of his truck, and a couple of spotlights began sweeping the field. Six floodlights suddenly came on from a light bar on top of one of the trucks. Junior laid down by a prairie dog hole and told Pop to get down. *Assholes. It's those protesters.*

"What the hell is going on?" Junior asked. "Did those sonsabitches see us?"

"I think so," Pop said. "Let's go back to the shop for now. We can come back tomorrow night." He began walking quickly out of the path of the spotlights.

"I'll be along in a minute." He crawled back to the truck, reached into the cab for his rifle, and then lay down behind a prairie dog hole. He took off his gloves and mask, had a quick drink, and adjusted his scope. *This'll be easy, like sitting ducks.* One at a time, he shot out the spotlights and then the six floodlights on the light bar. It took less than 15 seconds. Pop stopped when he heard the shots and the yelling began.

"Someone's shooting at us! Get away! Move!"

Both trucks drove away quickly. Junior walked back to the shop and caught up with Pop just as the red lights of two police cars shone across the road. Both the sheriff's car and a back-up highway patrol car stopped by Junior's truck. The officers climbed the fence, looked in the cab, checked out the back, shone flashlights around, and then drove around the property and up to the locked gate. The sheriff got out, and stood by his car. Over the crackly bullhorn, he issued a command: "Roy Corley, come and unlock this gate. Roy Corley, get down here now or we'll cut the lock."

Pop drove his truck to the gate, unlocked it, and all three cars drove to the shop. The red lights were still flashing as the sheriff ordered Junior to give him the .22 and lie down in front of the car. He cuffed him, rolled him over, and took the pint out of his pocket and tossed it aside.

"I told you not to discharge that firearm in the city limits," the sheriff said. "Now you've done it. We've got you for assault with a deadly weapon. Don't you know that's a felony? You're toast, *and* you're stupid."

"Fuck you. I didn't assault anyone," he slurred. "I just shot out some freakin' lights. They were messing with us."

"Are you drunk? We can add 'drunk and disorderly' if you want. You're going to jail, son."

That morning Pop had checked his horoscope. It warned that he might not be getting the full picture. There could be turbulent times ahead that would require his full attention. In addition, starting a new path would be a good use of his energy. He turned away from Junior, and looked toward the mountains. *What kind of son have I raised?*

"Look, sheriff," Pop said, "we've been under a lot of pressure. There are so many people around. You know he didn't mean anything."

"What were you doing out there?" the sheriff asked. "You were putting out that poison, right?"

"I have a right to poison those rodents on my own property."

"Maybe so, but Junior does not have the right to shoot at people and scare the hell out of them. He is drunk, and he could have killed someone. You know that, Roy. I'm going to have to take him in." The sheriff helped Junior up, and then he put him in the back seat of his patrol car and closed the door.

"I'm taking him to the County Detention Center. You can come down there after awhile and see about him, but I recommend you leave him in the drunk tank to cool off for the night. I'm confiscating his rife."

Mom walked up from behind some trees.

"What's all the commotion out here?"

"Junior's going to jail. He's drunk and he shot at the protesters."

"Is anyone hurt? Is Junior okay?"

"Everyone's okay. He just shot out some spotlights," Pop said.

"Mrs. Corley, you can come to the county lockup later and check on Junior. My advice is to leave him for the night. He's in real trouble." The sheriff and the highway patrolman turned off their red lights and headed down the driveway.

"This whole thing is getting out of control," Mom said, her voice shaking.

"Junior is no help," Pop said. "I asked him to help with poisoning and he ends up making everything worse. Why can't that boy learn?"

"He tries. I think alcohol keeps him from thinking straight. Deep down, he's really a good man."

"He's good at screwing up, and that's about all."

"You say he takes better care of the equipment than anyone else. He's good to his animals."

"Face it, we've raised a drunk, pure and simple. He was born that way."

"He wasn't born that way. He was born just like everyone else, sweet and innocent. He's troubled, and he needs our understanding and our support. He can work his way through this. Why are you always so negative about him?'

Increased sensitivity. Lots of stress. Horoscopes don't lie.

"He needs serious help. He needs to straighten up, and you need to quit making his life easy."

"I pray for him every day, and I know God is with him. It's just a matter of time."

"You can pray for him all you want, but he's got to decide to take better care of himself or something's going to come along and whack him good. You just can't keep tempting fate."

"If you would pray for him and stop putting him down, maybe he would have a chance."

Pop took a deep breath. "I know we're under a lot of stress. Please don't take this wrong. I care about Junior, but I'm fed up with his drinking."

"I know. So am I, but I'm not giving up on him and you shouldn't either."

After a sleepless night, Mom and Pop appeared at the County Detention Center and posted a $5,000 bail for Junior's release and a $1,600 check for repair of the trucks. The county prosecutor reduced the charges to "drunk and disorderly," "discharging a firearm in the city limits," and "willful destruction of property." According to the sheriff, Donald had come in a few moments earlier and told the magistrate judge they'd go along with the lesser charges if the Corleys would pay for the damage to the trucks.

"We don't have any animosity," Donald told Mom and Pop. "We just want things restored to how they were, and we want you to think about a land trust."

Pop felt small and embarrassed. He was worried Junior would smart off again. Mom squeezed Pop's hand.

"Thank you," Mom said. "We're aware this could be much worse for Junior. We will give your idea some consideration."

"We wish you no harm," Donald continued. "We all breathe the same air on this planet."

"Thank you for your kindness," Mom said. "We'll have a chance to talk again."

Pop chewed his lip. Junior wore that familiar pissed-off smirk on his face.

This guy Pressman is a fruitcake. Talk again—my ass.

Sunday morning was quiet at the Corley place. Mom was at church. Pop was in his shop, drinking coffee and leafing through travel magazines, and Junior was still asleep. The protesters had thinned out some, although a small group gathered at the main tent, singing quietly to the sound of a lone guitar.

Ida flashed her legs getting out of the car and walked straight toward Donald, feeling confident about her mission. Mom had filled her in on all the details of Junior's arrest, and Ida had decided it was time for her to do something before Junior and Pop made things worse. She knew her father and the stubborn darkness that could gather in his soul. Donald was a man, an attractive man. She smiled and tipped her head slightly, a move that made her blond hair shimmer in the sunlight.

"Hello, I'm Ida Corley." She put out her hand. "You must be Donald Pressman. I understand you're the leader here."

Donald took her hand with both of his hands and grinned. "Yes, I'm here on behalf of the Forest Guardians. It's great to meet you." He looked Ida up and down slowly.

Ida felt his fascination and straightened up just a little, so her breasts would rise against her green cashmere sweater. "Can we go somewhere and talk? I'll take you to lunch at The Garden."

"Sure," he said. "Let me get my jacket." Donald reached inside the tent and took his blue blazer off a wooden hanger. He put it on, arranged his collar, and smoothed his hair. "We can take my car."

It was just before noon, so they found a table easily ahead of the church crowd, and they both ordered chef salad.

"At least we have food in common," Ida said. "I wonder what else we both like?"

Donald smiled. His green eyes deepened from the light on Ida's sweater. "I suspect there are many things we both like. I understand you are a nurse, so I gather that life is important to you, as is healing. Right?"

"Yes, of course."

"Forest Guardians wants to heal the earth—to heal Mother Nature," he said. "Just like you, we took an oath to do no harm. We all breathe the same air on this planet, and every unnecessary death diminishes life itself. Don't you agree?"

"I agree, sort of. Sometimes death is a good thing, like when pain and suffering are too much. Sometimes people's rights are important, too. People have a right to eat, and we butcher animals every day." She motioned with her fork to the sliced ham on Donald's salad. "And we eat farm eggs before they are hatched," she said, waving a bite of hard-boiled egg at him. "People do have rights." She raised her eyebrows and smiled.

"People do have rights. The ham and the eggs come from farms, crops raised by hard-working people who bring food to our tables, a matter entirely different from killing endangered species. The Forest Guardians believe you shouldn't be able to kill prairie dogs so that you can have money. That's not right. There are other solutions." He reached over the table and touched her arm. "I told your dad and mom about a land trust that preserves everyone's rights, prairie dogs included. If you give the land to the land trust, then you can have a tax loss every year for the next five years. That offsets any income your mom and dad may have."

"We need the money," Ida said. "Mom and Pop don't have any income to speak of, except for the business, and they want to retire. He has worked all his life on our property. Pop won't be able to work much longer, and he's dreamed of this time for years. He has a right to sell it, and there are plenty of people who want to buy it. Why would we give it away?"

"You would give it to a land trust because you care about life and the sanctity of Mother Earth and all of her relationships."

"I care about the earth and I care about life and I care about *my* life," Ida said. "Mom and Pop want to sell the land now and share the money in the family so we'll all have a better life now. Can't we figure out some way to get along? This protesting doesn't help anyone." Ida wiped her lips with her napkin and smiled.

"You seem like a delightful woman," he said. But if you are coming on to me, you've got the wrong idea. Forest Guardians is my passion. I left a teaching job at UC Berkeley for the life I have now. Please understand. I'm dedicated, and for me, preservation of endangered species is a noble calling."

"Coming on to you?" Ida laughed. "You've got to be kidding. I have a steady boyfriend. I just thought we could get together again and talk some more." She paused. "Why did you join Forest Guardians?"

"Do you really want to know?"

"Sure. That's a big change."

"The short version? I was hiking with a friend in up near Lake Tahoe two years ago in May, and we came across a little fawn that had been shot in the gut with an arrow. He had chewed at the wound, and looked like he had been bleeding for a couple of days. He was lying on his side in some rocks in the sun and struggling to get up when we came upon him. I knew what I had to do."

"Put him out of his misery?"

"Right. His eyes were bright until I smashed his head with a rock. I watched the light in his eyes fade and something inside of me snapped. I realized I was living the wrong life. My life wasn't mine. I still dream about that fawn. We've got to find a way to heal the earth. Life is too precious."

"I admire men like you," Ida said. "It takes a lot of courage to commit yourself to something." They both got up, Ida paid the bill, and they went to his car.

Donald dropped her back at her car. Ida waved as she drove away. *It's a start. There will be more to come.*

Early Monday morning, a pickup truck with Bernalillo County decals parked at the gate and sounded its horn. A man got out, waited, and then sounded the horn again. Pop drove his truck down to the gate and got out.

"What's going on?" he asked.

The man answered his question with a question. "Are you Roy Corley?"

"You're looking at him."

"My name is George Farmer and I'm an extension agent with the county." He handed Pop his card over the gate. "Some folks found a couple of dead prairie dogs by the road, and there's been a report you're using prairie dog poison. Is there any truth in that?"

"Might be," Pop said.

"Mr. Corley, I need to see the poison. I have a court order." He handed Pop a document.

"It's up at the shop." Pop opened the gate and they drove their trucks to the shop. Pop had unloaded the Kaput-D from Junior's truck and had it neatly stacked on a pallet.

Farmer read one of the labels. "I'm sorry but you are using prairie dog poison that has been outlawed in New Mexico. It's only acceptable in some counties in Colorado, and it is for the black-tailed prairie dog, not the Gunnison. I'm going to have to confiscate this poison and have it destroyed. There have been too many secondary killings for it to be allowed."

"Can you do that? Just take it away? I paid good money for that Kaput-D. I bought it at the feed store in Bernalillo."

"You might have bought it a couple of years ago, but it was outlawed in December 2000, and you're not even allowed to possess it, let alone use it." George started loading the bags into his truck. He waited between bags, as if he was hoping Pop would help. Pop sat down by his bench and looked through a parts catalogue.

"That's it, Mr. Corley. Are there anymore bags anywhere?"

"Nope. That's all there is."

"Okay, I need to remind you to read that court order. It enjoins you against having Kaput-D on your property. Do you understand? If you're caught with any at all, it's a $10,000 fine and up to ninety days in jail." He waved his hand toward the protester's tents. "Those folks out there are looking for a reason to file charges."

Farmer drove down the driveway and Pop followed him to lock the gate. As Pop returned to his shop, Junior wandered up from his trailer.

"Who was that?" Junior asked.

"Why aren't you at work?" Pop asked.

"I called in sick. I've got a bad stomachache. Who was that?"

"That was the County Extension Agent. He had a court order to take all the Kaput-D. Seems it's now illegal in New Mexico."

"Well, sonofabitch. Now what are we going to do?"

"*You* are not going to do anything, dum-dum. We don't need things to get worse. I want you to leave this thing alone. Do you understand?"

"Yeah, I understand we're going to let some chicken-shit protesters tell us what we can do. Has that guy Pressman got you buffaloed?"

"No, but Jeff has an idea about the City Council and our attorney thinks it might work. They've worked out a plan with Mom to petition the City to stall on their prairie dog ordinance until next near. That would give Whitman and his bank time to buy the land and get started on their development."

"Could they kill the prairie dogs then?" Junior asked.

"Hell, I don't know. But Epstein said if we can sell the land, Whitman would have to figure out what to do with the prairie dogs."

"And who does this guy Pressman think he is anyway, God's gift to the earth?"

Farmer stopped his truck by the protester's tents, and Donald peered into the back of the truck and motioned to the other people. A rousing cheer filled the air as they saw the confiscated poison. Donald slapped Farmer on the back and shook his hand.

7

In the morning, Junior called in sick and then stayed home all day with what he figured was stomach flu. Mom brought over some soup and leftover stew from church. He drank a little soup, tasted the stew, and threw it down the garbage disposal. *Something about that church food tastes like crap.* Chewing Tums most of the day, along with regular nips on peach brandy, calmed his stomach. He drank himself to sleep in front of the TV and awoke early in a fetal position, clutching his stomach. *Damn, this flu is nasty.* After vomiting a few times, he was able to settle his stomach with a couple of glasses of milk laced with peach brandy. After about an hour, he finally felt normal again. He wanted desperately to get going on his plan, but he had to wait until the stores opened.

After whiling away the time by paging through a hunting magazine, Junior hopped in his truck with Popeye, drove to Ed's Sporting Goods on Menaul, and bought a new pellet gun. He chose the Winchester 1000xs with a 9x 32 scope. He'd just read that the rifle delivered a .177 caliber pellet at one-thousand feet per second at a range of three hundred feet.

"This one's the best for pest control," the sales clerk said. "It's quiet and accurate."

"Quiet. That's what I need. I've got hundreds to shoot, and I don't want any witnesses."

"Here's a couple extra boxes of pellets. You'll completely avoid the loud crack of the .22 rifle."

That evening, he set up where there was very little traffic and shielded himself from the road. He parked by the arroyo on the north side of the property, and he blocked the fence gate with his pickup truck so that no one could drive in. He assembled his wheelbarrow, tarp, a newly sharpened shovel, cooler of beer, a very bright flashlight, and then hid behind a large chamisa bush.

As the prairie dogs peeked out of their holes to begin their late-afternoon exploration, Junior shot at them. His upset stomach made him jumpy, and the prairie dogs seemed particularly agile. Their heads bobbed in and out of the holes in the waning light.

"Die, varmint!" he muttered as he fired. "Die, varmint!"

Darkness spread over the field, and Junior had missed every shot. All the beer was gone, so he finished the tequila and took one more shot at a gray head that had peered out of a hole. The creature squirmed and tried to get back in the hole. Junior grabbed his shovel, ran toward the writhing prairie dog, took a swing at it, missed, and fell down. He got up and chased the injured critter around the hole, whacking at it again. His shovel glanced off the dirt mound and hit Junior in the side of the leg.

"Oh, shit. You sonofabitch varmint!" he shouted.

The cut was deep and it gushed blood. Junior took off his shirt and tied it around the wound. He tried to stand up, but the shovel had sliced the tendon in his ankle, and his foot would not support him. His foggy brain was no help. He started crawling to the truck, dragging his injured leg behind him and vomiting beer and tequila. "Sonofabitch varmint."

Slowly, Junior made it to the truck, and pulled himself in behind the wheel. He took deep breaths and waved the shadows away, dark images of church scouts, tents, and campfires. He dropped his head on the steering wheel and passed out. And that was where Donald Pressman found him when he was making his nightly patrol around the Corley property.

Donald shined his flashlight into the truck, smelled the alcohol and vomit, and saw the floorboards covered with blood. Popeye was whining. Donald grabbed his cell phone and dialed 911.

"There's a man in a truck who looks dead," he told the dispatcher. "I think his name is Corley."

"Who are you and where are you located?" she asked.

"I'm Donald Pressman with Forest Guardians. I'm standing by a white Ford pickup on what I think is Guadalajara Street, just about a half-mile from a big Presbyterian church."

"Okay, I've got your location. Stay there."

The paramedics arrived and transported Junior to the University Hospital emergency room. He was alive, if just barely.

When Junior woke up, his foot was wrapped and elevated on a pillow. His mother stood over him. His leg hurt. There was an IV tube in each of his arms.

"You had a close call," Mom said quietly. "The doctor said you lost so much blood that you nearly died. You were lucky that fellow came along."

"What fellow?" asked Junior.

"That man Donald Pressman, the one with Forest Guardians. He said he would look in on you."

"I don't want to see anyone, especially that asshole. Tell the nurse," Junior said. "Where's Popeye?"

"He's at home in the trailer. I've been feeding him and Minerva."

"How long have I been here?"

"Two days," Mom said. "We've been very worried."

"Am I hurt bad?"

"You cut a tendon. The doctor said you'll heal, but it'll take a while."

"I remember I was killing those varmints. I hit myself with a shovel."

"It's not your job to kill the prairie dogs," Mom said. "Pop and I don't want you to get hurt. It's our problem."

"It's my problem, too."

"You've got to let this go and take care of yourself. You're sick. You need help."

"Five hundred thousand dollars is a lot of money. It'll change my life. I can finally get the hell out of here."

"You don't have to shoot them. There are other ways."

"Other ways?"

"Jeff and I are working with our attorney Epstein. He has an application before the City Council to postpone the new prairie dog ordinance."

"How would that help?"

"It would let our property sell before the law is passed."

"How long will it take?"

"Probably months."

"What does Pop think?"

"Pop is really impatient. He said he found a quick way, and he said to tell you he's taking care of things. He's stubborn, like you. I'm worried about both of you."

"Is he shooting those varmints?"

"He bought something called a Rodenator. It blows things up."

"Blows things up?"

"He got it for twenty-nine hundred dollars from a company in Idaho, had it FedXed yesterday. Pop said to tell you it's better than a rifle and you'd like it."

"Well, I'll be damned. Pop is taking action," Junior said. *If only he had done that five years ago, we wouldn't be in this mess.* His hands were shaking, and he felt like throwing up. He saw some strange shadows on the wall; they looked like spiders. Junior pushed his hands under his hips. He needed a drink.

The doctor came in, touched Junior's cast, looked in his eyes with his flashlight, and sat down next to the bed. "I need you to listen," he said slowly. "This is really important. Can you hear me?"

"Yes," Junior said. "What is it? Is my leg going to heal?" Mom walked over to the window, murmured a prayer, and sobbed softly.

"Your leg is your least worry. You have pancreatitis and you are approaching total liver failure. You lost a lot of blood. You almost died, and if you don't stop drinking, you will die soon."

"It's that bad?"

"Yes, it's that bad. You've had four units of blood, and I'm pumping you full of antibiotics. I'm hopeful you can get through this." He put his hand on Junior's chest. "Hear me. If you drink again as you have in the past, you will die. Your eyes are yellow. You are an alcoholic and you simply cannot drink."

Junior stared at the ceiling, watching little dots on the ceiling tile wiggle around. Tears flooded his eyes, and he began to shake. His leg hurt, his stomach was sour, and he felt like retching. If only he could catch a break once and a while, things would be different. "I don't want to die."

"I want you to sign yourself into the rehabilitation unit downstairs," the doctor said. "I've made the arrangements to transfer you, and they can treat your alcoholism along with your infections. You should plan on at least thirty days and maybe sixty."

"I can't miss work," Junior said. "I'll lose my job."

"I talked with your boss," Mom said over her shoulder. "He said he's been worried about you for some time and he'll keep your job open."

"Well, Pop needs me around the place, and someone has to take care of Popeye and Minerva," Junior said.

"We've got that covered too," Mom said.

The doctor shook his head and stood up. "This is probably your last chance. You won't live through another drunk." He handed Junior the clipboard with the self-admission forms ready to sign. "Here's a pen. You need to sign all the pages."

Junior looked at Mom. "What about the money? Who's going to pay for all this?"

"Our company insurance pays for up to sixty days of rehab for alcohol or drug addiction. The co-pay is twenty percent, but Pop says we're going to pay it. He says he doesn't want you around anymore if you're going to drink. He says if you don't get sober, you're fired, and you'll have to move out of the trailer. I've never seen him this way. He means it."

Junior's hand shook as he signed all the pages. The doctor picked up the phone, gave some orders, and within a few minutes, a nurse and a couple of attendants came in and began getting the bed ready to move.

"Are they moving me right now?" Junior asked.

"Yes, but don't worry, Junior. It's for your own good," said Mom.

The doctor felt Junior's pulse. "Your DTs are going to kick in soon so we need to get you moved out and medicated"

"I pray to God that you can stop drinking this time." Mom said. "Everyone needs you to stop. We can't stand it." Smiling, she put a paper bag on the foot of the bed. "I brought you fresh clothes." She turned abruptly and her elbow whacked his elevated ankle hard.

"Oww! Dammit, Mom, that really hurt!"

"Oh, I'm sorry," she said.

Junior saw her eyes squint, and her smile vanished just as quickly as it had appeared. She walked with Junior as they rolled his bed to the elevator and down to the second floor. It was a locked ward, dedicated to rehab. He looked around, heard the locks close, checked out his elevated foot, and threw up some blood into the pan resting on his stomach.

"Try to relax. Ida said she will be by to check on you."

"Godammit Mom," Junior shouted. "I told you I don't want to see anyone."

"Your sister is good support," Mom said. "She has a lot of faith in you, and she can watch your medications."

Mom used her handkerchief to wipe the tears from her eyes.

"I love you. I always will. I'll be praying for you." She turned and walked with the nurse toward the double doors.

"Who are you going to pray to? There's no one out there listening!"

Mom stopped, turned, "Someday you will come to know God."

Not likely. After all, the only way he knew anything about God came through those stupid Sunday school classes when he was a kid, that idiot woman teacher who made a big poster of God as a judge and embarrassed him when he couldn't remember Bible passages, and then there was Mom's constant harping about church and Pastor June's sermons.

Of course, he had to admit to himself that sometimes Mom's harping was accompanied by benefits. Mom did his laundry and often put casseroles, leftover food from the church, and chocolate chip cookies into his freezer. Sometimes she left a twenty-dollar bill on his dresser.

But except for that food and money, something had dealt him a bad hand. If there was a God, then God didn't care about him. He believed that God must not care because dark things came into his life—loneliness, despair, and bad luck, the stuff drinkers understand. *I'm a hard drinker, but not an alcoholic.* He couldn't focus his eyes. The tiny Winnie the Poohs on the nurse's shirt began to move around as she put a needle in his IV line. He saw himself as a little boy trembling in a scout uniform, and then Pooh Bear and Eeyore danced through the dark colors of his mind as he faded away for the night.

Mom stopped by Hobby Lobby on the way home. She leaned on her cart as she pushed it slowly down each aisle. She prayed under her breath and took her time picking out a new array of items. First, she got two tall yellow candles with dark blue Mexican pottery candleholders and a matching blue rippled-glass vase. She chose yellow and white paper daffodils and some light purple asters for the vase, heavy dark brown bookends that were replicas of stallions, and a brown walnut music box that played "How Great Thou Art" when the top was opened. Finally, she bought a cheerful brown-striped throw rug and a new stitched wall hanging that said "Welcome to this Home." In her mind, she had already added these new touches to Junior's trailer for when he returned from rehabilitation. When she got home, she put all the stuff in a brown paper bag, marked it "Junior's homecoming," and put it on the shelf in the garage with her other projects. These paper sacks full of decorations always gave her hope for how she might arrange the future.

8

Pop opened the box with a utility knife from the bench. His eyes lit up as he read the label: "Rodenator—Revolutionary Burrowing Rodent Exterminator." He'd found this device by searching through a new machinery magazine, *Earthmoving*, and had ordered one on the spot. *There's nothing like a new piece of equipment to tickle the soul of a working man.* He grinned as he paged through the instructions and figured he had this problem solved. No poison, no guns, and the book said the Rodenator was humane and legal in all states. He'd told Mom he was putting it on the company credit card and he didn't want any complaints. Assembly was easy. It was nothing more than an aluminum pipe with a curved nozzle on one end with a piezoelectric spark device, a hose that connected to a regular barbecue propane bottle, a carrying handle and a rack for the bottle, and a trigger with a guard. Pop admired the careful welding as he assembled the pieces.

The instructions said that propane is heavier than air, so the idea is to fill a prairie dog hole with propane, wait for it to settle into the tunnels, and then hit it with a spark that makes the explosion. The operator was encouraged to wear eye protection and turn to the side when he triggers the spark. *Wow, I wish I'd thought of it. This is one of those inventions whose time has come.*

Pop drove his truck to the Giant station, bought a couple of new propane bottles, and stopped at McDonald's for a couple of quarter-pounders with cheese and pickles. Mom thoroughly disapproved of fast food, but the hell with her: He needed energy for the task ahead. Pop picked up a newspaper and paged through until he found the horoscopes. *Can't be too careful.*

Capricorn said it was a good time to yield to the wisdom of your mate and to listen carefully to their guidance and judgment. It is not a good day to make waves in your relationship. So much for Mom. The Cancer horoscope suggested that today highlighted bold action and that all Cancers should stand ready to be surprised. *Yup, I'm on the right track.*

He finished a second order of fries, and tossed down the last of his chocolate shake. With any luck, he should be able to cover two acres a day and be finished in a long week. He didn't mind the work, and he hadn't felt productive for quite a while. *A man is worthless if he's not productive.* He just couldn't seem to get that fact through Junior's thick skull.

Mom ate lunch in the hospital cafeteria with Ida, and then settled into the hospital chapel for a couple of hours of Bible reading and prayer. As she drove up to the gate at home, she passed protesters carrying signs. She unlocked the gate, drove in, stopped in the house, and went out the back door toward the machine shed. She could see puffs of dirt and hear explosions from out in the field. Then she spotted Pop. He was sticking something into the ground, and after a few minutes passed, she heard a loud report and saw dirt fly.

"Take that, you little sonsabitches," Pop said. "This is my property, and it's time for you to die."

Boom. Boom. Boom.

Pop moved with a spring in his step, and the Rodenator made quite a racket. Soon, neighbors came out of their houses and wandered up to watch. Then more people seemed to come out of nowhere. They had been walking the property line on the Eubank side with their signs: "SAVE THE PRAIRIE DOGS," "PRAIRIE DOGS ARE ENDANGERED," "PRAIRIE DOGS HAVE RIGHTS." Donald Pressman had organized a dozen or so volunteers to walk the property lines in the daylight hours and to bring steady attention to the plight of the prairie dogs.

Several protestors shouted at Pop. "Stop the murders! Stop killing! Stop the murders! Stop killing!"

One protestor set up a telephoto camera on a tripod and started filming.

"Take that varmints! You are trespassers!" shouted Pop, unfazed by the indignant onlookers. Boom. Boom. Boom. He jumped over the holes and moved ahead as he waved off the protestor with the camera.

The sun was purple through the gray clouds to the west, and as it went down, the explosions made a yellow and bluish light as the dirt sprayed up from the blast of exploding propane. A gentle breeze pushed an acrid burning smell over the land. Mom stood by the house with her hands on her hips. Pop had covered about a hundred yards of perimeter. Mom shook her head as the news truck from KOB-TV drove up. The crew parked on Eubank, set up their antenna, climbed the fence, and came toward Pop. A woman in a suit, a cameraman, and a man carrying lights stopped in front of him.

"Oh no. "We're in for it now," Mom whispered. She moved close enough to hear.

"What are you doing?" asked the woman, whom Mom recognized as Karen Thomas—she was on TV nearly every night. The lights came on. The camera was running. Karen held a microphone toward Pop. He put his hand in front of his eyes as the lights blinded him. "I am exterminating a menace to my property," Pop said.

"Exterminating?"

"Yes, indeed. Exterminating."

"Is that legal?" she asked.

"Yup. I'm using my Rodenator. Guaranteed for two years. It's humane. The prairie dogs don't even know what hit them. They're dead from the concussion before they hear the noise. Legal and humane. Now, get the hell off my property."

"Your name is Corley, right?" she asked.

"Roy Corley, and this is my place. Now leave."

"You can't just walk all over this place and kill animals. You need a permit or something."

"Leave." He lunged at the cameraman with the Rodenator.

The woman and her camera crew hurried to their news truck and began to interview the protestors. Mom approached and held Pop's hand. Donald Pressman offered to be a spokesperson, and he talked about the new City of Albuquerque ordinance. He pointed out that the prairie dogs are an endangered species, and said they have a moral right to exist in the world of mammals.

"They're part of God's creation," he told her. "Almost ninety-eight percent of all the Gunnison and black-tailed prairie dogs have been killed by exterminators, hunters, and from loss of habitat from encroaching development. Their death upsets the balance of nature and all the other animals that interact with them—burrowing owls, black ferrets, coyotes, and birds."

"What can be done?" she asked.

"Well, the first thing is to stop killing them."

Mom pulled Pop along as they walked back to the house.

"I stopped by the hospital."

"Good. Is his leg going to be okay?"

"The tendon is cut. The doctor said it will take six weeks or so to heal. They have his leg wrapped up, to keep it still."

"I guess he lost a lot of blood. I should have gone with you."

"He had transfusions, and that part is okay now." Mom stopped by the porch, turned to Pop, and began weeping.

"Junior's really sick. The doctor said he has pancreatitis, and if he drinks again, he'll die."

"I didn't know he was that bad. Did you tell him what I said?"

"Yes. I told him you said he'd lose his job here and he'd have to move out of the trailer if he came home drunk. I think that helped him make the decision, but it broke my heart to tell him. He was really upset with you."

"Make what decision?"

"To go into alcohol rehabilitation. He signed himself in."

"I've done my best with that boy, but he keeps screwing up. Do you think he's going to be okay?"

"Ida says he's getting heavy antibiotics for his infection, and they'll keep him tranquilized for several days to get him through the worst part of drying out. She's checking on him a couple of times a day. The rehab doctor suggested we stay away for at least a week. Come on. Let's go in and eat something. It will do you good."

"Sure," he said.

Later, when they watched the ten o'clock news, they were shocked to see the final version of the story. KOB-TV had edited the piece so that Pop appeared to be a monster. Karen Thomas' producer had headlined the story "The Exterminator," and the segment replayed Pop's remark that the

Rodenator was humane just as an explosion blew dirt everywhere.

"It isn't fair," Mom said. They made you look like a murderer."

"They twisted everything. It's my property, and they can go to hell. You bet I'm an exterminator. Nothing wrong with that."

"I'm sorry for everything. This is a mess and we need to pray about it. Everyone at church will be talking."

"Look," Pop said, "fate has dealt us a tough hand today, but we have the law on our side. This is private property. We have rights, and I intend to stand up for them. You go ahead and pray if you want. Tell your so-called friends at church that gossip is a sin. See what they say about that."

The next morning, a city police car parked by the gate and sounded a siren. Two officers stood by the gate as Roy drove up and got out of his truck.

"Are you Roy Corley?" one asked.

"Yup. You're looking at him."

"We are here to serve you with a restraining order issued by a municipal judge that says you have to stop killing prairie dogs until there is a hearing." He handed Pop the paperwork. "Furthermore, if you are found killing any more prairie dogs, you'll be arrested for violation of the restraining order. Violation carries a penalty of up to sixty days in jail. You should appear in three weeks, with your attorney, at the address shown on the order for the hearing. Do you understand?"

"Don't you guys have better things to do, like arrest criminals?"

"We need to know if you understand the restraining order. Stay away from those prairie dogs. Do you understand?"

"Aye, aye." Pop saluted them and snapped his heels together. The officers drove off down the road as the protestors waved their signs and cheered. Pop drove back to the house and Mom came to the door. She took the paperwork and read it.

"They got a judge to issue an injunction against killing them until the hearing. If they succeed in proving their case, we can never kill these prairie dogs," Mom said with a sigh. "Well, that's it. Now we've got to find another path. This time, we're going to do it *my* way. Jeff and I have a meeting with Robert Epstein and a city councilor tomorrow, and you're welcome to come along if you'd like."

Pop raised his eyes to the Sandia Mountains, then turned around as

Donald Pressman waved at him. He turned to Mom, gritting his teeth, and whispered, "Let's keep an eye out for what's next. This guy Pressman has just begun. I've got a bad feeling about him. I don't trust Hollywood-guys like him."

Donald turned back to his crowd of followers and shouted, "Well, that ought to stop things for now. We can use the courts for a while, but we need to get ready for a long fight."

The next day, Pop drove Mom downtown to meet Jeff, Epstein, and Fernando Vigil, the Councilor for their district. Epstein had learned that Vigil was originally from a rural background in the South Valley, and was sympathetic to property rights. Rumors suggested he was at one time involved in cockfighting, but no one had ever proved it. Vigil's assistant ushered the four of them into a conference room. There was a bottle of water on the table for each of them. Pop opened his and took a sip. *Water in a bottle. Now who would have ever thought you could sell water in a bottle.*

"Thank you for seeing us," said Epstein. "Like you, we're advocates of property rights. Can you help us with the new prairie dog ordinance? The bank is afraid to loan money to the buyer."

Fernando Vigil glanced over at Roy with a twinkle in his eye.

"Are you 'The Exterminator,' the guy on TV last night?"

"That's me. I was trying to get rid of some rodents and they made me out to be a monster."

"As we say in politics, you lost that round. The media can ruin your life if you let them."

"We thought perhaps you could postpone the third reading for a while to study the issue further," Epstein continued. "We think this scenario is similar to water rights. The Corleys have had beneficial use of those fifteen acres for more than fifty years. So, it's not right that prairie dogs would suddenly acquire those rights. We think it was human habitat way before it was prairie dog habitat."

"That's an interesting argument," Vigil said.

"I think we could liken it to illegal immigration," Epstein added. "The Corleys were there first, enjoying the property rights Americans enjoy, and just because they wanted to, prairie dogs moved in. Maybe we shouldn't have the right to kill them, but we certainly have the right to move them away, like squatters."

Vigil inhaled sharply. "I understand the right to move them away, but I wouldn't push the illegal immigration issue. Where are you from?

"I worked for many years in San Diego."

"No surprise you have strong feelings about illegals, but around here many families have so-called illegal immigrants in their heritage. I think my grandfather was one."

"Sorry," Epstein said, ducking his head a bit. "I'll drop that line of argument, but we still think a man has the right to move squatters and trespassers off his property."

Vigil turned to Pop and grinned. "What do you think, Exterminator?"

"If we can't kill them, then I guess we ought to be able to move them."

"I remember something about a prairie dog ordinance in Santa Fe and developers moving them somewhere else," Jeff said.

"We looked at that," Vigil said. "The Santa Fe Ordinance that was passed in November, 2001, and it was based on the Boulder, Colorado Ordinance that was passed in 1999."

"They both allowed for relocation, didn't they?" Epstein asked.

"Yes. The relocation language in the proposed Albuquerque ordinance is the same."

"Yes sir. I was pleased to see the paragraph on removing any cloud on the title after relocation. That seems like an improvement."

"We borrow where we can, and we add as we need to."

"I was wondering about something," Jeff said. "The ordinance doesn't say anything about how we capture them or where we move them to. Are we free to use our own judgment?"

"Are you a Corley too?" Vigil asked.

"Yes sir, I'm Jeff Corley, the Exterminator's number-one son. I have a dental practice out on Montgomery." He smiled at Vigil.

"Do you make crowns?" Vigil asked.

"Yes, I make crowns and do restorative and cosmetic dentistry. Mom, smile real big and show Councilor Vigil your crowns."

Mom smiled at Vigil and blushed.

"That's a beautiful smile. Do you have any openings for new patients? I've got a couple of bad teeth and I've been looking for a good dentist for both me and my wife."

"Sure," Jeff said. "I'd be happy to help you."

"Are you expensive?" Vigil asked.

Epstein frowned at Jeff.

"I'm more reasonable than you might think. Bring your wife by the office and I can give you an estimate right away."

Vigil turned to Epstein. "Your argument about property rights and who occupied the habitat first is a good one. I like the idea of giving property owners the option of moving endangered critters to a more suitable location. The ordinance should also set standards for relocator companies and under what conditions." He turned to his assistant.

"Write up a short resolution asking for more study time on this ordinance. Let's give property owners the right to move these prairie dogs before the third reading comes back. I'll bet other councilors will support that."

"Yes sir, I think they will, although the news broadcast did not help."

"Mr. Exterminator," Vigil said, "I suggest that you do not attend the hearing. Mrs. Corley, I think you and Dr. Corley should be there. Be prepared to agree to move those prairie dogs and we'll see how the vote goes. Find a relocator who has some kind of track record. Restricting property rights is not a popular political position to take, so you should focus on that. And let me repeat, not a word about illegal immigration."

"Yes sir, and thank you for your help. We will see you at the next meeting."

Epstein and the Corleys gathered in the lobby.

"Well, I think we've got a shot," Epstein said. "You need to be careful about money and dental work, Jeff."

"I can figure on a new-patient discount."

"I'll start doing some research on moving prairie dogs," Mom said. "Jeff, could you get me copies of the Boulder ordinance? I'll bet there are folks with experience I could talk to."

Pop drove Mom home in silence. She looked straight ahead with her jaw set. Pop frowned and picked at his thumbnail.

9

On the way to work, Jeff stopped by the house and grabbed the message Mom left on the table. He called the number, and the phone rang eight times before a sleepy voice answered.

"This is Eddie with Prairie Dog Relocators."

"My name is Jeff Corley. I'm a cosmetic dentist here in Albuquerque, and we want to see about moving a large number of prairie dogs off my family property. Do you work in New Mexico?"

"Yes, but it will cost you more. I'll need gas money and money for a motel."

"How much do you charge for an estimate?"

"Well, I could come down this weekend. Let's say three-hundred for gas and a motel."

Jeff and Eddie made an arrangement. Jeff got an advance on his Visa card, and sent a money order by Western Union.

On Saturday after lunch, Jeff and Mom were having coffee when they saw a strange truck stop at the gate. To Jeff's eye, it looked almost exactly like a septic pumping truck.

"I think that's him," Jeff said, as he and Mom rose to walk toward the gate. The tank on the truck was bright purple and freshly painted. The tank was emblazoned with a picture of a prairie dog on its hind legs, along with the slogan: "Prairie Dog Relocators—Gentle and Humane." A tall scruffy man with a missing front tooth and a big smile got out of the truck.

"I'm Eddie. Pleased to meet you." He looked out over the field and smiled even wider. All Jeff could see was chamisa, clumps of grass, and prairie dog mounds, but Eddie's lips moved as though he was counting.

Jeff opened the gate and they headed toward the house.

"Wow, there's one helluva lot of prairie dogs here," he said. "Pardon my language, one helluva lot. I'd say roughly about fifteen hundred to two thousand." He took off his hat, smoothed his long hair back, and put his hat back on.

"Can you move them to a more suitable home?" Mom asked. "These prairie dogs have become a real problem."

"I'll bet they have. It's hard to tell whose land this is, yours or theirs. Normally I get twenty dollars each, but for this many, I could go down to ten dollars each."

"My gosh, that could be twenty thousand dollars," Mom said.

"I have expenses, and I have to find a place to put them, and that's not easy. There's not much rangeland left where people will allow them. I usually have to pay the people who take them."

"Are you careful with them?" Mom asked.

"Yes. Gentle and humane. That's me. The inside of the tank is padded with foam rubber two inches thick. I'll tell you what. I could set up and catch a few and you could watch."

"Could you walk around and check things out? We need to talk privately," Jeff said.

"Sure. I'll come back to the house in a little while."

Jeff and Mom went into the house, out of the bright sun, and called Epstein.

"We found a prairie dog relocator," Jeff said. "He seems legitimate—just a little strange."

"Is he licensed?"

"Not in New Mexico. He says he doesn't need a license here. He's got a truck with a capture tank, and he claims he's gentle and humane."

"Well, it'll look good with the City Council if we're proactive," Epstein said. "It can't hurt Fernando Vigil's resolution if we do something."

"I think we should try him out," Mom said toward the phone.

"I heard that, and I agree. Can he move some of them, to show our intent?"

"That's a good idea," Jeff said. "We'll let you know how it goes."

"Don't move too many. I haven't finished my research, and there might be some problem."

"We'll move enough to look good."

Pop walked into the house. "What's going on?"

"We're going to give this relocation guy a try," Mom said. "Now just let this be. We know what we're doing."

Pop nodded his head just as Eddie appeared at the door. Pop's mouth dropped open just a little.

"Well, what do you guys think?" Eddie asked.

Jeff stepped in front of Pop. "We would like to try moving a hundred prairie dogs now to see how it goes. We have a City Council meeting next week, and after that we hope to move them all."

Pop moved close to Eddie.

"How the hell do you do this, anyway? That's just an old septic tank pumper truck."

"It's not just any old truck. I'll set up and show you, but I can't give you the ten-dollar rate for just a hundred prairie dogs. I have expenses. I'll need twenty dollars each."

"Those rodents aren't even worth a penny each. Back when I was a kid, ranchers would pay us ten cents each to shoot those varmints."

"How about fifteen dollars each, cash, right when you're done," Jeff said.

"Okay, but I'm the one who gets to move the rest of them after your meeting next week."

"It depends on the meeting. If everything goes well, then you'll get the contract."

Eddie set up his truck near Eubank right on the fence line. Pop helped him fill a water tank and showed him where to drive. He announced his plan was to start at Eubank, move easterly, and mark the prairie dog mounds with cans of orange spray paint. Donald Pressman and about twenty protesters from Forest Guardians gathered by the fence, waving their signs and wearing their prairie dog hats. Mom and Jeff stood with Pop by the side of the truck.

"What's going on here?" Donald asked Eddie.

"Nice hat," Eddie said. "Got an extra?" A woman—Laura, from the church—put her sign down, dug a new hat from a satchel strapped over her shoulder, and tossed it over the fence to Eddie.

"Hot off the press," she said. It was light pink with a picture of a standing prairie dog on the front. The prairie dog had a tear running down his cheek with the words "Save Me" under the photo. On the white brim, it said, "ALL LIFE IS PRECIOUS," and the word "Precious" was pink, like the hat.

Mom rolled her eyes. Laura removed her hat and wiped her brow with her sleeve. Perspiration plastered Laura's blond bangs to her high forehead, so short that they looked like a skullcap that could be easily peeled away. Her fiancé Fred was sitting in the car, reading a magazine. He looked up and waved, as though he thereby fulfilled his duty to protect Laura. Mom blanched at Laura's frowning face and took a breath. She mouthed a prayer of gratitude. She felt her discomfort wane as she remembered that in the face of God, all are sinners. *We are all in this together and forgiveness is more powerful than hate.* She flashed a perfect smile at Laura. *I'll keep my mouth shut, be gracious, and turn this fat woman over to God for His guidance.*

Eddie admired the hat and shaped the brim with greasy hands. He put it on and grinned at Laura. "These folks have hired me. I'm a professional prairie dog relocator, and we're going to get started. Don't worry. I love these little critters, and I'm gentle and humane."

"It seems like a good compromise," Jeff said to the crowd of Forest Guardians. "We don't wish any harm to people or animals. We only want to live peaceably here."

"We don't think they ought to be moved," Donald said. He motioned to a young man who turned away and made a call on his cell phone. "This is their home. Moving them is too stressful. It destroys the ecosystem, their social organization, and their breeding cycles."

"In Boulder we move them all the time. They seem to do okay. Don't worry, man. I'm very gentle with them." Eddie began pulling a large hose out of a compartment under the truck. It was like the vacuum hose at the car wash. He hooked it up to a pump and motor mounted on the fender. Pop kicked his foot in the dirt as the sheriff drove up, his squad car's red lights flashing. Donald motioned to the sheriff, who loped up to the fence.

"What are you guys up to now?" he asked.

"We are moving prairie dogs," Pop said. "We can't kill them, so we are moving them."

"There can't be any harm in that," Jeff added. "This man is a professional and he will find them a new home."

The sheriff scratched his ear and took off his sunglasses. "I don't know of any laws against moving them," he said to Donald. "The Corleys are probably within their rights."

"The Gunnison prairie dog is an endangered species," Donald replied. "Remember, we do have a court injunction and we should wait for the hearing."

"With all due respect," Jeff said, "the injunction says we're prohibited from killing them, not from moving them." He glanced toward Mom and Pop.

"I think he's got you there," the sheriff said. "I don't have any legal reason to stop them."

Donald walked away, talking to his friend with the cell phone, and a couple of other protesters. Sweat formed on Laura's lip beneath the shade of her prairie dog hat. The afternoon sun shined on the wet back of her pink tee shirt, and she held her head high as though she was proud of how her tee shirt and hat matched. Her pink, round face closed in on a pursed smile. She glared at Mom, and Mom returned a smile.

Jeff sensed a temporary calm. Pop nodded at him. Jeff flushed at Pop's admiration, as though the warm sun had come out from behind a cloud. *Pretty smart.*

"I'm going to go ahead, then," Eddie said cheerfully.

He made some soapsuds with baby shampoo in a large tub that he'd unstrapped from the back of the truck. He put a small hose in the first prairie dog hole and hooked it to fittings on the tub and then to the outflow of the vacuum pump. He started the Briggs and Stratton engine. As the hole filled with soapsuds, prairie dogs peeked out, and Eddie vacuumed them up through the big hose and into the padded tank.

"The soap brings them out their holes and makes them slippery," Eddie said by way of explanation. "They slide real nice through the hose." There was a Plexiglas window on the side of the tank, and Jeff, Mom, and Pop watched the prairie dogs shooting out of the end of the hose and bouncing helter-skelter around on the foam padding. Then they settled down and huddled together, wet, soapy, and confused. The sound of their collective chatter came through the wall of the tank.

"I'm impressed," Pop admitted. "This could be a good idea. How did you find this guy?"

"I checked around," Jeff said. "I thought you'd like how this works. It's a great piece of equipment."

"If this wing nut can get these varmints moved, do you think Whitman will go ahead with the purchase?"

"I'm hopeful," Jeff said. "We have to get the City Council to go along with the delay. I've already asked Epstein to let Whitman's attorney know we're making progress."

Donald paced back and forth. Laura was wringing her hands, with Fred now at her side. Donald's friend walked beside him, matching his paces, as if to comfort him.

"I sure wouldn't want to be sucked through a hose," Laura said. Tears rolled down her cheeks and onto her prairie dog tee shirt. "I'll bet those poor little creatures feel trapped." She leaned back against Fred as he stood tall.

Donald put his hands on his hips as the sheriff drove away. Mom counted the prairie dogs shooting into the tank. They were up to twenty-five, as best as she could tell, and Eddie had sprayed orange paint on fifteen holes and one of his shoes. He stopped and adjusted his hat.

"Next time it won't be so easy," Eddie warned. "They'll be wary of me. I'll have to use a lot more soap suds, and it will take longer. Hey, tell that woman with the hats that the baby shampoo doesn't hurt their eyes. I've tried it on myself. It doesn't even sting."

Pop helped mix some more suds.

The sun was settling and ribbons of gray and pink streaked across the sky. Eddie shut off the pump. A cool gentle breeze made Jeff shiver. He felt strong and peaceful in the sudden quiet, and he could smell the baby shampoo and the wild sage crushed under Eddie's truck tires. He heard the feverish chatter and scratching of the prairie dogs in the tank. Jeff tipped his head back, hugged his shoulders, and watched bright orange shimmers chase pink streaks along two jet trails at high altitude. The streaks faded into white as they neared their source, airliners full of people headed to important places who had no idea about the significance of this moment at the Corley place. The image of his new Mercedes reappeared in his mind.

He thought that Betty would enjoy a weekend road trip. They could drive to Vegas. Maybe he should call her.

"That ought to be about a-hundred," Eddie said.

"Actually it's about a-hundred and ten," Mom said. They sure are busy in that tank. Looks like they're having a convention."

"I'll toss in the extra ten," he said. "It's been an easy day."

They went back to the shop and Pop counted out fifteen one-hundred dollar bills. "Here you go. Good luck with those varmints."

"Thanks," Eddie said. "I found a guy in Farmington who knows someone who has a home for them. I'm meeting them early tomorrow morning. Say, could I have a little extra for gas money? This truck is a real guzzler."

Pop gave him a couple of twenties. Jeff watched him count out the money. Incredible. Pop probably never imagined he would pay someone to move the varmints he and Junior shot and his father poisoned. Mom's smile suggested she was hopeful even after the appearance of Laura. Eddie jumped into his truck and smiled. *Maybe I should fix his tooth,* Jeff thought.

"Call me right after the meeting," Eddie called as he drove down the driveway.

Pop ambled down the driveway to tend the gate. The pink sky faded and the evening shadows fell over the land. The full moon peeked up over the eastern horizon and a hawk soared silently overhead. A prairie dog squeaked a warning and dove into his hole. "Damn, this might work," Pop muttered as he closed the gate and walked to the house.

As Eddie's purple truck drove by the Forest Guardian's main tent, Donald shone a flashlight on the license plate. Soon a car pulled out and followed the truck.

10

After Jeff went home, Mom sat quietly in her chair with a heating pad on her stomach. She chuckled to herself as she thought about soapsuds, the vacuum hose, chattering prairie dogs, and Eddie's purple truck. She and Jeff should have gotten involved sooner. They could have shielded her family from all the TV news and conflict. She could have controlled Pop and Junior's outbursts. And that Laura. She's so chubby. Poor girl.

As Mom looked out the window at the fading light, she felt a fresh breath of hope, and a peaceful feeling, her fickle old friend who often came in times of morning prayer. She let her eyes wander to the red lights that flickered on top of the radio towers on the mountain. The coming darkness made the lights seem to get brighter as they pulsed like an array of beating hearts. Strength came to her soul as she imagined a new tether of her protective veil tie itself to the highest tower. It held tight like an anchor of safety in a foreboding wind. Tomorrow she would prepare for the Valentine Sweetheart Dinner at church. She thanked God for the day. Her sleep tonight would be deep.

In the morning, Mom floated into the church kitchen on a soul full of joy. A new piney odor came from the stainless food preparation table. Who had been cleaning? The smell interrupted her sense of calm. Junior was safe in the hospital, and Ida brought a watchful eye to his health. What a relief. She could relax for a few days and allow herself to feel proud. She and Jeff brought faith and reason to their prairie dog habitat. Eddie and his relocator truck appeared as a solution. The City Council would provide more time after Fernando Vigil introduced his resolution, and in a month or so, they would sell the land and her plan would start fresh. Thank you,

Lord, for all your blessings. Thank you for bringing Eddie. He may be one of your ragamuffin angels. Mom turned on the lights in the kitchen, retrieved her clipboard, and turned her attention to her job as Hospitality Director.

The Valentine Sweetheart Dinner was an annual event sponsored by the Martha Circle of women as a fundraiser for their mission activities. Traditionally, over two hundred people came from all over the Northeast Heights. The food and entertainment were always good, and the dinner speaker offered remarks on the current mission outreach. The theme was "Love and Outreach," and the Martha Circle cleverly put the romance of Valentine's Day together with a mission focus. As June had said, it was a feel-good evening. This year, they had a goal of raising ten-thousand dollars for their Bosque restoration activities, a mission outreach that came out of June's sermons on global warming, hunger, and stewardship of the earth. The Martha Circle had come to believe, at the urging of June, "dominion over the earth" meant "take good care of what God has created." They had a specific goal of planting willows and cottonwoods in an area of the Rio Grande Bosque that fire had leveled. The church Scouts joined in with building plans for park benches and trails; some would become Advanced Scouts. The Scouts would present the colors at the dinner, and the Scoutmaster, the son of Junior's Scoutmaster, would introduce the Advanced Scout candidates.

Mom was in charge of food service and table decorations, and LeAnn formed a committee from the Martha Circle to help. As Mom bustled aimlessly around the kitchen, she felt a mild sense of dread about Laura and her work with the Forest Guardians. It made her uneasy to think about LeAnn's reaction. Laura was complex, and the past few years had taken its toll on her life. Losing a father in her teenage years must have made some deep wounds. Mom put her hands on her hips and smiled cheerfully as LeAnn came in the door pushing a cart full of food and cases of soft drinks.

"Well look at you," Mom said. "You're already a day ahead. Is there more food?"

"The van is packed full and we need a couple more carts. I found sales on nearly everything at Costco. I'm so proud. I'm two hundred dollars under budget."

LeAnn's overly sweet voice sounded saccharine.

"Let's review the menu," she said. "The list says we have about one-hundred tickets for fajitas and one-hundred for the curried chicken breast. That should make things easy."

"I checked the list before I went to Costco," LeAnn said. "New potatoes were on sale. I had to buy frozen vegetables, but I found huge bags of squash medley with pimentos. They had the hundred and fifty chicken breasts ready, but we'll have to slice fifty for the fajitas. The beef was already sliced. I just love to go to Costco."

"Are we still okay with the chocolate raspberry swirl cake for dessert?" Mom asked.

"I think it'll be great. I still remember the last time you made it."

"Is the Martha Circle committee still doing table decorations?"

"They'll be here Wednesday noon to set up," LeAnn said. "They got a little carried away, but they captured the theme. Each centerpiece is a round scrap of Astroturf with an open Bible turned to Genesis. There's a little stand with a cutout picture of the earth from space, and heart-shaped candies with scripture references surround the Bible. Chocolate hearts make a circle around the whole thing. Kind of cute, don't you think?"

Mom cringed at all the mixed colors: orange and red peppers, green guacamole, beige corn tortillas; white chicken breasts with a reddish curry and yellow lemon sauce, a yellow and green squash medley with red pimentos. Then, top things off with brown new potatoes with chives and parsley, dark brown chocolate cake with a maroon raspberry glaze, and a piece of plastic-green Astroturf with an open Bible and a blue and white earth-from-space photo, multicolored candy, and a pile of dark chocolate. Oh well. Just let it go. The Martha Circle means well.

"Have you heard about the speaker?" LeAnn asked.

"No, who is it?"

"June is going to given an introduction about stewardship of the earth, and then the head of the Forest Guardians has a presentation about the web of life. Then the Scoutmaster will present the Advanced Scout candidates, you know, the boys that are building the benches."

Mom sat down and rifled through the grocery receipts.

"The Martha Circle had a great idea, don't you think? Laura is part of the group now, and she's been designing the Forest Guardian's graphics. It was a great coincidence. I haven't seen her so happy in a long time. A God-thing, you know."

"I need to get started on the cakes," Mom said. "It will take about five big sheets. I want to have enough for seconds." Mom dragged mixing bowls out of the cupboards and put them up near the mixer. LeAnn made room in the huge refrigerator for the meat and frozen vegetables.

"I need to talk with you about something," LeAnn said. Mom thought she was going to ask about Junior, so she turned and smiled, prepared to tell LeAnn that he was safe.

"Laura's coming over to talk with you in a few minutes. She wanted me to be here."

"What about?"

"It's about her wedding. She has something to say."

The sound of the food mixer filled the silence until Laura came in the back kitchen door. She was wearing a pink tee shirt with a prairie dog photo. Around the photo, white script said, "PRAIRIE DOGS ARE GROUND KITTENS." Her pink hat matched. *My God, that cap makes her look like a child.*

"There's been some changes." Her voice filled the room, brassy and piercing. Mom's ears hurt. She sat on a kitchen stool, folded her hands, and smiled at Laura. *A gentle voice turneth away wrath.*

"And what changes might those be?" Mom asked softly.

"First of all, I don't want you to cook for my rehearsal dinner, and second, I don't want you to cook for my wedding reception."

"I'm certainly willing to step aside," Mom said. "I just wanted to be helpful."

Laura put her hands on her hips and frowned. "I don't think a church hospitality director should be killing animals, and I don't want to have anything to do with you. It's murder."

Mom looked at LeAnn who was staring at the floor and peeling potatoes. They should just be washed, not peeled. New potatoes are better cut in half with the skins on. Poor Laura. She's so covered up with anger she's going to spoil her wedding. One of the overhead fluorescent lights hummed, sputtered, and went out.

"Besides that," Laura said, "almost the whole Martha Circle agrees with me and they're going to fight you in court. You just want the money. You don't care about those ground kittens at all."

Mom felt a quiet rumble near her colostomy bag. She sniffed inside her jacket. Nothing.

"Now, you know that we hired a relocation company to move the prairie dogs to a more suitable habitat. You saw it with your own eyes. The fellow is gentle and humane."

"He sucked them through a hose, and it interrupts their breeding cycle. That's not gentle. They're all traumatized."

"Please try to understand. I want my children to get along. I want my family to be happy. It is my deepest prayer. You and your mother understand. We've been through a lot together, and we've supported each other. Please, it's about my family."

"I don't want you touching my food. That's all there is to it." Laura slammed the door as she left. Through the window, Mom saw Fred standing by the car holding the door open.

LeAnn touched Mom's hand. "I'm sorry. I've got to support Laura on this. She's my daughter."

Mom wiped a tear away as June came in the kitchen. "Everything going well for the Sweetheart Dinner?"

"We're on track for that," Mom mustered a smile. "But we just had a little conflict about Laura's wedding."

"Is Laura here?" June looked around.

"She just left," LeAnn said. "She doesn't want Mom to cook for her wedding because she says Mom is murdering animals, you know, the prairie dogs."

"Yes, I've heard the controversy is heating up. Is it true that the Martha Circle is planning on political action in court?"

"That's what Laura suggested," Mom replied.

"Mercy. This is how church splits happen," June said. "We've got to find a way to leave these conflicts outside the church doors. This is God's house, and it needs to be a place of solace for everyone. I'm sorry. This must feel like quite a rejection."

"I don't really mind. I can step aside for the wedding. I'm sure LeAnn and the Martha Circle can take care of things. I have the menus ready to go."

"That's gracious of you." June turned to LeAnn. "What is this doing with your friendship? I would imagine you feel pulled between Laura and Mom."

"After all we've been through with Laura's dad, I've got to support Laura on this one. You understand, don't you?"

"I think you need to support your daughter, but remember Mom has been your spiritual companion for years. You can't walk away from that. You need each other."

"Can we pray together?" Mom asked.

June bowed her head.

"I don't think so," LeAnn said. "This is deeper than prayer. This is blood."

June looked up, bewildered. June always had an answer, but silence covered the kitchen like a passing shadow as LeAnn walked down the hall to the bathroom.

"What's going on?" Mom asked. "Did I just lose my best friend?"

June held Mom's hand. "I think there's something else at work here. Let's go to my office."

June and Mom prayed together for peace in the church and for God's grace to promote understanding among his children. They also prayed for Mom's faith and her health.

"Thank you," Mom said. "I always feel better when we pray."

June settled back in her chair. "I didn't realize how much this prairie dog issue is heating up," she said. "I hear there are protesters camped out by your house."

"Yes, and we've been served with a restraining order to keep Pop from killing prairie dogs. The Forest Guardians claim endangered status for the prairie dogs, but Jeff came up with a way to relocate them. We talked with a City Councilor about postponing the hearings on the prairie dog ordinance until we can get them all moved. Our attorney thinks we have a good chance. No one gets hurt that way."

"Sounds like a reasonable plan to me," June said.

"Laura is working for the Forest Guardians and she was with the protesters the other day. They think we should give the land to a land trust and leave the prairie dogs alone. That would leave us without any money, and Pop is getting too old to keep working. Junior is in the hospital now. It's a mess, but I'm hopeful about the City Council's vote."

"Junior is in the hospital? I didn't know."

"He got pancreatitis. The doctor thinks Junior should say in the hospital for a while until he's better and to get some help with his, you know, drinking."

"Is he in alcohol rehabilitation?"

"I guess that's what they call it. We can visit when we are invited."

"Will they let a Pastor visit?"

"I think so, but that's not a good idea. Junior doesn't think much of the church. It would probably upset him."

"You let me know when it might be appropriate. In the meantime, how are you doing? Is it well with your soul?"

"There's one bright light. Jeff met a girl and I think he likes her."

"What's her name?"

"Betty. He met her in the dental chair. He fixed her front teeth and put her picture up right beside mine." Mom smiled.

"That sounds promising. I know you worry about him."

"Yes. You said there might be something else at work with Laura. What did you mean by that?"

"Tell me what you think it could be," June said.

"Sometimes I wonder if I'm supposed to suffer for other people. Have you ever felt that way? My faith is strong, and I seem to have courage. Do you think God may be calling me to carry the burdens of others, like Laura?"

"I think you can provide comfort and spiritual support, but I don't think you're supposed to suffer for her. I was thinking more along the lines of loss and grief. We may understand better in the light of her father's death and her inability to grieve. I need to call upon your compassion for that."

"Do you think Fred is too old for her?"

"Who am I to judge? They seem comfortable together."

"When I met him in Bible study, he reminded me a little of LeAnn's husband. It may have been that he's so quiet. You can't tell what he's thinking. I hope he takes good care of Laura. She needs somebody."

"Thank you for your compassion."

"Can I ask you something else?"

"Sure."

"I was wondering...do you think evil might be working here? I'm a faithful servant, and all I want is what God wants, a peaceful family. I pray for that every morning, and here I am in a horrible mess. Maybe God can't do anything about it. Pop thinks that sometimes." Mom stood up and paced around the office.

"From what I can see, your problems come from people, not from God."

"Could it be the Devil or wicked little minions or something like that?"

"Let's think about this. We both believe there are evil forces that God fights all the time. We know darkness and brokenness nourish the worst in people and blinds them to God's Holy Spirit. I guess in that sense we could say evil forces are at work. To me, it seems more like ignorance and fear."

"I see that, but I don't know why Laura and the protesters and my children are all so afraid. Lord knows, I can see the ignorance, but it still feels like a dark power that stops me from making peace in my family."

"Most people are afraid of change, even change for the better," June said. "In my experience people project their private fears onto changing situations. Maybe Laura sees the lost love of her Father in the eyes of prairie dogs. Maybe the protesters see the comfort of their childhood ties with the earth threatened. Maybe the Forest Guardians fulfill the need to escape a deep loneliness through their community. I think evil is the power that feeds and sustains our fears, and faith is our best weapon. As a Pastor, I've seen how faith and hope can resolve conflict, and I've seen how stewardship always yields better solutions. For me, that's how we fight evil."

"Why does God let this go on? He could stop it. We could move ahead. He loves us, He wants the best for us, and He's the most powerful force in the universe. What is He waiting for? I'm tired of watching my children suffer. I can't carry it all."

June stood up. "Think of it this way. God gave all the people around you a free will, and He promised they would always have it. People do things all day, and every night God looks down on His children, shakes His head, and uses His power to make the best of what He sees. That is the grace of God, and we have to trust it."

"Thanks, but I have to admit my faith is shaken. I think God should do something about all this." They walked to the door.

"Oh, there's one other thing. I need to ask you to step aside as the Hospitality Director for a while, at least until this prairie dog situation resolves. I'm afraid all the strong feelings are going to split the church.

Could you lie low for a couple of months? Of course, I expect to see you in worship."

"Who would take the job?" Mom asked.

"As you said, LeAnn and the Martha Circle can fill in, at least until this situation gets settled."

They hugged and Mom walked slowly to her car. She felt like all her energy had drained out onto the ground and left a wet trail behind her. Upon arriving home, she fell into bed and slept soundly until Pop woke her up.

"Are you okay?" she heard him ask. "Your horoscope said today's a bad day for relationships."

Mom rubbed her eyes. "I got very tired. The people at church are involved with our prairie dogs, and it really bothers me."

"You never take naps in the middle of the day. I thought maybe you were getting sick again. Are you sure you're okay?"

"Laura doesn't want me to cook for her wedding reception and June wants me to give up my hospitality job until our prairie dog problem has been solved. People in the church are taking sides. I can't even trust LeAnn. It's a mess."

"Those church people are all gossips." Pop looked downcast and sullen as though he was containing his anger. "They're supposed to be your friends. Come on, let me take you out to dinner."

Mom and Pop went to Little Anita's for Mom's favorite chicken enchiladas and then to Ben and Jerry's for some ice cream. Pop was a good listener, and he helped Mom get to bed early for a night of needed rest.

"I've got to take a skip loader to Espanola tomorrow, so I'll see you when I get home. It could be late," he said.

"Thank you for a lovely evening. You know I really do love you."

Pop pulled a cover over her and closed the door.

In the morning, Mom sat in her chair praying and musing about her time with June. She felt sad and adrift, not like her cheerful self last night. In her reverie, a thought arose suggesting that other peoples' moods, especially Pop's, often controlled her sense of happiness. She shouldn't let that happen.

It didn't seem right, although it could be a part of the journey of suffering she had to take for the redress of the tiny life she had snuffed out. She was only sixteen then, and her mother had arranged it with their old family doctor. No one else knew, and she and her mother never spoke of it. Sometimes she imagined the child would have completed her family, brought balance to the unbridled trio she had raised, and made them healthy. Although, honestly, if that child had been born, a little girl she imagined, she probably would not have married Pop. He wouldn't have found a single mother attractive, so there you go.

No, this is my life, and I will rely on God to make the journey as painless as possible. I'll pay my dues until my cleansing is complete. Thank you God for this day. May I rejoice and be glad in it.

11

Danny Sandoval took two chairs in the back row of the City Council Chambers, one for himself and one for a tan puppy on a blue and white bath towel. The puppy gnawed on a rawhide chew toy, and the room hummed with noisy people. Short and dark-haired, Danny had smooth light brown skin. His square face was well proportioned and his chiseled features framed a gentle bright smile and blue eyes. Danny exuded vigor, and gave the impression of a man who carries an inner strength wrapped with a happy disposition. He'd tied his jet-black hair into a short ponytail, and his nametag said, "Danny--Vet Tech."

Ida came in, looked around at the packed room, and headed toward the only chair left, the one with the puppy. She was dressed in a pink and gray jogging suit and scuffed pink tennis shoes. She tied her hair in a ponytail that flopped out the back of a white baseball cap that said "Foxy Lady." She flashed a smile at Danny and pointed at the puppy. "Is that chair available?"

"Sure." He moved the towel and puppy to his lap and kissed the puppy on the nose.

Ida sat down and lowered her jacket zipper a little, revealing her sports bra. She knew the art of casually revealing herself, and she felt affirmed as he noticed her shape. "I sure feel hot and stuffy in here," she said. "Where in the world did all these people come from?"

"It's a big crowd because of the long agenda," Danny said. "There's a thing about a prairie dog ordinance and the Albuquerque animal shelter budget is up for renewal."

Ida surveyed the room. She saw Jeff and their attorney Robert Epstein in the front row with Henry Whitman. Mom sat behind Jeff, and Pop was noticeably absent. Donald Pressman and his coterie of supporters from the Forest Guardians dominated the room. They looked like a platoon of soldiers with their matching prairie dog hats and tee shirts. Ida noticed a few neighbors and a dozen or so people from Mom's church. *This does not look good.*

"Why are you here?" she asked Danny. "Oh, my name is Ida."

"Hi, I'm Danny. I'm going to speak in favor of increasing the spay-neuter budget for the animal shelter. And you?"

"My brother is trying to get the City Council to postpone the new prairie dog ordinance."

"How come?"

"My folks are trying to sell their land and there are prairie dogs on it. The new ordinance is holding up the sale." Ida moved back as Danny leaned toward her.

"Why do you have a puppy here?" Ida asked.

"He's a visual aid for my speech." He took two three-by-five cards out of his shirt pocket and held them up to Ida. "I'm going to use the puppy right at the end, you know, for effect. He's a terrier-spaniel mutt from the pound, and his name is Lucky."

"For effect?"

"Over his lifetime, he can father over three-hundred unwanted puppies if he's not neutered. The operation only costs thirty-five dollars and it's a simple couple of snips." He turned Lucky over and showed Ida his little balls.

"Yes, I know about testicles. I'm a nurse." She searched Danny's face to see if he was teasing her.

His cheekbones framed the bluest eyes she'd ever seen, a royal blue magnified by clear liquid. *No problem with dry eyes for this man.* He wasn't teasing.

"It's really very important. We have to euthanize two-hundred cats and dogs every week."

"My God, two-hundred a week?"

"Sometimes it's more in the summer. We fill a pickup every Friday, and we take the bodies to the land fill." Ida put her knees together as he leaned over and showed her a large photo of a three-quarter ton pickup full of plastic bags. "I'm used to hospital work, but this makes me queasy."

Danny held Lucky up to his face and they touched noses. "Someone dropped him off on Monday, just in time for my speech. He talks to me, you know."

"Right. I'm sure he talks to you," Ida said.

Danny put Lucky up to his ear, listened, and then said, "Yes, I agree."

"What did he say?" Ida smiled.

"He said you're beautiful and that your socks don't match."

Ida looked at her feet. Her socks were both pink, but from different pairs. She felt a tinge of self-consciousness, a feeling she hadn't had for years. It was as though Danny had seen too much too soon.

"Would you like to hold Lucky?" He handed the puppy and the towel over to her.

"No thanks." She reached out and petted his head. "I really don't know much about dogs." She smelled an odor that reminded her of the geriatric floor at the hospital. A gavel sounded from the front and everyone stood up for the pledge of allegiance. The gavel sounded again.

"Because of unexpected travel, we don't have a quorum tonight," the Chairman said. "I'm canceling the meeting and rescheduling it for one week from today, same time and the same agenda. I apologize for your inconvenience. We stand adjourned."

"That's disappointing," Danny said. "I was all set." They both stood up.

"The delay is hard on our case," Ida said. "It gives the Forest Guardians time to gather more supporters."

"Hey, do you want to get some coffee?" Danny asked. "There's a Starbucks across the street."

Ida noticed they were exactly the same height, and his smile made wrinkles by his eyes. His breath smelled like spearmint tic-tacs, and his tee shirt was light blue, old, and soft. Bet he sleeps in it. Slender with muscular arms and shoulders, he probably weighed twenty-five pounds more than her one-thirty. He was in his early thirties, and there was no wedding ring. Except for his height, all the signs were good, but his gaze was intense. He didn't leer. She would've been comfortable with that. He didn't stare and hold eye contact too long like her last doctor boyfriend, creepy-eyes. Yet he seemed to notice things that might be foreign to her, and that made her uneasy. Was her mascara all gone? She casually sniffed in the direction of her armpit.

"Sure. I've got some extra time since there's no meeting." She extended her hand. "I'm Ida—last name is Corley," she said, "intensive care nurse at University Hospital."

"And I'm Danny Sandoval," he said. "I work for the animal shelter. You've met Lucky." He shook her hand and then touched Lucky's paw to her hand.

"Nice to meet you both," she said.

Ida ordered a half-caff, non-fat soy latte and Danny ordered an Americano. They sat by the window and watched the crowd come in.

"That's Donald Pressman," Ida said. "He's head of the Forest Guardians and those people are his supporters. They stopped my father and my brother from getting rid of the prairie dogs on our land. They even got a court injunction after my father was on the news."

"They killing them?" Danny asked.

"Sure. They're varmints, you know, just like rats." She wrinkled her nose. "Just like rats. That's what my dad says."

"Do you have to kill them? Can't you figure out a way to move them? Maybe out on a prairie where they would be happy?" Danny gazed out the window and took a deep breath.

Ida was aware he hadn't looked at her breasts. I wonder if he's gay.

"We've moved a few, and we're giving that a try. My brother says that's a good option, but there are hundreds of them on our place, and the Forest Guardians say it's too disturbing for their breeding cycles. They want my folks to give the land to some kind of trust and leave the prairie dogs alone."

"I hate to see people kill animals," Danny said. "We are connected to them you know, and whenever we kill them, we lose a little bit of ourselves." He glanced at the photo of the truck full of bodies. "There's got to be a better way."

"The Forest Guardians say we should give our land away, and I just can't see that. They are asking my family to give away three-million dollars for a bunch of rodents. That sucks."

"Wow, we could fund the animal shelter for six years with three-million dollars."

"You're not very supportive," Ida said. "That's our property and our money."

"Sorry. I guess I care more about animals than money." He shifted in his chair, put Lucky up to his ear, and listened. Ida smiled and asked, "Is he saying something"

"Yes. He says your heart is beating fast and you smell like rain and lavender. He says you make him so excited he might pee." Danny grinned.

"It's time for me to go." She knocked over her cup as she stood up and turned away from him.

"I guess I'll see you next week," he said. "Same time, same agenda."

"See you Lucky," she said over her shoulder. Ida felt somehow exposed as she jogged to the parking lot by the City Hall. If I ever seen Danny again, I'm going to tell him that Lucky talks too much. What a jerk.

Jeff, Mom, Epstein, and Whitman's attorney Francisco gathered in the hall outside the City Council chambers. They waited until the crowd left the building.

"What just happened in there?" Jeff asked.

"Sometimes things are too hot for a quorum," Epstein replied. "From what I can gather, Fernando Vigil needed more time to get things together. I suspect he called in a favor. No quorum, no meeting."

"Does that bode well for us?" Mom asked.

"I think where he's headed is to give us a chance to move some of the prairie dogs. That's all we need, just a little time," Jeff said. "By the way, Vigil brought his wife by for an appointment. She needs a couple of crowns."

"I'll talk with Mr. Vigil this week," Epstein said. We're going to argue first that the Corleys had beneficial use of the land as a home and business before the prairie dogs moved in and took over."

"Remember," Jeff said, "nothing about immigration."

"Don't worry, I got it," said Epstein.

"Second, we'll argue that if we have a chance to relocate them to a more suitable habitat, then everyone will come out just fine. In fact, the prairie dogs will be better off in a wilderness area and not so close to traffic and congestion. They belong on a prairie. Third, we need to mention the gross receipts tax and the building permit fees that will come from the development. I don't want to push on that, but I will mention it. The

Councilors are aware of the financial impact of the development."

"Do you think they'll postpone the vote?" Mom asked.

"All they have to do is give it another thirty days," Epstein said. "That should be easy."

"Then can we sell the land?" Mom asked.

"I talked with the bank's attorney and the title company," Fred replied. They said if we can close in the thirty-day period, and if the property is exempt from the ordinance, we can go ahead. If we get a postponement and move the prairie dogs, then the fifteen acres will be grandfathered in."

"When would we have the money?" Mom asked.

"If they vote for a postponement, we can get the sale organized in less than a week and you will have your money within two days," Epstein said.

Mom turned to Jeff and opened her arms. Jeff looked at the ceiling as they hugged and Mom whispered, "Thank you. I've always had faith in you."

12

The nurse offered Mom a chair in the private visiting room adjacent to the rehab unit.

"You should limit your visit to about fifteen minutes. Junior's doing well with his pancreatitis, but drying out from years of alcohol abuse makes him rattled."

Mom glanced at her watch. "Sure."

"You should prepare for some hostility." The nurse left through the door to the hallway. It locked.

Mom smoothed her skirt and flipped idly through an outdated celebrity magazine.

She looked up and saw Ida through the small window in the other door—the one to the patient ward—and heard her keys as she unlocked it and came into the room.

"Hi, how are you doing? I checked on Junior. He'll be out to see you in a little while."

"How is he?"

"He's alive and stable, and I think he's through the worst." Ida sat down next to Mom. She paused for a moment and then asked, "How are you? I'm worried about your health."

"I'm very tired. I don't have much energy. Do you know that your pink bra shows through your white scrubs?"

Ida glanced down at an almost imperceptible hint of pink. "I don't think much about it."

"White underwear would be more appropriate, and you really need a size larger shirt."

"Don't start in on me. These are my work clothes. Sometimes I change a couple of times a shift. The emergency room is messy."

"It's as though you are advertising your body for sale or something. Modesty is much more attractive. I hate the way men look at you."

Ida stood up and paced the visiting-room floor.

"What's going on? You seem way upset. Aren't you here to see Junior?"

Mom shook her head. "You just don't understand. Right now there's so much to be unhappy about, and I'm having a hard time."

"I'm sorry for all the pressure on you. I really am. But please don't take it out on me." Ida sat down again and held her mother's hands.

"I wouldn't take it out on you if it didn't come from you. I pray every morning that you would find a modicum of modesty. I didn't raise a tramp, and I want you to be wholesome."

Ida dropped her mother's hands and stood back up.

"Oh for Christ's sake," she said with an exasperated sigh. "I have all my clothes on, I'm not wearing much make up, and I'm at work. No one is complaining."

"Are you wearing one of those thongs?" Mom continued, all but ignoring Ida. "I don't see any panty lines, and those pants are skin tight."

"That's enough." Ida turned to leave. "I'm done."

Before she could make her exit, though, a nurse unlocked the patient door and Junior shuffled in. Both she and Mom turned to greet him.

Junior's sunken eyes peeked out from his gaunt face as he mustered a slight smile. It appeared as though it hurt to move his face. Mom smiled back to cover her shock, and tried to hug her son. Junior stood wooden, his arms remaining stiffly at his sides.

"How are you doing?" Mom asked.

Junior slumped into a chair.

"How do you think? I feel like death warmed over," he said.

"They say your infection is getting better and you're through the worst part. Pop says to tell you hello." Mom looked away, to keep herself from staring at his shaking hands.

"Tell that sonofabitch I haven't had a drink for eight days."

"That's great. I'll tell him. I know you can do this. I have faith in you."

"What about Popeye and Minerva?"

"I'm feeding them every day, and they stay around the trailer. I've been giving Popeye a rawhide in the morning. I know they miss you."

"Do they have fresh water?"

"Yes, of course. Guess what? I have some good news about the land. We filed an appeal with the City Council to postpone the ordinance for a while, to give us a chance to relocate the prairie dogs. A man came and took about a hundred of them away so we could show we mean well. Our lawyer thinks if we can get the postponement, then we can move them all and our land sale won't be affected. We have the meeting next week, and we could have the money within a week after that."

Junior looked at Ida.

"Jeff and Mom have been managing all this," she told him. "They've met with Mr. Vigil, one of the councilors. Jeff is working on Vigil's teeth. Whitman's lawyer is working with our lawyer. It looks good."

Junior brightened for a moment, but his smile faded just as quickly as it had appeared. His eyes drooped and he wiped saliva from the side of his mouth. He braced himself with the chair's metal arms and pushed himself up.

"I'm going to take a nap," he announced. He waved feebly at Mom and Ida and opened the door to the ward.

"He looks horrible," Mom said as soon as the door closed. "Do you think this rehabilitation will work?"

"From what I can tell, Junior's really scared. He knows he almost died."

"What do they do with him?"

"As soon as the infection is under control, they'll start with group work, and they'll assign him a sponsor, a recovered alcoholic who can be his companion and get him on the right track."

"He seems so tired, and he's lost at least twenty pounds."

"They'll keep him zonked out with Librium for a while. That'll help with the shakes and hallucinations."

"I worry so," Mom said. "He's angry, and he seems afraid of other people. I keep urging him to try church again."

"You need to get off of that church stuff and leave him alone. It's as if you have him tied to you with a string. He's a grown up, and he has some issues to work out. The last thing he needs is pressure from you about church."

"Why is he so angry? It's like he hates everyone."

"He has some serious issues. He probably *does* hate everyone, including himself."

"But, I don't understand why. Is it something Pop did?"

"You really don't know?"

"No, it's always been a mystery. Sometimes I think it's because Pop is so strict with him. I try to make up for it." Mom stood up and stared out the window. She and Ida had not talked like this for years, and she didn't want to ruin it. She sat down and held Ida's hand. "Do you think I make up for it?"

"Oh," Ida said with a sigh. "You really are clueless. You've put it out of your mind, haven't you?"

"What? What have I put out of my mind?"

"The church Scouts. The youth group at church. Mr. Cunningham."

"I remember. That was the summer after Junior finished sixth grade, but what about it?"

"He quit the church Scouts."

"Yes, Pop said he was a girlie boy and a quitter. I hated that."

"Mom, that assistant troop leader, Cunningham, was a child molester. He went with the boys on that camping trip to the mountains, up by Jemez Springs. Then he moved to California. They found out later he had abused Junior and two other boys."

Mom's head dropped into her hands. She took deep breaths and sobbed, her entire body shaking. Ida put one hand on Mom's shoulder the other across her own eyes.

"Oh God, you really didn't know," she whispered.

They sat still for a couple of long minutes, as though posing for a statue. Then Ida pulled away and stood up.

"The Scoutmaster called and called," Mom said, "but Pop said he didn't want anything to do with Junior's quitting. It was up to Junior to fix it. He wouldn't let me return the calls."

"Come on, pull yourself together. It was twenty years ago. There's nothing you can do about it now." She handed her a tissue from her pocket. "What Junior needs now is for you and Pop to leave him alone. The group therapist will call you when it's time for a family session."

"There's got to be something I can do."

"You need to leave him alone. He needs time." Ida hugged Mom. "I've got to go back to work. Go home and rest."

Ida started toward the hall door and stopped suddenly when a nurse unlocked the door. "The Corley family is in here," she said, ushering in a young man with a ponytail, holding a puppy under his arm. He grinned.

"Hello," he said to Mom. "I'm here to see Junior Corley. You must be his mother, and oh, hi there," he said to Ida. They were both startled.

Ida threw a wide-eyed smile at Danny as she slid out the door and bustled down the hallway to the Emergency Room.

"Yes. I'm visiting my son. He has pancreatitis, and he's getting better."

"Oh, that's good."

"Yes. Do you know him?"

"My name's Danny Sandoval and I volunteer here at the rehab center. They assigned me to be Junior's sponsor, you know, to help him through the next month or so."

Mom stuck out her hand. "I'm Janice, but everyone calls me Mom. What do you do to help him?"

Danny shook her hand and said, "I'm a recovering alcoholic and I walk alongside Junior and encourage him. He's going to need someone to talk to."

"I can tell you a lot about him," Mom said. "And I want very much to help."

Danny shifted the puppy to his other arm.

"I think it would be best if you stayed away for a while, at least until the counselor calls you for a family visit."

"Yes, that's what my daughter said."

"Your daughter?"

"The nurse that just left. That's Ida, our middle child. Junior is the youngest, and their brother Jeff is the oldest." Mom took a small notepad from her purse, wrote down her phone number, and handed it to Danny with a shy smile. "You can call me anytime and keep me informed."

"Everything Junior and I talk about is confidential," Danny said gently. "Right now he needs someone he can trust who will help him be accountable." He stood up to leave, adding, "Nice to meet you. I'm sure we'll see each other again. Tell Ida that Danny and Lucky say hello." He pointed at his puppy.

"Do you know her?" Mom asked. She tipped her head to the side.

"Lucky and I met her once at a City Council meeting. I've got to go. Hope to see you again."

Danny opened the door with his key and ambled down the hall toward Junior's room. Tears formed in Mom's eyes. This could be the start of losing Junior forever.

On the way home, Mom stopped at Hobby Lobby. She leaned heavily on the cart, her stomach gripped by a sharp pain, and moved slowly through the paper flower and basket aisle. She picked out a tall green wicker basket, some white Easter lilies, a handful of green ferns, and several purple crocuses. She imagined a verdant centerpiece for the Easter dinner she would prepare. Junior would be there, sober and pleasant, Pop would be proud and smiling, and Jeff and Ida would talk about their work. She found a sense of peace thinking about how Jeff would handle the relocation issue with the City Council. This Easter would be a true celebration, and the money would be in the bank in everyone's new accounts. Her constant pain softened as she thought of Easter Sunday and offered little breath-prayers, like "God help me."

13

Tension held in the air like static electricity waiting to spark. Mom, Jeff, Bob Epstein, Don Whitman, and Francisco Romero sat at attention in the front row. Jeff had reviewed all of the presentations, and despite the constant presence of needling protestors, he felt good about the evening. An engineer friend had prepared displays of aerial photos of the land and neighborhood, showing all the developments nearby. From the displays, it was clear the Corley property was ideal for a mixed-use development.

Donald Pressman, a couple of young protestors, a strange little man in a safari shirt holding a notebook, and scores of supporters gathered in the remaining seats.

The women from the Martha Circle at Grace church sat together. June sat in the back. LeAnn and Fred sat together. Ida stood by the door near a couple of reporters, and Danny stood at the podium summing up his plea for more money for the animal shelter. There was an easel featuring photos of the truck full of euthanized animal carcasses, and he held Lucky with one arm.

"Money for spay-neuter programs is the answer to all the killing," he said. "Please give it a try. Thirty-five dollars can prevent the birth of over three hundred dogs that would have to be killed." He approached the five City Councilors and held little Lucky up for them to see.

One Councilor reached out, smiled, and scratched Lucky's ears.

"Thank you for your consideration."

The Councilor made a motion to increase the animal shelter budget by fifty-thousand dollars for the rest of the year, and the motion passed unanimously.

There were no seats, so Danny joined Ida in the back and leaned against the wall with a grin of relief on his face. He kissed Lucky on the nose. Ida shifted her feet and smiled at him.

The Chairman rapped his gavel.

"Next on the agenda is the Corley request to postpone the final reading and adoption of the Prairie Dog Ordinance, Ordinance number 2002-4. Is the applicant represented?"

"Yes," Jeff replied. He set up the display of the property, and Bob Epstein approached the podium. He explained the circumstances and insisted that the Corleys cared about the prairie dogs and wanted to have an opportunity to move them to a more suitable habitat prior to the enactment of the ordinance.

"We've already moved over a hundred of them," he explained. "We have retained the services of a professional relocator, who is safe and humane and has a good deal of experience. He's reputable."

In addition, Epstein argued, the Corley family had been there for well over seventy-five years with their contracting business on the land. Their domicile and business location surely predated the existence of the prairie dogs. He looked straight at Fernando Vigil when he said, "The Corleys had provided sanctuary for the prairie dogs over the years, and now they need to move them to a safer place away from the pressures of encroaching civilization."

"It is also a question of property rights," Epstein added. "The Corleys' property rights include the beneficial use of their land for their home and business, and also the right to sell. To buy and to sell real estate in New Mexico is a basic property right. We surely cannot overlook that right."

"Thank you," the Chairman said. "Mr. Romero, you are listed here as next."

Francisco Romero walked to the podium. There were boos and catcalls from the crowd. The Chairman rapped his gavel. "We'll have order in this hearing, or I'll ask the audience to leave," he said. "Proceed."

"I am Francisco Romero, attorney for Henry Whitman, the prospective developer of the fifteen acres in question. We have been working with your Planning Department on our master plan for a mixed commercial and residential development with open spaces and recreation areas. The fifty homes should provide five-hundred thousand dollars in permit and impact fees, and one-hundred-fifty thousand annually in property taxes. The commercial and retail space could easily provide over one-million dollars per year in gross receipts taxes. Of course, the developer will pay for the water and sewer extensions, and the development will generate ten-thousand dollars a month to Albuquerque Utilities. We calculate that the return flow credits to the basin will free up substantial water rights. Albuquerque is a progressive community, and this development will be state of the art.

"If I may, I want to direct your attention to the aerial photo of the property. You can see that it constitutes infill. There are homes and developed areas surrounding it. It thereby meets the infill recommendations of the Planning Department, and they are prepared to recommend approval of our master plan.

"Thank you for your consideration. We believe the Corleys should have a chance to relocate the prairie dogs before the ordinance is passed and thereby be grandfathered in as exempt property."

Two of the Councilors nodded their heads as they leaned over and whispered to each other. Jeff felt elated and held Mom's hand.

The Chairman then asked for comments in opposition. "If you have signed up, then you can speak, and you are limited to three minutes. I will keep the time."

A parade of speakers lined up.

Jeff rubbed his chin as he remembered a time years ago when he was thirteen and women from the church gathered at a council meeting. Mom helped organize them, and Jeff was in tow. They overwhelmed the councilors with arguments why the church should be allowed to open a pre-school, even though they did not have adequate parking. After an hour, they obtained a variance, and the pre-school is still operating to this day.

Although the women tonight were different, they somehow seemed the same. Jeff could almost see a plan take shape: impassioned women, one by one, earnest as Sunday morning, forming a wall of righteousness, all covered with sentiment—clearly the most effective and annoying force in every church. Soon female emotions would cloud the councilors' minds, a force few decent men can resist. He hoped the men stayed focused.

LeAnn escorted a tremulous elderly woman to the podium.

"It's high time we stopped killing things," she said. "God created everything on this earth, and, well, every living thing has a purpose. We have to stop killing things." She sobbed softly. LeAnn nodded at Donald, and escorted her to a seat.

A tall woman with long hair and a green dress stood up. "Mr. Chairman, Councilors, my name is Ruby Jo Chandler and I am a member of the Martha Circle at the church. I arise before you to object to killing prairie dogs or moving them." She took a breath and looked straight at Councilor Chavez.

"When I saw that big purple truck and the hose sucking those wet little ground kittens out of their holes—their homes—it was like, well, I couldn't help but think of a rubber hose sucking a live embryo from the womb of Mother Nature. It was horrible. We cannot allow this wanton disregard for life. Please vote against this motion."

Councilor Chavez seemed shaken. It was as though Ruby Jo's plea had thrown a switch in his mind, making the vague idea of life-rights, the right to be alive, turn into the clear idea of a right to life, the anti-abortion mantra of conservatives in the crowd.

The next woman stood at the podium. She looked like an overweight Meryl Streep.

"Mr. Chairman, Councilors, my name is Flo Miller, and I endorse Ruby Jo's remarks. I want to add that these little babies are delicate. When you disturb them, their moods change, and experts agree that you interrupt their breeding. They are fighting against extinction, and then you come along and break up their families. I'm sure they don't feel like breeding after being torn from their homes. I urge you to vote against this motion."

The Councilors listened for almost an hour to passionate pleas to save the prairie dogs and to leave them alone so they could thrive in their homeland. LeAnn was the last speaker. She stood up with an air of resolve—lips pursed and chin up. She threw a glance at Mom, unfolded her papers, and grabbed the podium with both hands.

"Mr. Chairman, Councilors, my name is LeAnn Cooper, the presiding President of the Martha Circle at the church. I represent most of the women, and I can tell you we are voters. We stand united in opposition to killing prairie dogs for money, and that's what the Corleys are doing.

They might as well put a price on each one of them, mothers, fathers, and babies." She shuffled her papers and adjusted her glasses. "They just want to get the money from the developer, and they don't care what happens to these little ground kittens, even if they become extinct. They just want the money so they can buy motorcycles, cars, and motor homes and go on trips, and buy new bedroom furniture. We think it's horrible, you know, to kill for money." She paused for a moment as Donald nodded at her.

"If there are two-thousand prairie dogs out there and the Corleys get 3 million dollars, that's fifteen-hundred for each one. Kill one prairie dog and get fifteen-hundred dollars. I think you can see what's going on here. All the women at church urge you to vote against the motion."

The Chairman called for a recess, and after ten minutes, he called the room to order.

"Can someone please sum this up?" the Chairman asked.

Donald arose and argued that all life is precious, that the Gunnison Prairie Dogs claim endangered status, and that moving them disturbs their culture and their breeding cycles. In addition, he suggested that the prairie dogs were likely on the land long before the Corley family bought it. Therefore, they had prior rights.

"Mr. Chairman," said Fernando Vigil, "we've heard all sides of this issue, and I would like to offer a motion."

"Go ahead, Mr. Vigil."

"I move that the final reading of Ordinance 2002-4 be postponed for sixty days."

"Is there a second?"

"Second."

"Is there discussion?"

The Councilors looked at each other and remained silent. Jeff held Mom's hand and winked at Bob and Francisco.

The door opened and Laura scurried over to Donald, waving a folder.

"Wait," she said. "Wait."

Donald looked quickly at the open folder.

"Point of order, Mr. Chairman," Donald said.

"What is it? We are about to vote."

"May I approach? You gentlemen must see this." He smiled at Laura, who was beaming in her matching prairie dog hat and tee shirt.

"Come on up."

Donald put a glossy photo of a family in front of each Councilor. The photo featured a father, a mother, and two teenage children, each with a .22 rifle, each holding a dead prairie dog by the tail. Their smiles revealed a moment of family pride.

"What is this?" the Chairman asked.

"These are some of the prairie dogs that the Corleys relocated with their supposed reputable relocator. We followed the relocator truck. He sold the one-hundred prairie dogs to a man in Farmington who took them to the Double X Ranch in Wyoming. The Double X Ranch sells weekend prairie dog hunts for shooters."

Donald handed out copies of a full-page ad from a shooters magazine.

"This is surely not safe and humane," he said. "This 'relocation' story is a sham. The Councilors have been duped."

Laura raised her eyebrows at Jeff and smirked. Mom dropped her head in her hands. Jeff looked at Bob Epstein, who appeared bewildered.

Fernando Vigil took note of his fellow Councilors. Three were shaking their heads over the photos and frowning. "I want to withdraw my motion."

"Does the second approve?"

"Yes, Mr. Chairman."

"Motion withdrawn."

"Could we please take a short break to consider the new information?" asked Vigil.

"Okay, I'm calling a twenty-minute break."

The crowd cheered, and Donald hugged Laura. The Martha Circle surrounded her with hugs of congratulations.

Mom sobbed with her head in her hands, and Jeff huddled in the corner with Bob and Francisco.

"What the hell are we going to do?" Jeff asked.

They followed Fernando Vigil into the hall and moved to a doorway.

"What the hell *is* this?" he asked Jeff.

"A total surprise. I swear. We had no idea. I'm sure the relocator is legitimate. I'll bet he didn't know either."

"This looks bad," Vigil said. "Do you have a Plan B?"

"We can promise to monitor the relocation," Jeff said. "We can follow the prairie dogs to a suitable destination and provide photos."

"Folks aren't going to trust you, but we can try," Vigil said.

Jeff sat down and held Mom's hand as the Chairman called the meeting back to order.

"Let's give the Corleys a chance to reply," he said.

Epstein stood at the podium. "The Corleys had no idea of the unfortunate outcome, and they believe the relocator didn't know either. He would not have gone to so much effort to be gentle and humane if he knew of the ultimate result.

"We are willing to monitor and to guarantee safe delivery of the relocated prairie dogs, and we will provide photos. We can assure you this will not happen again.

"In addition, and with all due respect, I want to remind you of the Corley's property rights, and the fact that they have provided a sanctuary for hundreds of prairie dogs for decades. This is a property rights issue."

The Chairman asked Donald if he had anything to add.

He came to the podium. "Mr. Chairman, Councilors, we believe the prairie dogs occupied the property before the Corleys bought it, and we think we can prove it. I submit to you that the prairie dogs have inalienable life-rights, and that their life-rights are precursors to the Corleys' property rights.

"Please allow me to introduce Dr. Chuck Pentoff, Professor of Biology from New Mexico State University. He is one of the foremost experts in the world on the Gunnison prairie dogs."

A short, slender man stood up, a man in his early forties, wearing a tan safari shirt with large pockets and beige hush puppies. He shifted the cell phone case and small pair of binoculars that hung from his belt, then approached the podium with the manner of a teacher who spent a good deal of time waiting for people to ask intelligent questions. There, he straightened the horn-rimmed glasses on his nose, which seemed too large for his shiny, balding head.

His stance suggested he was always right.

Jeff, Bob, and Francisco glanced anxiously at one another. The three men now realized that Donald had choreographed the entire evening.

Laura waited outside for her dramatic entry, and Dr. Pentoff just happened to be in the crowd. Jeff took a deep breath and swallowed hard. He had underestimated Pressman.

"May I address the Council?" Dr. Pentoff asked.

"Yes, please."

"I'm Dr. Chuck Pentoff and I've been retained as a consultant by the Forest Guardians. They believe that the prairie dogs lived on the land, as a full and undisturbed homeland, prior to Corley's ownership. Frankly, I'm not sure if this is true, but I do know how to find out."

"How would you do that?" the Chairman asked.

Mom squeezed Jeff's arm. He could tell from her face that her stomach hurt and she was horribly distressed. Something had changed, and the room smelled moldy.

"It would take some time. Basically, I would attempt to find out by monitoring the language of the prairie dogs."

"They have a language?" the Chairman asked with a skeptical laugh. "You mean you can understand them?"

"Yes. They have a rudimentary language. Their language evolves over generations. I can likely tell from their language development how many generations have lived there and for how long."

Jeff raised his eyebrows and nodded at Epstein.

"Mr. Chairman, if I may," Epstein said. "We would like to proceed with safe and monitored relocation. How long the prairie dogs have lived there is not relevant to the issue at hand."

"I think it might be," said Councilor Chavez. "As Councilor for this district, I have an obligation to be fair to everyone. After all, this idea of life-rights could have a bearing. Both people and animals have a right to life."

The women from the Martha Circle cheered and clapped.

Chavez continued, "Would you be willing to share the cost for Pentoff here to settle this question? It could have a long-term bearing on our Ordinance and certainly affect our vote."

Mom squeezed Jeff's arm.

"Mr. Chairman, Councilor Chavez, we would be willing. However, I would like to begin relocating the prairie dogs before their breeding season in May."

"You'll have time later, if that's the option we choose," Chavez said. "We have to find out who was there first. Dr. Pentoff, can you find out in thirty days before our March meeting?"

"I need permission to set up on the Corley land and to stay there for the month," Pentoff said.

"I'll help you get started," Jeff said.

Chavez made a motion and it passed. Dr. Pentoff was to provide a report to the Council by the next meeting, and they would go from there. It was clear to Jeff and the attorneys that who lived on the land first would now be the determining factor in the Corleys' request for postponement of the Ordinance 2002-4. Somehow, the issue had moved politically from property rights to right-to-life issues. Mom and Jeff looked straight ahead and stood tall as they walked out. June tried to offer a comforting word, but Mom ignored her. The Martha Circle women gave each other high-fives all around.

Ida listened from the back of the room, watching Donald smile and work the room. As the crowd disbursed, she sank into despair. She felt helpless as she heard Jeff attempt to negotiate, and Danny's continual happy whispers annoyed her. Why did he have to stand right there with that smelly dog? Didn't he understand what was at stake here?

"I don't believe this happened," Danny exclaimed. "They approved enough money for the rest of the year for the spay/neuter program. I didn't think they would listen to me. Isn't that great?"

As Mom and Jeff left, Ida folded her arms and stared at the floor. She had a premonition that the land was never going to sell, and she was stuck here in her life.

14

Danny rushed out the door with Ida behind him. "Hundreds of unwanted dogs and cats will be prevented. Imagine. I think it was the photo of the truck full of dead dogs, don't you?"

"Congratulations," Ida said flatly. She caught up to him.

Danny slowed down. "You know, it's been nearly five years, but I can see the promises working. This is surely a new happiness, and I did in fact know the right thing to do in this situation. Yup, God is doing for me what I couldn't do for myself."

"Five years since what?"

"Since I quit drinking."

"Oh, I didn't realize you had a problem."

"Yup. I help the rehab folks and sponsor drunks. It's my service work."

Donald and Dr. Pentoff walked ten yards behind them. Donald called out.

"Ida, wait just a minute. I'd like for you to meet Dr. Pentoff."

They stopped. "Hello," she said. She extended her hand and Pentoff shook it with a limp grip, perhaps just being polite.

"I was thinking." Donald said. "We had a good conversation before. Would you accept another invitation for lunch sometime? I'd like to take up where we left off."

Ida smiled, folding her arms in front of her. "I think the stakes have been raised. This time it will have to be dinner at a nice place."

"Fair enough. I'll call you next week and we can decide on a place."

"Nice to meet you," Dr. Pentoff said.

"Me, too." Ida smiled. "It's always exciting to meet smart men."

Ida and Danny hung back as Donald and Dr. Pentoff walked ahead.

"I was wondering. Did you by any chance see my brother while you were at the hospital? His name is Junior."

Danny stopped and turned. "Yes, I did."

"This is too weird. How do you know Junior?"

"Seems like a huge coincidence, but God always has a plan, don't you think?"

Ida tipped her head. "Are you his sponsor?"

Danny smiled. "Yup, I'm just getting to know him. He's pretty fucked up about now."

"Fucked up. Is that your professional opinion?"

"I'm not a professional, Ida, but I do know drunks, and Junior is fucked up, pure and simple."

"He's angry, I know that," Ida said. "I can't believe you're working with him." She touched Danny's arm. "Sometimes he calls me, but he's been under a dark blanket for years, and I don't really know him anymore. You know he almost died."

"He's young. I think he's got a chance," Danny said. "He can get through this and get some time under his belt. It will be a new life, that's for sure."

"What do you think he needs the most?"

Danny started walking, and Ida kept pace. "I really shouldn't say."

"I'm used to keeping medical information private. It won't go beyond us."

"Most of all? I think your mom and dad need to leave him alone for a while so he can see his way clear. They're stones around his neck. They pull him down into a dark place."

"I tend to agree. They can be hard to be around. I always feel judged or ignored."

Danny was quiet for a moment, then said, "Hey, I feel like celebrating. Would you like to go to Scarpas for a pizza? I'm thinking hamburger and pineapple."

Ida wrinkled her nose. "I hate pineapple. I'll just get a salad."

They took separate cars, and met at Scarpas. Danny motioned to a quiet corner, and the server ushered them to the table and lit the candle. They ordered—his pizza and her salad.

"Do you think that Donald guy knew about Laura's horrible photo?" Ida asked.

"You bet," Danny said. "I think he directed the whole thing, just like a movie."

"Really?"

"After I talked, I saw a chart he had on the table. I think he even helped write the church women's speeches."

"What a jerk. Jeff sure did look surprised," Ida said.

"I think he caught everyone by surprise," Danny pulled a piece of pizza loose from a string of cheese.

"I'm glad Pop wasn't there. It would have been a bad scene. Pop's pretty outspoken. Sometimes his support doesn't help. What about you? Does your father support your dog rescue efforts?"

"My father's dead."

"Oh, I'm sorry. I didn't know."

"Yeah, he died in a motorcycle accident when I was a senior. That Pressman guy is wily. When you're up against someone like that, you've got to use everything you've got. No holds barred."

"You're right. Jeff wasn't prepared. He should have covered that relocator better."

"Who could have known? It was probably innocent. He just sold the prairie dogs to a guy in Farmington who was supposed to turn them loose."

"He turned them loose all right, and now they're targets for shooters or already dead."

"I think Jeff just needs to get the rest of them moved somewhere safe— not a big deal."

"It might be too late. You heard the councilor. That guy Pentoff thinks the prairie dogs were there before my grandfather bought the land."

"He's still got to prove that, and they have to get by the 'private property' issue."

"We'll watch Pentoff closely. Ida put her hand on her chin. "He seems like a wimp, don't you think? I hate the idea of him on our property—for a month for Christ sake."

"Your situation is going to be okay. Just relax," Danny said.

"And how do you know that, Mr. Man-of-the-world?"

"It's like my situation. I just kept doing the right thing, and I turned the outcome over to God. Tonight God did for me what I couldn't do for myself."

Ida shifted in her seat and looked down at her empty salad bowl. "What do you think God did for you?"

"I think he nudged things just a little so the vote was positive and now thousands of lives will be saved."

"You're weird. You just happened to pull that councilor's heartstrings with those photos and by having Lucky with you. It was a good move."

"That's what I mean. I did the work and God took care of the outcome. Tell your family to get prepared and then turn those prairie dogs over to God. It'll work out. You'll see."

Ida wiped her mouth with a napkin and stood up. "I've got some things to do," Ida said, her eyes narrowing. "Starting with that wimp Pentoff."

Danny grabbed the check. "I've got it, my treat."

"Thanks, but I still think you're weird."

"How so?"

"I think I need to control my own outcomes, and so do you."

"Whatever, but it's going to wear you out."

As they walked to their cars Danny said, "I think I'll take that as a compliment—you know, that you think I'm weird."

Ida smiled.

"Hey, I've got an idea," Danny said. "Would you like to have a tour of the animal shelter?"

"Why not?" Ida said. "I wouldn't mind seeing where you work."

"How about tomorrow?"

"Sure. Tomorrow's fine. I work a day shift. Come by after three." Ida got in her car, and drove off waving. She wondered why she'd been so impulsive. This guy was definitely not her type.

Danny picked her up after work, and they toured through the clamor and the smells.

"These are the ones they've picked up and been able to identify," he said, gesturing to a cage filled with yelping dogs. "They call the owners to come and get them, but sometimes they don't come. They have to buy a city license and have current rabies shots. It's forty-five bucks."

"Where do they go if the owners don't pick them up?"

"Down that hall over there. That's death row. After two weeks they're killed and taken to the landfill."

Ida stepped lightly on the wet floor and stopped at a door. "What's in there?"

"That's the cat house." Danny smiled. "They rotate them to the front adoption cages for a couple of weeks, and then the unlucky ones are killed."

"This is horrible. I can see why you're happy about the budget increase."

"Want to take a kitten home?"

"I don't think so. I'm never home."

That night they went to dinner and saw *The Bourne Identity* with Matt Damon. Danny smelled like Old Spice and fabric softener. He probably put too many softener sheets in the dryer. She was pleased, however, that his blue eyes revealed a hint of lust. He dropped her off at her apartment. Maybe there's a friendship in the making.

The next afternoon they walked for a couple of hours on the river Bosque trail. Danny was a good listener, and Ida talked openly about her disappointment over the prairie dog fiasco. They went to the Flying Star for some soup, and split a huge piece of chocolate raspberry layer cake. Ida let Danny put a forkful of chocolate icing into her mouth.

"That is way too sweet." She smiled and wiped the side of her mouth.

"You deserve it," he said. "It's time for a good life. You've been hopping around too long."

"Hopping around?" Ida frowned. She thought he was criticizing her, like Mom would.

"You know, jumping from one thing to the next, and then moving on again. I think you need to slow down and really savor every day. Maybe you're missing something."

When Danny stopped the car to drop her off, Ida impulsively invited him in for coffee, although for the life of her, she couldn't imagine why. Too late now. She unlocked the door and turned on the lights. Danny looked around, and stood with his hands in his pockets.

"What would you like to drink?" she asked.

"Have you got a Diet Pepsi?"

"Sure, but I'm going to have a vodka tonic. That won't bother you, will it?"

"No, that should be okay," he said.

Ida mixed herself a drink, and poured him a Diet Pepsi. "Cheers."

They sipped their drinks for a moment, and then Danny took hers from her hand, put both glasses on the counter, and stood in front of her.

"What are you doing? I was drinking that."

He put his hands on each side of her and backed her up to the counter. He stood close enough to be nose to nose. Maybe she should be afraid.

"I want to see your eyes," he said.

She let him gaze into her eyes for a moment and then turned away. "What did you see?"

"I saw a very lonely soul in there," he said as he held her face with both hands. He kissed her gently under each eye, and then kissed her softly on her lips. Their mouths lingered for a moment as she put her hands on his forearms, ducked her head under one of his arms, and moved to the side. She picked up her drink and drained it. "I don't think I know you well enough to talk like that."

"You let me kiss you," he replied.

"But that's different. What do you want, anyway?"

"I want to get right to the truth," he said. "The truth stops a lot of nonsense, don't you think?"

"Okay, I am lonely sometimes, and so is everyone else. I have a lot of friends, though, and my work keeps me busy." Ida steadied herself. She thought they would hang out, laugh, and maybe someday have a roll in the hay, but she didn't expect this. Danny was too direct. "Aren't you ever lonely?" she asked.

"Sometimes I'm lonely and sometimes I feel really crowded." He pointed a finger to his temple. "It's dangerous for me to be alone with this monkey brain. Know what I mean? It's weird. I feel sad when I'm alone and I don't like to be around people, present company excepted of course." Danny chewed his upper lip. "Sometimes all I know to do is pray."

"You pray?" *Oh no, not like my mother.*

"I ask God to take away my worry and resentment. When I feel crowded, it's usually from self-pity or my impatience with people. You know, 'poor me' stuff. I have to find peace somehow, and praying works better than drinking or doing drugs."

"Are you, well, do you still have a problem with alcohol?"

"I can't drink," Danny said. "I'm an alcoholic, but like I said, I've been five years without a drink or a drug. Don't worry though, I'm harmless. My real problem now is lust." He grinned.

Ida poured some vodka and tonic in her glass and added a couple of ice cubes. "Are you sure my drinking doesn't bother you?"

"I do fine with Pepsi, but thanks for asking."

Ida excused herself. She went to the bathroom and splashed water on her face, studying her eyes in the mirror. She couldn't see what Danny saw, but noticed some sadness. She refreshed her lipstick, ran a brush though her hair, and touched a hint of jasmine behind each ear and on her throat. As she came back to the living room, Danny was checking her books and reading the titles.

"You read novels," he said. He raised his head and face as though he smelled the jasmine.

"Yeah, I like fiction like John Grisham. His stories are exciting—nothing too heavy. Did you read *The Firm*? Tom Cruise was great in the movie."

"Great movie. Lately I've been reading things I read in college. I think I missed a lot because my consciousness was normally altered, as they say."

"Like what?"

"Now I'm reading Flannery O'Connor's short stories. Last month I finished Steinbeck's *East of Eden*, and I'm about half way though Fox's *Sermon on the Mount*." He paused. "What in the world is that wonderful smell?"

"It's jasmine. Did I put on too much?"

"No, I like it. It smells warm and sexy." He moved close, took her hand, and walked slowly toward the bedroom.

As if a gentle wind was pushing her, Ida tipped her head and allowed herself to be led. Danny looked around, turned on a night light, and then sat down on her bed as if it were his. He had an air about him that made her wonder if she had known him for a very long time.

She sat beside him, embarrassed because she was sitting there and because the bed was so rumpled. "I didn't make the bed this morning."

Danny put his face down in the sheets and took a deep breath. "It's okay with me, the bed smells like you, warm and spicy." He smiled and kissed her gently.

"So, just like that—we're going to bed?" Ida asked.

"I figured you wanted to. Did I misread something?"

Ida felt puzzled and realized she must have revealed her curiosity about having sex with this gentle, funny man who loved puppies and worked at an animal shelter. This was a far cry from the group of upwardly mobile doctors, the place she normally searched for her ideal man. There was something mysterious about Danny, but she couldn't figure out what it was. It was as though he was from another country or another time.

"No, you didn't miss anything." She took a breath and began unbuttoning her blouse. Might as well get on with it. Danny undressed quickly and slipped under the rumpled sheets. He held up the sheet for her to join him. Ida decided to finish undressing slowly so he could watch, an action she understood, and then she slipped in bed beside him. She stretched her arms over her head, pointed her toes, and felt almost mischievous. *At least we're through the awkward part.*

"I have an IUD," Ida whispered. She had a passing thought about STDs, but figured since he was so healthy, he must be okay—a foolish thought for a nurse. *Oh, what the hell.* Danny kissed her gently and slowly.

His hand traced the lines of her throat, her breasts, her hips, and held her face with a feathery touch that felt commanding and strong. His breath smelled like sweet cloves, and his tongue felt silky as he explored her tongue and lips. She felt a little flushed and smelled a hint of citrus in his hair as she moved her body to fit against his. She wasn't used to being with someone who was her same height, but it felt comfortable to her when they gazed into each other's eyes, something she normally avoided.

They held each other for a while, and he stroked her back as he kissed up and down her neck. Ida fondled his body until he was ready, and then eased onto her back and used both hands to help him enter her. She scooted down slightly and prepared herself to respond. Ida was good at this and knew how to please a man with her Kegel squeezes and thrusts. Ida remembered the time when a doctor, after vigorous sex, fell on his back out of breath and told Ida she was truly an Olympic sexual athlete and deserved a Gold Medal. She liked that. It made her feel competent and high on the scale of womanhood, an athlete in the art of love.

Danny dismissed her preparation as he slipped his hands under her hips and arranged her exactly to his liking. The balance had shifted, and he was in charge. He moved slowly and deeply. She was surprised at her rush of natural body fluids. Deep breathing filled her lungs and tightened her stomach muscles. She yearned to draw closer. Normally she used KY lubricant from the nightstand drawer, a graceful one-handed ritual she'd mastered to preserve the mood, but not now. This was the first time she could remember her body responding this way.

Danny didn't stop, although he occasionally slowed way down and pressed his body to hers as he tenderly kissed her mouth and then her breasts. Ida looked into his eyes and he smiled.

"Relax," he said, "just let yourself go."

Then he lifted her hips up off the bed, slid a pillow under her hips with a surprising show of strength, and began a deep and persistent movement. As he moved faster, she felt as though he was taking her over, possessing her, making her obey him as his hands completely controlled her upward movement. Her mind filled with vivid colors and jasmine smells as she reached and grasped with her swollen labia and pushed ferociously against him, flesh on flesh, rubbing herself back and forth and slowly losing consciousness of anything but swirling rainbow colors and silky fabrics rippling in the wind. A soft moan started quietly from a place under her stomach, gained momentum as it entered her lungs, and filled her throat with a sound that came alive on the edge of crying. The light from colors going by at warp speed swept her mind away for a few seconds and put her down in a new place.

"Oh my God," she shouted. "What's happening to me?" The moan erupted as she threw her arms out wide and arched upward. "Oh my God."

They lay quietly for a while, tracing each other's bodies with gentle fingers.

"You sure do have a nice apartment. Thanks for asking me to come by."

Ida slapped his chest and laughed. His joke helped her cover up the strange new feelings she was having about her body and about his taking over. She felt a warm shiver as she thought about obeying his gentle commands. *This woman on this bed is truly not me. And this man beside me, well, who knows anything about that.* "Who are you really?" she asked.

"I'm just a guy who loves your smell," Danny replied. "What you see is what you get. Just a guy."

"No, I mean who are you deep down?"

"Deep down I'm a man full of lust in search of a life of sanity and a God of my understanding."

"I don't feel lonely." She put her hand on his heart. Danny got up on one elbow and looked into her eyes in the dim light.

"I don't see any loneliness in there now," he said. "Can you see lust in my eyes?"

"No, your eyes look peaceful, like you don't want anything."

"How about that. No lust, no loneliness."

"Do you want to sleep here tonight?" Ida asked.

"I didn't plan to, so I've got animals at home to feed, and I've got to be at the shelter real early. I'll take a rain check, though." Danny got dressed and Ida stood up by the bed, looking around for her bathrobe.

"My God you're beautiful," Danny said. "When God made women, he used you as the gold standard." Ida faced him, smiled and posed with her hands on her hips, and then turned to check the closet. She grabbed a pink robe and wrapped it around herself, feeling mildly embarrassed about her display.

"Do you want some coffee before you drive?"

"Sure. I could use a cup."

15

Chuck Pentoff arrived at the Corley place early Monday morning in a gray Dodge mini-van. Pop and Jeff stood by the gate to meet him. Mom and Jeff had explained the issue to Pop, and Mom made him promise to be helpful. Jeff felt awkward about the turn of events, promised Pop he would check his horoscope, and put on a confident face as he swung the gate open. Chuck stepped out of the van. His pith helmet made him appear ready for a safari. He wore new hiking boots and camping pants from REI with the price tag still on the back pocket.

"I'd like to introduce my father, Roy Corley," Jeff said. "Everyone calls him Pop."

"Hello, I'm Chuck Pentoff—it's fine to call me Chuck. We're going to be spending a good deal of time together for the next month."

Pop shook Chuck's hand and pulled him off balance, close to his face.

"What the hell do you do for five-thousand bucks a week?" He let Chuck pull his hand free.

"Well, sir, I study Gunnison prairie dogs, their social behavior, and their language. I'll be keeping daily notes, and I'll prepare a report in about three weeks."

Jeff put his hand on Pop's shoulder. "How can we help?"

"I'm going to find a suitable spot to set up, and then I'll need electric power to my tent. And I'll need a bathroom and a shower. I'll be cooking in the tent."

"You can use Junior's place for that," Jeff offered. "He's away for the time you'll be here. I'm sure Pop can move the generator nearby."

Chuck shook his head. "A generator is too noisy and polluting. I'll need you to run power from somewhere."

"I can run the power from the machine shed," Pop said.

"Okay, then. I'll leave my car here and scout around for a while. Can you show me how to get to the bathroom?"

"Walk down the road to the trailer by the house," Jeff said. "I'll meet you there and unlock the door. I need to make sure Popeye knows who you are so he won't bark."

"I gather Popeye is a dog?"

"Yes, Junior's companion. He stays at the trailer."

"Please keep him away from my tents. He would be an uncontrolled variable in my study. We do not want anything affecting the outcome. This is science, you know."

"We'll make sure Popeye stays away. He doesn't like strangers anyway."

Chuck walked around, studied the property, and settled on a spot near the top of a rise about fifty yards from the trailer and hidden by a large chamisa. It was one of their childhood shooting spots. Jeff, Pop, and Junior used to hide there in the early evening and shoot prairie dogs with .22-rifles. Jeff helped set up two camouflage tents: one family-size tent for Chuck and his listening devices, and the other, smaller tent for amplifiers and other equipment. Chuck strung wire to five different mounds with active prairie dog holes, about seventy-five yards apart from each other. He hooked up a series of small high impedance microphones to each wire and hid them near the holes. The wires terminated at an amplifier and digital recorder set up in the equipment tent. He put a small mixing board, earphones, and his laptop computer, a printer, and another screen in the other tent, and arranged small speakers, chairs, and a thick foam pad for his sleeping bag. At the large tent opening near the door, he drove a stake in the ground, mounted a small platform, and attached binoculars, a telescope, and his digital camera.

"This is quite an affair," Jeff said.

"I'm very thorough in my work, and I'm hoping to publish the results. I'll have video recordings, still photos, and sound recordings of everything I observe. After all, I am the expert in prairie dog language in the United States and maybe the world. It is a heavy responsibility."

"Okay. What's next?"

"Let's get the power hooked up and you can help me test everything."

Pop came back from Summit Electric with a couple of boxes of 8-3 underground wire. Pop had fashioned two 4-plug receptacles, and together they ran the wire from the tents to the machine shed. Pop had a spare 50-amp breaker, and he hooked up the wire and snapped on the breaker.

"This stuff is expensive," he said to Chuck. "I'm going to take it off the five-thousand a week you're getting."

"Sorry, Pop. Expenses for supplies to get me started will be your cost. I'm sure you can use this wire for something after I'm gone."

"Well, you've got power." Pop threw up his hands and walked to the house, muttering. He dragged his left foot as though it hurt more than usual.

Jeff and Chuck tested each of the microphones, and Chuck checked out the digital sound and video recorders. Everything worked. Images from the binoculars and telescopic lens on the video recorder filled the computer screen. Chuck could switch between the holes or display them all at once on a split screen.

"What happens now?" Jeff asked.

"I think I've identified the main entrances to five different coteries. There will be about twenty-five prairie dogs in each coterie, and there will be a dominant male and a couple of his favorite females that we'll need to identify. Then I'll listen, record, and identify their distinctive sounds. If the sounds match from the different coteries, then we can conclude we have a distinct word that communicates throughout the community. My work takes incredible patience, but that's what good scientists have, endless patience. Excuse me. Bathroom break. I'll be back in a few minutes."

"Where were we?"

"Endless patience, recording words," Jeff said.

"Yes. Each generation of prairie dogs lives three to five years. If a culture of prairie dogs is relatively undisturbed, they seem to come up with a new word every three or four generations. We will see how many words we can identify in the next three weeks. I'll be conservative and calculate that each distinct word represents twenty years. I'll assume that they had no words at all when they first got here. Therefore, for example, if I can identify six distinct words, then I will conclude they have been relatively undisturbed in this homeland for six times twenty, or one-hundred and twenty years. The key is to identify the words. The rest is logic."

"I gather you know some prairie dog words?"

"Yes, that was part of my doctoral dissertation, 'Prairie Dog Linguistics and the Sexual and Social Organization of the Mammalian *Cynomys gunnisoni.*' "

"Do you provide a lot of consulting?" Jeff asked.

"Actually, no. This is my first consulting job. Normally I teach and do private research on the Gunnison and other endangered species. I assure you, however, I will be objective."

"Are you married? You're going to be gone quite a while."

"I'm married, but we don't have any children. My wife Lola supported me all through graduate school. She's excited and has her eye on a new home. This job will help with the down payment. She might visit one weekend. I told her I'd take her to the Santa Ana Star Casino."

"The casino?" Jeff smiled. "That's surprising. I thought you were a scientist."

Chuck laughed. "We first met in a casino," he said. "I like to play poker and Lola plays the slots. She can sit by the one-dollar slots for hours. One weekend I won sixty-eight hundred dollars at the poker table."

"I hope you don't lose your consulting fee."

"Don't worry, I promised Lola we'd save it for the down payment. Besides, I have to focus on publications. I'd like to move to an associate professorship."

Despite the friendly conversation, Jeff found himself imagining ways he could question Chuck's study if it turned out badly. He was beginning to see serious flaws. The prairie dogs that first arrived could have already had five or six words from other habitats nearby. There could have been natural migration over the years. It was likely they were disturbed by floods through the Domingo Baca Arroyo. Independent variables existed everywhere. Pentoff seemed too eager. Surely, Donald Pressman knows it would be awkward to defend Pentoff's work in a courtroom, and the best thing to do is to cooperate and see what he discovers. He's probably not going to find much anyway. Jeff smiled to himself. *Maybe he'll find a prairie dog word for "get me the hell outta here, I want to move."*

Jeff sat on the porch with Mom and Pop, and the three of them watched Chuck drive down the road to get supplies.

"This should work out okay," Jeff said. "It's very unlikely he's going to prove anything."

"It's damned inconvenient," Pop muttered.

"If Councilor Chavez had just kept quiet, our motion would have passed," Mom said. "And that Laura, she sure did have her night in the spotlight."

"Chavez has got us between a rock and a hard place," Pop sighed. "There's not much else we can do. Another twist of fate."

"I'll take Chuck some leftover food from church," Mom said, seemingly eager to change the topic. "This weekend, I can make him some turkey sandwiches and bake some blueberry muffins."

"That would be nice, but don't overdo it," Jeff warned. "We don't want to appear we are trying to influence his scientific study."

"Maybe there's a prairie dog word for 'gimme a blueberry muffin,'" Pop said. A grin crept across his face.

"Maybe so," Mom said. She smiled at Pop and clasped his hand.

When Jeff left after dinner, he saw a light come on in the tent and a small blue flame from the camp stove outside. Chuck was cooking supper. Down the road, the Forest Guardians sat around a small campfire and sang songs. Tonight was a new moon, so it would be very dark. Clouds moved in and brought a gray dusk to the fifteen acres. The night smelled stale, and Jeff felt trapped and wary. A hawk dove toward a prairie dog hole and Jeff heard a disturbing sound: "aaach, aaach; aaach, aaach." It sounded to Jeff like a small child screaming for help.

16

On Saturday morning, after Chuck's first week, he invited Mom, Pop, and Jeff to visit his tent and to see the progress of his research. They followed the path Chuck had worn from the tent to the trailer. Mom handed Chuck a basket of blueberry muffins, and they sat down on folding chairs in the main tent. Chuck moved an easel and foam board for his presentation. He had put up an array of photos.

"Thank you for the muffins," he said. "I'm eager to give you a preliminary report."

Mom felt uncomfortable in the steel chair, and her stomach hurt. Easter was early this year, falling on the last Sunday in March. It was only four weeks away, and she dreaded the possibility that another big failure would invade her Easter table and bring disappointment to her children. Pop's manner was sullen, and Jeff seemed tired and cheerless. Mom folded her hands together on her lap and smiled to hide her building annoyance.

"First, I want to report that I'm making good progress," Chuck said. "These photos appear to be the dominant males for each of five coteries. The male typically has three or four favorite females. They are polygamous, you know. The survival rate is not good for prairie dog pups, so they have many offspring."

Mom stared at the array of photos. Each male was standing up and facing the camera as though he was posing. For rodents, they were kind of cute.

"How did you get these photos?" she asked.

"Oh, I have a telephoto lens on my digital camera. I transfer the video to my computer, and then I can print individual frames. They're quite clear, don't you think?"

"They're great photos," Jeff said. "They'll look good in your publication."

"I hope so." He pointed to his computer screen. "These are photos of the favorite females for each of the dominant males. Typical communication styles involve male-to-female and female-to-male. In addition, there is often female-to-female chatter. The males don't communicate much with each other unless they are sending out a warning to everyone."

"Have you found any words?" Pop asked.

"I think I've found two, but I need to observe for a while longer. I want to be objective. Unless I find the exact same sound in all five coteries, then I do not give it the status of a word. I'm fairly certain about the word 'aaach, aaach.'"

Pop shook his head. "What the hell does *aaach, aaach* mean?" he asked as he raised his eyebrows at Mom.

Chuck pointed to the photos. "I've observed that each of the five males screamed out that sound and dove into their holes whenever a hawk flew nearby. I think the sound means 'danger.'"

"Maybe it means 'hawk,'" Jeff said. He smiled at Mom, hoping she'd be amused by his comment. Instead, she just looked troubled.

"No, I don't think so. They also screamed 'aaach, aaach' when a coyote came near, and when an owl landed on a cedar branch nearby. I am almost ready to conclude that it means 'danger'. I have recorded each male screaming 'aaach, aaach' more than five times. I am going to use ten times as conclusive evidence."

"How do you tell these males apart?' Mom asked. She leaned over and studied the photos. "They all look the same to me."

"The one on the left I call Topper. He has a white tuft on his head, and he gets up as high as he can on any nearby mound of dirt. I gather he likes to be on top. He has probably always been a natural born leader. The next one I call Big Al. See, he has bigger than normal flanks and chest. He probably weighs five or six ounces more than the other males. In the human world, he would be your football-player type. The next one I call Skipper. He's nervous and hyperactive. He turns around often, and he mutters and chatters. I am sure his mother thinks he is a real motor-mouth. This one is Little Ed. He's clearly smaller than the other males. He's slender and quick. If you look carefully, you can see a badly chipped front tooth. He probably chipped it in a fight with a bully when he was little."

"What about the fifth one?" Pop asked.

"Well, I've not named him yet. He's darker brown, has a thick neck, and scampers with an unusual gait. I think he once had a broken leg. I've seen him with six different females. He's a real ladies' man."

Mom shook her head back and forth. She looked at Jeff and rolled her eyes.

"Have you identified the females?" Jeff asked.

"I have. There are too many for names." He scrolled through photos on his computer. "I call Topper's females FT1, FT2, and FT3. The letters stand for 'Female,' and 'Topper,' and the '1, 2, and 3' stand for the order of his favorites. So FT1 means Topper's number-one female. I have done the same for the others."

"How do you know which female is the favorite?" Mom asked.

Chuck glanced at Jeff. He pursed his lips. "I'm not sure how to say this scientifically. Let me try. I count the number of breeding encounters for each male. Being polygamous, each male clearly has a choice. When the encounters with one female reach double the number of encounters with the next female, I conclude one is the favorite and the other is second."

Mom blushed. "Have you identified any other words?" She held her stomach with both hands. She felt tired.

"I have recorded a number of instances of the sound *'eeek, eeek'* during their breeding encounters. I think *'eeek, eeek'* means 'breeding' or 'sex,' but I didn't notice it right away, so I have to go back through the recordings and watch more encounters. As I said, each male will have to say *'eeek, eeek,'* at least ten times before I conclude it is a word."

"Do they say *'eeek, eeek'* when they start breeding or when they are finished?" Pop asked.

"From what I can tell, they say it a number of times throughout the breeding event," Chuck said. "The sound is quite clear. The *e's* are always the long vowel sound. It is as though they know the English letter *e*."

"So from your theory," Jeff said, "if *aaach, aaach,* and *eeek, eeek* are indeed words, then you would conclude this culture of prairie dogs has been here for about forty years."

"Yes, that's correct. There are a number of other sounds, but I haven't identified patterns yet. This week, I focused my attention on danger and sex, so to speak." He grinned at Jeff. "Excuse me." Chuck walked down the path to the trailer.

"This isn't going well," Jeff said. "His science is weak, but it plays well with the political folks. There is a lot more here than first meets the eye. I'm surprised."

"What should we do?" Mom asked, folding her arms over her stomach. She felt as though someone had opened a valve in her soul and her dreams were flowing out.

Chuck came back into the tent.

"Thank you for your report," Mom said. "We'd better get going. Let me know if you would like some more muffins or something."

"Sure, and thank you for your hospitality."

Pop, Mom, and Jeff filed out of the tent. Jeff's head drooped.

Suddenly, Pop turned around, back toward Chuck. "Say, I think you should name that other male Hopalong."

"Hopalong?"

"Yeah, since he's crippled. You know, he sort of hops along."

"Will do," Chuck said.

Ida worked a long weekend and began a four-day break on Tuesday. She spent most of the day with Mom. Mom was in distress, and since the discussion at the hospital, she felt a renewed sense of compassion. Mom's colon surgery was only six years ago, and she was worried something was up.

"Is your pain worse?"

"It isn't so much that it is worse, it just never stops. It wears on me."

"Do you take your pain pills?"

"I take Tylenol, but I don't want to take that other stuff. I get foggy and I don't feel like doing anything."

"Does anything else help?"

"If I'm able to do my prayers and meditations, it seems to dull the pain."

"You know it's time for another CAT scan. There may be something going on in there, and we don't want to ignore it."

"I know, but Easter is coming up, and I'm looking forward to our family dinner. This year, I'm going all out, and we're going to have a turkey and a ham. Junior will be home by then. He likes scalloped potatoes, and your father likes creamed green beans with mushrooms. I'm going to bake that corn bread with molasses, and a couple of cherry pies. Do you want that spicy stuffing for the turkey, the one with green chile?"

"Whatever you cook will be fine, and I will be there to help."

"Will you wear that green outfit, the one with the white blouse and jacket? It makes you look so professional."

"Sure. I know Easter is important to you." She feared there might not be another Easter.

Mom seemed worn and anemic. The sparkle in her eyes dulled more often. "I'm worried Dr. Pentoff is going to find proof that the prairie dogs were here first, and that jerk Chavez is going to buy into that whole thing. He could make sure the ordinance is passed, and we'd be stuck."

Ida put her hand on Mom's shoulder. "I know. Jeff told me all about it. I'm worried, too. Have you talked with Bob Epstein?"

"I called him. He said our best chance is supervised relocation, so he's investigating. He says he's concerned the Councilors have this whole business about prairie dogs having 'life rights' mixed up with the right-to-life issue. It gets confused with church and everything."

"I don't trust those church people," Ida said, "especially that Laura and her friends. They'll do anything to stop you. Why does she seem to hate you so much?"

"I have no idea." Mom sighed wearily. "Maybe it's because of the money. LeAnn said one time that we were killing prairie dogs for money, and that was against God's plan."

"See you before long," Ida said. She drove part way down the road and parked. Then she got her flashlight, found the path, and walked to the tent to visit Chuck.

"Hello, anybody home?" she called out.

"Yes, I'm here. Lola, is that you?"

"It's Ida Corley. We met at the City Council meeting?"

"Oh, yes. Come on in." Chuck arranged a chair. He had been watching breeding encounter videos, and he closed his laptop screen. "Would you like something to drink?" he asked.

"I'll have a beer."

"Sorry, I don't have any alcohol."

"Coffee?"

"I can't drink coffee or anything with caffeine."

"Okay, how about a Sprite?"

"Sorry, it's carbonated. Would you like tea? I have decaf peppermint."

"Sure, peppermint tea it is." Ida surveyed her surroundings. On a makeshift shelf, Chuck had a few pots and pans, cups, a couple of plates, and an array of pasta, boxed rice, boxed mashed potatoes, a couple of acorn squash, and a bunch of bananas. His foam mattress featured a doublewide sleeping bag and pillows with green flowered pillowcases. His clothes hung neatly on a rack, and he had a couple of folding cubbies with wheels that were full of books and papers. One battery lantern was on, and his laptop computer hummed. Photos of prairie dogs and labels covered a foam board on an easel.

"Excuse me," Chuck said. "I will be right back."

He took a flashlight and headed out on the path to Junior's trailer. Ida opened his laptop and watched videos of prairie dogs copulating and squealing *eeek, eeek*. She closed the laptop and stirred the mint tea that was heating on the single-burner camp stove. She saw the flashlight approaching, and sat on the bed with a cup of tea. Ida undid her ponytail, shook out her hair, touched up her lipstick, and slipped off her sweatshirt jacket. Her cleavage made soft shadows above her spaghetti strapped tank-top. The tent seemed warm from the heat of the equipment.

"Sorry, sometimes I have to attend to things quickly," he said.

Ida pointed to his array of bland food. "Do you have an intestinal disorder?" she asked. "You know, I'm a nurse, and it's safe to talk with me about things."

Chuck studied her face in the light of the lantern, and Ida thought she saw him look down at her breasts. She leaned forward. "I put the teapot on the shelf. It seems strong enough."

Chuck poured himself a cup of tea and sat down on a folding chair.

"I have to watch my diet. They say I have an irritated intestinal problem."

"Irritable bowel syndrome?" she asked.

"That's it. I do okay if I eat five or six small meals and stay with soluble fibers. I can't have alcohol, caffeine, or anything fatty. If I eat fried foods, I'm miserable for a couple of days."

"You know, I have a dietician friend who runs an IBS Diet Clinic on the weekends. If you'd like, I could give you a referral. Maybe she would have some diet tips that would be helpful."

"That would be nice. I'm always looking for relief."

"I'll tell her you are going to call." She cleared her throat. "What were you watching on your computer?"

"I've been making digital videos of male and female prairie dogs in their breeding rituals." He pointed to the male photos, and then he explained about their names, their polygamous nature, and their favorites. "I think I've made a new discovery," he said. "I'm certain that *eeek, eeek* is their word for sex or breeding, but upon review of the tapes, I think I've found another way of identifying the favorite female. My first way was to count the number of times a male would choose a certain female, and I think that remains a dependable method. However, I've also noticed that when a male is with his favorite female, his squeals of *eeek, eeek* are much louder. That discovery would be a scientific breakthrough and would be worth a publication by itself."

"Wow, can I watch?"

"Sure," Chuck said. "It is a good idea to have another observer." He brought the laptop over to the bed and sat down next to Ida. He started the video with Big Al over again. He had edited the tape, and had compiled enough breeding encounters to show that Big Al had chosen FA1 twice as often as FA2, and had chosen FA2 twice as often as FA3. There were over twenty-five breeding events.

"My, that Big Al is quite a thruster," Ida said.

"They get moving quite fast," Chuck said, focusing on the screen. "There are spermatozoa present all the time, so each thrust carries the opportunity of impregnating the female, so the deeper the better."

"Does the female always raise her tail and back up like that?" Ida asked.

"Most of the time they're compliant that way. On occasion, he'll pin her down and force her."

"Is that one the favorite?"

"Yes, now listen and try to remember how loud Big Al squeals. Okay, now this one is FA3. Doesn't he seem quieter?"

"Definitely, almost as though she is not as exciting as FA1. He doesn't seem to be thrusting as hard, either."

"Now, check this out. This is FA2."

They listened carefully to 'eeek, eeek.' Ida moved her face close to Chuck's.

"That's quieter than FA1," Ida said. "I'd say you're on to something here."

"Do you realize what this means? I may have discovered a means of ordering what I have called serial polygamy. The louder squeal may correlate with the female that could be genetically predisposed to the healthiest litters of pups. I could have stumbled on a way of helping to repopulate the Gunnison species and address their endangered status."

"Don't you mean we have discovered something? I am an observer as well." Ida smiled at him, reached up, and touched his nose. "I don't know, maybe FA1 is just a better lover, and Big Al loves her body."

"These male prairie dogs are not discriminating that way," Chuck said. "I think it is evolution at work."

Ida moved closer. "Have you ever thought of being polygamous?"

"I'm sure Lola wouldn't approve." He stood up and poured some more tea.

"Let's see. You are the male called Chuck Pentoff, so Lola would be FP1, right?"

He laughed aloud. "Yes, I guess that would be right. Are you suggesting that if I were polygamous, that you would be FP2?"

"Well, I guess it would depend on how loud you squeal." She laughed, stood up, and moved in close to Chuck. She took off his glasses and began unbuttoning his shirt. "Watching these videos has made me all hot and bothered."

"We shouldn't be doing this. I am not polygamous, and you are my client's daughter. This would destroy my scientific objectivity, and it's a conflict of interest." He pushed her hands away. "Let me have my glasses."

Ida took his hand, stared into his eyes, and slowly backed up to the mattress. She reached over and turned down the light. The muted light in the tent made shadows play on the walls from the videos of the prairie dogs copulating on the computer screen. The night was quiet except for their breathing and Big Al squealing, "eeek, eeek." Chuck had the twenty-five encounters running in a loop, so they continued to play, and their images flickered.

Ida pulled him gently down on the mattress, lay beside him, nuzzled in the nape of his neck, and let her hair flow over his face. She slowly unbuckled his belt, and Chuck let her slip his pants down to his knees. Ida gently stroked him with both hands. She covered his face with a pillow, paused, and touched him lightly, teasing him with first one hand and then the other. Without warning, Chuck jerked and ejaculated.

"It's okay," Ida said. "Just relax. I know what to do." She cupped her hands underneath. She probed around gently. Nothing. Undescended testicles? Cryptorchidism?

"Where are your balls?"

Chuck jumped up, pulled up his pants, and turned up the light. He closed the top of the computer.

"It is time for you to leave."

"Do you realize you could be at risk for testicular cancer?"

"Yes. I had surgery when I was twenty. It is not your business. You need to leave."

"Well, thank God. I worry about medical issues. I am interested, Chuck, and I want to learn more about your study. You have a powerful intellect."

"Thank you, but you really must go. You may visit again, but only in the daytime. That is a rule we must live by. I am not polygamous, and I know I am right about that."

"Bye. Hope to see you again." Ida put on her jacket, turned on her flashlight, and made her way back to her car, shaking her head, and smiling. This was the first man she'd ever met who's a premature ejaculator, has irritable bowel syndrome, lost his balls, and thinks he's always right. Wonder what his wife is like. At the gate, she stopped and checked her cell phone. The picture of Chuck was a little dark, but her computer would lighten it.

There was a missed call and a voice message. "Hello, Ida, this is Donald. Please call me back. I have made reservations for Saturday night if you are available." *Things are finally going my way,* she thought. *One down and one to go. Here comes my new life.*

She dialed his number. "Hi Donald, this is Ida."

"Hey, is Saturday night okay?"

"Sure, I'm available. Where are we going?"

"Is the Prairie Star nice enough?" he asked.

Ida laughed. "Sure, I've never been across the river with you. It could be fun."

"Okay, I'll pick you up at your apartment about 6 pm."

Ida spent Saturday afternoon cleaning her apartment. She put clean sheets on the bed, showered, and washed her hair. She chose a green skirt and a green scoop neck top that matched her eyes. Pearl earrings and a matching pearl necklace highlighted her light touch of makeup, and a hint of pink in her lipstick matched the pink bra that showed when she leaned forward. She blotted her lips as the doorbell rang, and she opened the door.

Donald's tan face and light hair framed his dark brown eyes. He wore a crisp blue blazer over a silk shirt with an open collar. The shirt was out, and his slacks were beige with sharp creases. Ida stepped back from his bright smile. Only Mom had teeth that nice, and it had taken Jeff months to create her smile.

"Please call me Donald. All friends do." He surveyed her apartment.

"Sure, would you like to have a drink?"

"Oh, I don't think so now, since we're driving across town. Can't be too careful, you know. Maybe later. We should go."

Ida grabbed a black sweater, and they walked to Donald's car. They drove in awkward silence. As they passed the Santa Ana Star Casino, Chuck Pentoff and a woman passenger pulled into the parking lot in his gray Dodge van.

"That looks like Pentoff and his wife," she said.

"Where?"

"There, pulling into Santa Ana. Maybe they're on a date."

"Would you like to go to the casino after dinner? It can be fun."

"Maybe, unless something else comes up. Been thinking about anything besides prairie dogs?"

Donald smiled. "You know, I love being a political activist, but someday I want to go back to teaching. Maybe someday I'll settle down, but not yet."

"I want more than anything to go on for my Master's Degree. Selling the land will really help with that."

"There are other ways, you know. I'll bet you make it happen."

Ida felt as though they made a good couple, or at least a convincing one. Strangers turned their heads as they walked by. Although they disagreed about the prairie dog issue, she felt warmth between them, although, admittedly, it was more like the friendship of a brother than the heat of her time with Danny. Donald was pleasant enough, though, and she wondered if he had tan lines or if he sunbathed in the nude. She looked forward to what she needed to do.

"What is it that you wanted to talk with me about?" she asked Donald.

"Well, it's a little awkward, and it has to be absolutely private. I would be more comfortable talking in your apartment."

"Okay, but let's stop at the casino for a little while."

Donald stood by Ida as she played a couple of dozen hands of blackjack. Ida felt exhilarated as she won a few hands, and turned and hugged Donald. He picked her up and spun her around when she doubled down on aces and won both hands. She cashed in three-hundred dollars in chips, and felt excited about what was to come.

"Okay, let's go," Ida said. "I'm dying of curiosity."

At her apartment, Donald sat at the kitchen table with coffee, and Ida made a gin and tonic for herself.

"I need you to promise this is just between us," Don said. "I want to make a serious proposition."

"A serious proposition?" Ida sat down and leaned forward. She followed his eyes to her scoop neck and her cleavage.

"Very serious," Donald said. He put his hand on the back of her hand and scooted closer.

"I have a donor to the Forest Guardians that will give me a million dollars."

"A million dollars? For what?"

"Well, he wants this prairie dog problem to be solved. He is proposing that the Forest Guardians purchase five acres of your land for one million dollars, and that your parents, in turn, give the remaining ten acres to a land trust. He'd put the five acres he buys into the trust, too. That way, your folks will have their retirement money, and the land trust will preserve the prairie dogs in perpetuity."

"That's what you wanted to talk with me about?"

"Yes, I thought that we get along well, and you would be the one to talk with Mom and Pop and your brothers."

"Why didn't you just talk with the lawyers?"

"Well, I have an intuition about you. You're very smart, and as a nurse, you've become pragmatic and focused on healing and solving problems.

You're the right one to bring it up, and I want this to work out. You see, Ida, I trust you. You're a good woman."

A good woman? She was accustomed to being a beautiful woman, a highly desired woman, a free and liberated woman—but a *good* woman?

"Will you talk with your family? It could be a good solution. I think Chuck Pentoff's report will make the City Councilors vote against your application, and that could stop your sale altogether. This way, you could withdraw your application, and your folks would have a million dollars."

Ida sat up straight. "I'm not sure about that," she said. "I think Chuck Pentoff may not conclude what you think he will."

"Will you at least talk with Mom and Pop?"

"I'll talk with them tomorrow. Is that it? Is there anything else you want to talk with me about?" Ida's voice turned chirpy.

"That's it, except I want to thank you for a lovely evening. I enjoy being with you." Donald stood up and hugged Ida briefly. "Call me soon and let me know what they say."

Ida walked him to the door. She felt manipulated or tricked, but she couldn't put her finger on why. He had been truthful. He had looked at her body. Yet her bed remained undisturbed, and she was to carry a solution to the heart of the problem, a proposition of a different kind, a compromise.

Ida called Mom right after church and said she'd like to meet with Mom, Pop, and Jeff. Mom arranged an early dinner, and at five o'clock they sat down and Mom offered a blessing.

"I met with Donald Pressman," Ida said immediately after Mom's amen. "He wants me to ask you something."

"It's probably best to work through the attorneys," Jeff said. "I'm a little uncomfortable about that."

"I know. I said the same thing, but here's the deal. He has a donor who wants to buy five acres to put in a land trust if we'll give the other ten acres to a land trust. Then the prairie dogs will stay here forever. He'll give us one million dollars."

"No way, Jose," Pop said. "I'm not giving any land to anybody."

"Wait a minute," Jeff said. "You and Mom could put away the million dollars, and with your Social Security and Medicare, you could retire and be comfortable for the rest of your lives. This could be a good idea."

"You kids wouldn't get anything until we die," Mom said, "and then it would only be what's left over. I don't like the idea at all."

"Then it's settled," Pop said. "Call Mr. Hollywood and tell him no way."

"I've been thinking," Ida said, "first we should see what happens at the City Council meeting. Chuck might not find enough words. They could vote to postpone so we could work on relocation."

"Oh, we got a letter today," Mom said. "They moved it up a week because of the conflict with Holy Week."

"Let's wait until then, and I'll tell Mr. Pressman we'd like him to keep the offer open until after the Council meeting."

"Do you think he will?" Jeff asked. "I'd hate for Mom and Pop to lose the opportunity. If Pentoff's report proves those prairie dogs were here before the Corley family bought the property, then he probably wouldn't want to go ahead."

"I can at least find out," Ida said.

As she got into her car, she saw a light in Pentoff's main tent, and a woman outside. Apparently, Lola was there for the weekend. Ida felt confused and scattered. It was as though she was standing under a waterfall, wet, and disheveled. *I need to call Danny. I need someone I can talk to—someone I trust. Trust? Wow, I guess I trust him. Where in the world did that come from?*

"This is Ida. How have you been?"

"I've been busy with the new budget and all the reorganization at the shelter," he said. "I thought about calling, I miss you. Sorry I've been out of touch."

"I'm feeling lonely and confused," she said. "Can we meet somewhere? I want to talk with you about some things."

"I can get away right now. Shall I drive up to your place?"

"Sounds great. Could you stop and get some ice cream? I want something sweet."

"Rocky road coming up. See you in an hour or so."

They sat at the kitchen table with big bowls of ice cream. Ida made coffee. She talked nonstop for an hour about her confusion over the land, her folks, her brothers, Donald Pressman, Pentoff's report, and the City Council. She left out the part about Chuck and the photo.

"I wish I could see my way clear," she said. "I'm not sure what we should do, I mean there's a lot of money involved."

"Maybe we should focus on the big picture. The land's not going away. Eventually they'll move the prairie dogs away. The pressure for growth is too strong. Just accept how things are. It'll be fine."

"I suppose so, but we're all ready for a new life. With the money, I can do whatever I want. Jeff can get out of debt, and Junior can move away, and start over somewhere else."

"The last thing Junior needs is money. A drunk with money is a disaster waiting to happen. Would you like to pray?"

"No, Danny, I'm too scared. Can you just hold me for a while?"

They moved into Ida's bedroom, undressed, and stretched out on the bed. Danny pulled her close and held her while she cried herself to sleep. Sometime in the night, Ida awoke and nuzzled her face into Danny's neck. They made love gently. Ida sat on the edge of the bed.

"Right now I feel safe," she said, "but my mind is jumping all over the place."

"There's a lot going on in there," Danny said. "Let's pin things down. What are you the most worried about?"

"I'm afraid Mom is getting sick again, that her cancer is out of remission. She's in pain all the time, but she doesn't say much."

"Can they treat it?"

"She had surgery six years ago, but I'm doubtful they got it all. The chemo put things on hold for a while, but I'll bet it's spread again. Mom looks anemic. I want her to get a CAT scan, but she's decided to wait for a while. I think she's afraid to find out."

"I'll bet this whole prairie dog fiasco has her super-stressed."

"There's that, and she's upset about the church. They've asked her to step aside for a while with her volunteer work. She's always been in charge of hospitality, at least until a couple of weeks ago. Now her friend—well, ex-friend—LeAnn, is supervising, and her daughter has most of the women in the church helping the Forest Guardians."

"You know you can't fix any of this, don't you?"

"Come on. There's a lot I can do. If we sell the land, everyone wins." Ida slipped under the covers and moved close to Danny.

"Why don't you guys just take Pressman's offer and be done with it? I thought the main thing was your folks' retirement."

"Mom is convinced the money will fix our family. She's all but told me that. She wants us to be happy. I'm afraid it's her dying wish."

"I don't know. I don't want to offend you, but maybe not getting the money will fix your family." Ida pulled away and sat up. She held the covers up over her breasts.

"What the hell do you mean by that? What do you think I am, some kind of gold-digging whore?"

"Hear me out. You and your brothers are grown up, but you're all tied up with Mom. To me, it looks like one big knot. Think about it. Most people are on their own before they're twenty, and Mom is still doing Junior's laundry and focused on your and Jeff's problems." Ida pulled the covers up over her head and lay down.

"Don't you feel smothered sometimes?" he asked. "Junior does."

"Just be quiet. I don't want to think about it anymore," Ida said, "I want to go to sleep."

"Okay, but let me ask you one more thing. What do you really want? Don't just say 'the money,' because we both know it's more than that."

The sound of their breathing filled the room for a full five minutes before Ida sat up. "What I really want is my Master's degree, but I can't get it without the money."

"Sure you can."

"Okay, you're so smart, how do you recommend I pay for it?"

"You could work part time, cut back on expenses, find a cheaper place to live, and go to school part time. It's not rocket science. People manage." Danny reached out and held her. "You don't need all that money. Lord knows you're a grown woman. You can make it on your own."

"I don't know. I think I'd be too scared."

"How about this idea? You could give up your apartment and move in with me. We could share living expenses."

"You would do that?" Ida said.

"Open your eyes. We trust each other, we feel safe, you're not lonely." He paused. "I think we're an item."

17

Junior's counselor called Mom and suggested a Tuesday evening family meeting. Her pain brought an irritable mood, but she soldiered on and arranged things with Jeff, Ida, and Pop. The counselor ushered them into a private room and then brought Junior. It had been nearly four weeks since anyone had seen him. Junior was gaunt and slender, but he had color in his face, and his eyes conveyed a sense of peacefulness. His hands were steady, and he glanced at each person without his eyes darting around. Mom stood and tried to hug him as he backed away.

"Hello," he said.

"You look like you'll live," Pop said, offering his hand. "It's good to see you."

"You been blowing up any prairie dogs?" Junior asked.

"Nope. I'm staying in the background. Better that way, I guess."

"The City Council meeting is tomorrow night," Jeff said, "and the vote looks good."

"I realize this prairie dog issue is what's up for the family, but we need to turn to the matter at hand," said the counselor. "Junior has been working with a sponsor and has been attending two AA meetings and group therapy every day. He has completed all his antibiotics and the pancreatitis is gone. He has twenty-four days of sobriety, and we're here to see how we can best support his discharge from rehabilitation. This is a critical time in the life of this alcoholic. He'll be returning to all the circumstances that brought him here in the first place. We need to talk about some things."

"How can we help?" Mom asked. "I've cleaned the trailer, and there's food in the refrigerator. I threw out all the alcohol I could find."

"That's not what he means," said Ida.

"What does he mean?"

"Excuse me, Ida. Let me jump in here. Mrs. Corley, we are here to discover the best way you can help, but we are going to find that out from Junior.

"He knows what he needs to do. Junior has agreed to attend ninety AA meetings in the next ninety days and to check in with his sponsor every day. His employer has offered to take him back, and Junior has promised to go to work every day without fail."

"You still have your job with me," Pop said. "The equipment always needs maintenance and you stopped drinking. The deal is still on with the trailer, so you can come home."

"Are Popeye and Minerva doing okay?" Junior asked.

"I've fed them every day," Mom said. "They seem happy, but I'm sure they'll be glad to see you."

"Whatever you need, Junior," Jeff said, "just let me know."

"Same for me," Ida said. "If you want, I can come by and give you B-12 shots. I understand that helps with the craving."

"I'm going to take charge for a minute here," the counselor said.

Junior gazed at the floor.

"This could be the hard part. We know alcoholism involves the whole family. In his group therapy, Junior has identified some issues, and he's now going to tell each of you how you can support him. Your job is to be truthful, and to say whether you can comply or not. Does everyone understand? This might be an odd approach, but I think we need to clear the air."

Junior took a deep breath.

"Okay, Junior, it's your turn. Let's start with your father. Tell him what you need, just like you did in the group."

Junior raised his head in Pop's direction. "I feel worthless when you call me dum-dum. I need you to stop doing that. I feel angry when you continually interrupt me. I want you to stop." Junior looked away and cringed.

Mom felt as though she needed to hide. She was afraid to look at Pop.

"I can do that. No 'dum-dum' and no interruptions, but you have to say interesting things." To Mom's surprise, Pop actually grinned. "I guess dum-

dum can get old after a while, huh?" Junior nodded, and his face relaxed.

"That wasn't so bad, huh? Now, your mother. Go ahead and tell her what you need."

Junior gazed at the floor.

"Go ahead."

"I can't even turn around without you being there and doing something. You're in everything, and I feel like a five-year-old child. It really makes me angry. I want you to leave me alone, and I want you to stay out of my house unless you're invited. And I want you to quit mentioning church. I don't want anything to do with that church."

Tears formed in Mom's eyes, and in her mind, she prayed that God would help her. She felt shunned, as though all of her efforts over the years counted for nothing, nothing at all.

"If that's what you need, I guess I can stay away."

"I don't mean stay away from *me*. I just mean I need to be treated like an adult, like you would treat someone at your church."

Mom nodded her head and took a tissue from her purse.

"I have a professional recommendation. There is something you could do that will help both you and Junior."

Mom dried her eyes. "I'm willing to do most anything."

The counselor handed her a pamphlet. "Here is a list of all the Al-Anon meetings in Albuquerque. People who love alcoholics need help too. You should find one where you are comfortable and go at least two times a week. Can you do that?"

"I think so. That's what my pastor thinks I ought to do too."

"I can put you in touch with some other women if you would like. They would be glad to take you to a meeting and help you get started. Shall I have someone call?"

"That would be fine."

"We're on a roll here. Now, your brother," said the counselor.

"I have a lot of respect for you, but you're not always right, and I do have good ideas. Just because you went to college doesn't mean you're superior. Your 'leader of the family' attitude really pisses me off. I know more about running the business than you do. I want you to respect me or at least pretend that you do."

Jeff closed his eyes and took a breath. "Okay, I can do that. There are many things I admire about you, but I never tell you. I'm sorry for that."

Junior turned toward Ida. "Sometimes you're like Mom and it pisses me off. I'm afraid to tell you because you're so strong and so beautiful. I'm uncomfortable around women. It's like you're on a pedestal and you like it up there. I just want you to be my sister, you know, a friend. Please do not make medical observations and comments about me. When you do, I feel dead, like a bug pinned to a board."

Ida looked confused. A sour irony seized Mom as she absorbed Junior's comment that Ida was like her. *Of all things, Ida like me? Junior has it wrong. We are different as night and day.*

"You've got it," Ida said. "No more medical observations or comments. I'll work on being a friend."

"At the risk of being patronizing, I'm going to ask each of you to tell Junior what you heard and how you are going to respond."

They each repeated Junior's request.

Junior stood up, and started for the door. Then he came back, shook Pop's hand, and did a group hug with Mom, Jeff, and Ida.

"When should I pick you up?" Mom asked.

"I have a ride home with my sponsor. I'll be busy. I'm working on something, but I'll see you for Easter dinner on Sunday."

"Okay. By then we should be set to sell the land and put the money in the bank," Mom said. "We have Jeff to thank for that."

Dr. Chuck Pentoff walked into the City Council meeting with his wife Lola by his side. As they passed the door, Ida stopped Chuck, and handed him a folder with the photograph. Ida's loose hair, shadowed cleavage, and one hand framed Chuck's turgid penis. For a cell-phone photo, it was remarkably clear.

"I thought you would like to have this for your report," Ida said. She glanced at Lola. *Okay Lola, here we go—now let's watch him squirm.*

Chuck smiled, took the folder without looking, and they sat down in front next to Donald. Ida watched from the back as Chuck looked in the folder and stiffened. His face turned pasty white. Casually, he covered the folder with other papers.

The Martha Circle from Grace church was out in force and dressed in matching tee shirts and hats. June and other church leaders took seats in the back, and many of the Corleys' neighbors were scattered throughout the room. Mom sat with Jeff, Pop sat in back with his Caterpillar cap on, and Ida stood by the door with her arms folded over her warm-up jacket. Ida felt strong. This was it. She had talked with Don, and he'd agreed to keep the million-dollar offer open until after Easter. They wouldn't be accepting it, though. From Chuck's reaction, the Corley land sale would happen within the week.

The Chairman spoke. "This meeting shall come to order. We have a quorum present. The matter before us is the Corley request for the postponement of Ordinance 2002-4 regarding prairie dogs. You may begin."

Jeff stood at the podium with Bob Epstein and addressed the Council.

"Mr. Chairman, councilors, my remarks will be brief. We request that the ordinance be delayed for sixty days so we can relocate the prairie dogs from our property to a new and more appropriate habitat. We are prepared to photograph all aspects of the relocation, use a licensed and experienced relocating company, and guarantee safe passage to an appropriate habitat. We have retained a veterinarian to accompany the relocation company to insure a healthy transition. In addition, we'll file affidavits and photographs with the council assuring that the relocation occurred as promised. This is the best solution for the prairie dogs and for all concerned."

Bob Epstein moved to the podium. "Mr. Chairman, councilors, I have only one legal point to make. Although I'm sure the Forest Guardians are prepared to address the issue of who inhabited the land first, according to real estate law in New Mexico, animals do not have property rights. In fact, the question of who lived on the land first is legally irrelevant. It might be interesting science, but it's clearly not material to this issue. The Corleys provided sanctuary to the prairie dogs for decades, and now they simply want to move them to a better place. This practice fits with both the Boulder Colorado Ordinance passed in 1999, and the Santa Fe Ordinance adopted just four months ago. Both cities have determined that relocation is humane and helps to sustain the prairie dog population."

"Thank you." The chairman glanced at the Councilors.

"Mr. Chairman," said Fernando Vigil, "In the interest of time, I'd like to make a motion to get things started."

"Go ahead."

"I move that Ordinance 2002-4 be postponed for sixty days, that the Corleys clearly document their prairie dog relocation procedures, and that their property be exempt from the ordinance."

"Second," said another Councilor.

"It has been moved and seconded. Are their questions?"

"I just want to highlight something," said Vigil. "The Boulder City Council and the Santa Fe City Council have spent months on their ordinances, and I don't think we need to reinvent the wheel here. I urge the adoption of my motion." He looked over at Jeff and Bob Epstein as Francisco Romero approached the podium.

"Mr. Chairman, Councilors, I am Francisco Romero representing Henry Whitman, the prospective developer of the property. I would like to offer an observation. The City will receive gross receipts tax income in the first five years sufficient to hire a dozen new police officers, and purchase a dozen police cars, a new fire truck, and a new ambulance. Public safety certainly rises above the simple relocation of a few prairie dogs. I urge you to vote for the Corley request."

Donald stood up and raised his hand.

"Mr. Pressman," the Chairman said, "do you have a question?"

"Yes, Mr. Chairman. We want to question the issue of life-rights. We believe the prairie dogs lived on the land first, and thereby they acquired life-rights, the right to exist undisturbed in their sacred habitat. Neither Boulder nor Santa Fe considered the issue of life-rights. The Forest Guardians and the Corley family shared the cost of a scientific study by Dr. Chuck Pentoff, noted expert on the Gunnison prairie dog. We would like to hear his testimony now."

Bob Epstein stood up. "Mr. Chairman, even though the Corleys helped pay for the Pentoff study, we believe the results are irrelevant to the issue. Prairie dogs do not have property rights. This is a matter of law. None of us is above the law."

"What about life-rights?" Councilor Chavez asked. "Life is above the law. Surely, they have the right to life. I for one want to hear Dr. Pentoff's testimony. We've come this far, and we need to hear what he found out." A cheer went up in the crowd. The Martha Circle chanted, "Right to life, right to life, right to life."

The chairman rapped his gavel. "I'll have order in this room or I'll dismiss the audience," he said. "Please proceed with your presentation."

Chuck straightened his tie. Donald Pressman arranged a couple of easels so that both the Councilors and the audience could see. Chuck turned and looked back at Ida. She smiled, stared at him, and shook her head back and forth. She glanced at Lola and felt alarmed to see Lola's face broadcasting pure hate. Chuck took a breath, lifted his head high, and began.

"Mr. Chairman, Councilors, members of the audience, I am Dr. Chuck Pentoff, an expert on the Gunnison prairie dog. I have conducted an intensive scientific study of the prairie dogs on the Corley property. I have studied their language, and I have concluded that their community contains at least eight distinct words. If I had additional time, I believe I could find a few more words. This is a mature prairie dog culture with a history of hundreds of generations. They have become part of the land. By very conservative estimates of twenty years for a word to evolve, the discovery of eight distinct prairie dog words means the prairie dogs have lived in that habitat for at least one-hundred sixty years, well before the time the Corleys bought the property in nineteen thirty-two." Chuck walked to the front and handed each councilor a copy of his study. On the easels, he had posted photos and names of all the dominant males, including Hopalong, and a list of the words. In addition to *aaach, aaach* (danger), and *eeek, eeek* (sex), he had discovered *uhaaa, uhaaa* (food); *thaaa, thaaa* (peaceful); *eoooo, eoooo* (pain, suffering); *waaak, waaak* (water); *yaaap, yaaap* (good person); and *yuuuk, yuuuk* (bad person).

Chuck turned and stared intently at the crowd, but he focused on Ida.

"You must understand. Moving prairie dogs interrupts their breeding, and there's no doubt about my conclusion. The prairie dogs were on this land first. The Corley family came later."

"Thank you, Dr. Pentoff," Chavez said. "I guess that settles the right-to-life issue." A muffled murmur arose from the crowd. A man and a woman in the back waved signs that said "GOD GAVE CREATURES A RIGHT TO LIFE."

Ida unfolded her arms. She looked at Mom and Jeff, glanced at Pop, and again felt hate coming from Lola. She stared back at Chuck. He smiled. *That sonofabitch thinks I'm bluffing. He thinks I'm not going to do anything. I wonder if he's told Lola?* Suddenly, it dawned on Ida. Chuck had called her bluff. What could she do? If Lola already knew, then he was safe. If Lola knew, then the photo just made Ida look like a whore giving Chuck a hand job. *That sonofabitch.*

Councilor Chavez whispered to a councilor, said something to another, and then said, "Mr. Chairman, I call the question."

"Any further comments? "

Epstein arose.

"Mr. Chairman, Councilors, I want to remind you that according to the law, prairie dogs do not have property rights. A yes vote would be overturned in court."

"Any other questions? There being none, all in favor of the motion?"

Two voted yes.

"All opposed?"

Two voted no.

"And the Chairman votes no. The motion fails."

The crowd jumped up and cheered. June rushed over to Mom, Pop stormed out of the room, Jeff helped Mom stand up, and Ida stood with her mouth open. Donald rushed to congratulate Chuck. "Well done," he said. "Well done."

That bastard, Ida thought. She turned to leave and wiped the tears from her eyes. She felt someone come up from behind and take her hand.

"No big deal," Danny said. "Let's get some air. It'll be okay." He held Lucky in his other arm. "Lucky says you smell good and your ponytail is too tight."

18

The glum mood in the Corley kitchen settled on Mom. Her stomach hurt, she felt weak, and wondered if God had abandoned her. She had attended Sunrise Easter services with Jeff, stepping lightly with him on her arm, but try as she may, she could not summon her sense of worship. The music was beautiful, the liturgy was perfect, and June gave an inspiring message. She even took a moment to pray privately with Mom. However, for Mom, the awkward glances from her church friends and the childish smirk on Laura's face chased God right out of the sanctuary. Was she losing her faith?

"How much do we owe our attorney?" she asked Jeff.

"About ten-thousand. He says we have a good chance for an appeal in District Court. He's convinced the City Council acted illegally."

Ida sliced some more potatoes. "Mom, we still have Donald's offer to consider. He called again to tell me the offer is still good. He said his buyer might be willing to look at a counter-offer, something a little higher."

"Maybe you should consider it, " Jeff said. "It sure would give you and Pop a breather, and Pop could sell his equipment. You could take a cruise to Alaska or something. You deserve a comfortable retirement."

"I don't know," Mom said. "Pop and I made a decision to share our estate with you kids before we die, and that's what I want. I want you to have the opportunities we didn't have. Did you hear anything from Betty? I had such high hopes."

"She and her husband got back together and they moved to Ireland for a couple of years. Her company has a plant there."

"I'm sorry, Jeff. Well, at least she has a pretty smile."

Pop walked into the dining room. "Do I hear you talking about Pressman's offer? There's no way I'm going to give my land away to anyone. The rule is you buy and sell land, you don't give it away."

"I checked with a tax attorney friend of mine," Jeff said. He said the one-million dollars is really worth one-million, one-hundred fifty thousand because the gift of land would offset the capital gains on the five acres. That's a pretty good deal, Pop, and they might go higher."

"I'll tell you what," said Pop. "We made a promise to Junior, so let's wait until he gets here, and we can talk about it again." Pop's horoscope urged him to stay flexible, release his sense of humor, and be ready for surprises today. Mom's horoscope indicated that a spirit of cooperation could be coming her way and she should seek allies. It warned that a stubborn outlook would be counterproductive.

Junior came in about 4 pm, and they all sat down for dinner. Mom had prepared a beautiful table with two bouquets of spring flowers and rainbow ribbon gathered in loose swirls as a base. Everyone dutifully bowed as Mom offered a blessing.

"Dear Lord, thank you for this Easter Day and for the resurrection of Jesus Christ. Thank you for His life that sets for us the example of how to live. Thank you for His sacrifice that He might someday forgive us for our sins. Keep us strong as we face the disappointments and setbacks in life, and forgive those who persecute us. Bless this food, and bless our family. Amen."

The food was delicious, and Mom felt a wave of pride lift her mood as her children enjoyed their dinner. The chatter among them was light-hearted, and Jeff even managed a joke about Dr. Pentoff and his names for the prairie dogs.

"He even named one of them Hopalong," Jeff said. "I guess it was because of his crippled leg, but all I could think about was Hopalong Cassidy, that cowboy on TV when I was a kid. Remember? I had a lunchbox with his picture on it."

"He got shot in the left leg in 1935," Pop said. "That's how he got the name Hopalong."

"How in the world do you know that?" Ida asked laughing.

"I've seen all his movies," Pop said. "I was the one who named that male Hopalong. I didn't know Pentoff would use it."

"You named a prairie dog?" Junior asked.

"Yeah, he's the crippled one, and he's a real ladies man. Sort of reminded me of myself." He grinned and took a bite of turkey.

"What in the world has gotten into you?" Mom asked.

"I don't know. Things just seem funny today. Jeff, go ahead and tell Junior about the offer from Donald Pressman."

"Pressman has a large donor for the Forest Guardians, and they've offered a million dollars for five acres if Mom and Pop will give ten acres to a land trust. All fifteen acres would go to the trust. That way, Mom and Pop would have the money, and the prairie dogs stay. He said it can happen right away."

"It would be up to Mom and Pop. It's their land."

"I want you kids to have the money from the ten acres," Mom said. "Pop says he's opposed to giving land away to anyone, so I think we'll turn down the offer. I'm tempted to take this whole thing to court. Epstein says we have a good case."

"They're looking for a counter-offer, and I think they will go higher, maybe to a million and a quarter," Ida said.

"I think it's up to Mom and Pop. I used to want the money in a bad way, but I don't think I'm ready to handle it. I have to keep my life simple. You shouldn't do this for Jeff, Ida, or me. You should think about yourselves." He glanced at Jeff who was nodding his head.

"Say whatever you like, but I'm not signing anything that gives away the land my father gave me," Pop said.

"That's it. Ida, please call Pressman and tell him we are not interested in his offer and there will be no counteroffer."

"Okay, but I think you're making a mistake."

"I've been thinking about something," Junior said. "I was sitting out there on a mound of dirt the other night and watching the moon. Orion was bright in the sky, and I was wondering what else we could do with this land. An idea came to me. What would you think of a park? We could charge people to come and see the prairie dogs. That would serve them right for all the hassle they've caused us. Wouldn't that be great?"

Everyone stared at Mom. She tilted her head to the right and planted her feet. When she tried to smile, her face felt brittle, as though smiling would crack her skin. She licked her lips, top and bottom. "You don't want our money?"

Ida reached into the neck of her light blue sweatshirt and pulled up the pink strap of her bra that had slipped down. "I'm worried about you, not the money. Does your stomach hurt?"

"Not too much, but this whole thing is such a mess. Look out there. Look. Everything's so tattered." She turned her back to Ida, raised her hands to the sky, and clenched her fists. "What in heaven's name do you want from me?"

Ida put her arm around Mom and hugged her. "Relax. Take a breath. It's going to be okay."

"You think so?" She pushed away. "Can't you see? This whole place is falling apart. Jeff's debt is crushing him. Junior's stuck here. You can't go to school without the money."

"There might be a way."

"How?"

"I can share living expenses with a friend and get some student loans."

"With a man?"

"Danny. He's a good friend. We would be roommates."

"I'll bet."

Mom bent over slightly and held her stomach. Tears ran down her face, and she wiped them with a tissue from her pocket. "You don't know how tired I am. I don't think I have another project in me. I can't stand this." Her eyes darted to Pop, pleading.

Pop rubbed his knee on his bad leg and waved his hand. "I've said for three years I want to retire and travel, remember?"

Junior stepped closer to Pop, grinning. "You've worked every day of your life. I know you. One trip, and then you'd be back here driving the loader or the D-6."

Pop gazed out upon the land. Flashes of reflected sunlight from the windshield of the loader blinded Mom, and she covered her yes. "You said you're tired. You're tired of all this, aren't you?" Mom's voice sounded desperate, as though she was pulling against the years of attachment Pop and his father had with this land. Would he just wither away if he retired? Could she deal with his casting about, his searching? She couldn't stand that.

Pop shook his head, and the hint of a smile appeared on his face. "I don't know about a park. Sounds like a lot of work."

Turning toward the mountains, Jeff narrowed his eyes. "There's nothing like it anywhere in Albuquerque. It could be a draw for school kids. He bit his thumbnail. "I'll bet it would make money."

"It would take thousands of dollars to even begin." Pop took a pencil and a small notepad from his shirt pocket and began writing.

"Hold on," Mom said. "I don't think there's time."

"Time for what?" Junior asked.

Mom ran her fingers through her hair. "Time to build the roads and things."

Pop spoke up. "I figure we'd need a couple hundred thousand."

Jeff smiled. "There's no mortgage on the land, right Mom?"

"It's free and clear. What are you thinking?"

Junior put his hand on Pop's shoulder. "Work is your life. Like you always say, this land isn't going anywhere. We could always sell it later if things don't work out."

Lights sparkled in Pop's eyes, bright lights that drew the gray darkness from Mom, like two strong magnets.

"What the hell," Jeff said. "I could see a few more patients and help with the costs. Let's roll the dice."

"Not so fast," Pop said. "There's a lot to think about."

Junior opened his hands, gesturing to the shed. "Want to look at a design? I've got some drawings inside."

Pop took Mom's hand. "Let's go see. It could be fun." She allowed him to lead her. He walked quickly. "I'm not that old, for God's sake. I could build access roads, lay water lines, and put in power. Junior and I could build a concession stand and maybe even a main building."

Mom had not seen him this animated since the time he decided to build the machine shed. What in the world was going on?

Ida caught up with them. "You guys could put in park benches and observation stations. We could even mount some telescopes like Pentoff did." She cocked her head like a little Irish setter puppy. "I'll bet Donald and his donor would be interested in an investment. Do you mind if I asked him?"

"Not so fast," Pop said. "Let's look at drawings first."

They gathered around the drafting table as Junior sketched out his ideas. He pointed out trails, park benches, picnic areas, observation posts, a concession stand, and his ideas for a Corley Education Building with scale models of prairie dog underground habitats.

"Seems like we're on the same page," Ida said. "How about a first aid station?"

Jeff pointed. "Good idea. Right there by the concession stand."

Pop put his hands on his hips, leaned back, and laughed out loud. "Ida, go ahead and talk with Mr. Hollywood and see what he has to say. I'd like to sell those protesters tickets to see our rodents."

Mom sat down on a sawhorse and placed her hands carefully beside her. The hum of her children's voices sounded like a choir as the family's approval settled upon Junior. She could finish her days on the land without all the development. She could make lunches for Pop, Junior, and the workers. Her friends at church would flock around and congratulate her for her wisdom. June could relax about a political split at Grace church. Like divine inspiration, Junior's park idea formed a new heady dream in Mom's soul, a dream of a verdant landscape with happy children, a gazebo outside for weddings, and her family working together. "You guys put together some estimates, and we'll go from there. I'm going back to the house and clean up the kitchen."

Pop helped her to stand up. "Mom will have the final say. She's been keeping the books for thirty-five years."

Junior beamed. "Maybe we could see our way clear to give the Sheriff a couple of free tickets."

"Come on, I'll go with you and help," Ida said.

As they walked by Junior's truck on the way back to the house, Mom glanced into the pickup bed. The light from a rising moon shined on two empty vodka bottles in a pile of garbage. She quickly pointed to the moon, ignoring the bottles. "It's such a beautiful night. This is the best Easter dinner ever."

19

Junior had learned some things in rehabilitation, but they remained fuzzy and illusive, in need of practice. In April, however, he learned without a doubt that few things in life astound us like an idea whose time has come. It shines in the arms of its mother like a new baby. Together, mother and baby float on rising clean water, making their way over every obstacle, as though God's will was at work or the stars aligned themselves just so. Junior tapped into a spiritual vacuum and everyone wanted to be near the excitement. New opportunities dripped off the idea daily as it stood tall in the sunlight, waving to a thousand fathers. The prairie dog park gathered up Junior and defined his purpose.

"You see, when you surrender, God takes over and does things you can't begin to do by yourself," Danny said. "No matter how exciting this gets, I don't want you to get a big head. You've got to stay with your meetings. Don't worry. I'm going to be with you."

"No one really cares much about what I have to say," Junior said. "Except now, and all of a sudden I'm in the spotlight. I don't know if I can handle it. I feel weird."

"Get the plan down, and get things focused. Then you can move aside."

Junior kept sketches and ideas in the machine shed, and people came by and put sticky notes on the drawings. Jeff met with the City Planning Department about the idea.

"It's private property," said one planner. "You can pretty much do what you want in terms of recreation. Since it's a business, we need to see plans for the buildings, but if they are temporary, we don't need much, just the location and materials."

"Should we get ready to go?" Jeff asked.

"We'll hurry on our end and we'll recommend conceptual approval at the next City Council meeting," said the planner. "I think they'll be relieved."

Jeff talked with Mom and Junior, and Mom told Ida and Pop. Initial estimates suggested that a three-hundred thousand dollar investment would result in income sufficient to pay the mortgage, cover repairs, maintenance, and provide staff. Everyone pitched in with ideas for income or cost savings.

Mom brought the idea of a white gazebo, covered seating, and outside weddings among new flowerbeds. June agreed to perform weddings there if asked.

Ida insisted on a first aid station, and after talking with Danny, she recommended a drop off kennel for unwanted dogs and cats. Danny convinced the humane shelter to help with the expenses of operating the drop off facilities.

Pop suggested that Junior rework the main access and change it to Eubank Avenue to save paving costs. Also, he thought the walking trail should be serpentine, and that two applications of crusher fines would drain well and would save money over the cost of blacktop.

After talking with Mom and Pop, Jeff and Bob Epstein met with Fernando Vigil, who said he could easily support the change in plans. The Councilors would rally around the park idea. In fact, he insisted that he be the master of ceremonies at the dedication.

Ida shared the news with Donald over lunch. He assured her of support from the Forest Guardians. As it turned out, the Forest Guardians needed an Albuquerque office, and he said he would check with the Board about leasing space in the park's Corley Education Building.

"I think I can be helpful. This turn of events brings tremendous energy. I'll bet we can lease an office and pay for all the tenant improvements. I'm also willing to talk with my donor about putting up money for a mortgage for construction. If he had some sort of covenant in the documents about the use of the land, I can imagine he would loan the money at a very low interest rate. After all, he was willing to make an outright gift."

"Thank you," Ida said. "I'll share the news with Mom and Pop. Pop doesn't have you at the top of his list, so it might take a while for him to treat you decently."

"I'm not worried about that. It won't take long after we make a new start. Tell him we can lease space and likely, we can provide construction money at a low rate. Then I'll find a time to talk with Mom and Pop before the approvals from the City Council. Councilor Chavez wants to help with the dedication."

"I'll talk with them soon, and I'll talk with Junior. I think I can smooth things over."

Later, after visiting with Mom and Pop, Ida gathered everyone together in the machine shed.

"I guess this is good news," Junior said. "You're grinning from ear to ear."

Ida shared the prospect of the office lease and the mortgage for construction.

Pop put his hands on his hips. "Sounds like Mr. Hollywood wants to help. Do you think we could stand him as a neighbor?"

"I think we could get used to the rent," Mom said. Her impish grin returned.

"I don't like mortgages," Pop said. "Mom says we can afford it though, and if the rate is lower than she figured, well then all the better. I think I can get used to Mr. Hollywood having an office."

"Junior," asked Mom, "have we got room for a softball diamond and field? The churches in the neighborhood need one, and they've agreed to share the cost of construction in exchange for the youth programs and the men's groups having use of it. They said they could pay a lease amount for the land and take care of all the maintenance."

"We've got room for that and plenty more," Junior said. He began sketching in a location for the softball field and bleachers.

"How about an archery range?" Mom asked. "The church scouts from Grace and the troop from the LDS church asked if they could build and maintain an archery range on the back corner, near the arroyo. They would charge a user fee and share the proceeds to help with the park expenses. Some boys would get their Advanced Scout award for building the range."

"Can do," Junior said. "The impossible might take longer."

Over the weeks that followed, a number of organizations asked to run the concession stands, but Junior wanted the Corleys to run concessions, scheduling, and tickets. Those are the profit centers.

The City Council meeting moved through the approval process in a matter of minutes. After hearing the support of neighbors, the Forest Guardians, and people from the churches, Councilor Vigil made the motion to approve and Councilor Chavez seconded the motion. The vote was unanimous.

"Good luck with the Corley Prairie Dog Park," said the Chairman. "It sounds like a fine solution to a difficult problem."

A zoning approval came the next week, and Junior and Pop put together a schedule of activities. Mom, Jeff, and Ida took Bob Epstein with them to meet with the donor from the Forest Guardians, and they worked out a mortgage at three percent interest. The Forest Guardians insisted on a clause that required the mortgage to be due upon sale of the land or upon a change of use from the Corley Prairie Dog Park. Bob Epstein worked through further details regarding estate planning, and they signed the mortgage the next week. The groundbreaking ceremony featured the Corley family, the City Councilors, and the Forest Guardians. Throngs of neighbors attended along with June and the Trustees from Grace church, the women from the Martha Circle, the Bishop from the LDS church, youth Scout Leaders, Danny, and Junior's AA home group. Never had the Corley land hosted such a conglomerate of folks. Pop told Junior he thought he saw Big Al, Skipper, and Hopalong standing just outside their holes.

After the dedication, Pop and Junior walked back to the machine shed. Pop pointed to the prairie dog mounds in the dusk.

"I think that's Big Al there, and that's Hopalong over there," he said. "I don't see Skipper or Little Ed. I haven't seen Topper for several days."

"Pop, I think I hear something, a quiet sound. Sort of like *Thaaa, Thaaa, Thaaa*. Do you hear it or is it just my monkey brain playing tricks?"

"Yeah," Pop said. "I hear it too. I think it's Hopalong. Pentoff said that was the prairie dogs word for 'peaceful.' Maybe they know we're not going to shoot them."

"Maybe so."

"I want to ask you something."

"Something about the park?"

"No. This might really piss you off," Pop said.

Junior stopped and folded his arms. "Go ahead."

"Mom's worried. She told me something last night, and she was crying."

"And?"

"She said she saw vodka bottles in your truck on Easter. She's been afraid to say anything. Are you drinking again?"

Junior let his arms drop to his sides, and he took a breath. "No, I'm not. I cleaned garbage out from under the trailer and there were some empty bottles. I even found some more behind the washer and dryer. I think the place is clean now, but who knows where I might have hidden bottles."

"Good. I'll tell Mom."

"Tell her next time she's worried, she needs to ask me herself. We've got to stop being afraid of each other."

"Will do. In the morning, let's start bright and early. I want to lay out the walking trail and stake out the building sites."

"Sure. See you in the morning."

Pop washed his hands in the utility room sink and sat down at the table. Mom made chicken breasts and pasta with mushroom sauce, a tossed salad, and fresh cherry pie. Mom's face was relaxed, as though she was floating on a cloud of grace.

Pop bowed his head, and Mom prayed. "Thank you Lord for this day and for the new life we have ahead. Thank you for our family, and may we use the food before us as energy to serve your Kingdom. Amen."

"Quite a day," Pop said. "Junior says he's not drinking. He was just cleaning up garbage from around the trailer. That's where the empty bottles came from, you know, from before."

"Thank God," Mom said. "Was he angry that you asked? I don't need to make him upset."

"I don't think so. He said if you're worried again, just ask him. He wants you guys to be able to talk."

Mom cleaned up the kitchen while Pop read, and then she showered and put on a nightgown and robe. She barely noticed her pain.

"Are you going to bed early?" Pop asked.

Mom smiled. "I was thinking about it, but I hate to be alone."

"How about some company?" Pop asked.

Mom's face flushed as Pop approached her with a sweet tenderness. He was gentle, focused on her needs, and his attention reminded her of when he was much younger. After a moment of shared pleasure, Pop pushed up on his hands, smiled into Mom's eyes, and said, "*Eeek, eeek, eeek.*"

Mom laughed aloud and tears filled her eyes. "What in the world are you doing? Should I call you Hopalong?"

20

Excitement came over the land, as though a throng of hummingbirds had discovered a fresh stand of penstemons. Pop, Junior, and Jeff stretched yellow construction-zone tape around the entire property, and strung pink survey tape to separate the prairie dog habitat from the areas of construction. Reluctantly, they had allowed Donald to review plans, and agreed to restrict visitors to interpretive trails at least fifty yards from any prairie dog activity. Jeff and Mom dreamed up the idea of watching stations with coin-operated telescopes.

Pop and Junior surveyed the centerline of the serpentine trail around the habitat, and they staked out the sites for the Corley Education Building, concessions stands, and a golf cart enclosure. Donald, through the Forest Guardians, agreed to lease an office space in the Corley Education Building. They would also have a kiosk featuring information about endangered species and ways of living that support the earth and all living things.

The building permit process was painful enough to drive Junior to drink. After a difficult night and extra meetings, he turned the plans over to Danny. The process required dozens of meetings with City staff. Danny talked them out of issuing an early grading permit so Pop could fire up his motor grader and level the main visitor roadway and the parking lot. It was another two weeks before Junior could start work on actual construction. After a drenching rain for a day, good weather, good fortune, and a bright sunrise peeked up over the mountains.

Mom drove to the construction trailer with lunch.

"Turkey sandwiches and potato salad. Great lunch," Junior said. "I feel alive again, and I can taste your food." He smiled at Mom.

"I haven't seen you guys work together like this for years," Mom said.

"Junior's a good hand," Pop said. "He's already done the layout work on the concrete. He can do the work of two good men."

"My boss will be here in two days with our concrete crew," Junior said. "They'll have the foundations and slabs poured by the end of the week, and I have framing packages scheduled to be delivered on Monday. I'll do the layout early, and the framing crew will hit it by 9 am if the weather's good."

The days passed marked by progress and evening tours. Jeff came by every evening, and Ida came on her days off. Mom got in the habit of having a light dinner ready for everyone late in the evening.

"Look," Junior said. "These classrooms will open into the hallway here, the bathrooms open out here, and the offices open out to the portal on the west side." He walked ahead of the rest of the family, pointing out features of the building and grounds. He often had to slow down so Mom could catch up. One evening, Pop drove up with Mom in a golf cart. "This cart is Mom's. She can get around faster and see more." The cart was light beige to blend with the earth, and it had a long whip antenna with an American flag on top and a light green pennant underneath with a picture of Hopalong and two kissing prairie dogs.

"Where in the world did you get that picture?" Jeff asked.

"Epstein made a deal with Pentoff to buy photo rights," Pop said. "We are going to use them for plaques on the trails and for stuff in the concessions stand. It was Mom's idea. She got the rights to all of the Pentoff photos."

"Do we have drinking fountains?" Mom asked.

"Yup," said Pop. "They're at every watch station, by the concession stands, and outside the Corley Education Building."

"I'm sure we forgot something, but it hasn't come up yet," said Junior.

Mom spent a couple of hours a week with June in pastoral counseling. She told June that the park construction and her health would keep her from resuming the Hospitality Director position.

"I think it's best if we leave things as they are," Mom told her. "People have gotten used to LeAnn and the Martha Circle taking care of things."

"I wish you would reconsider," June said. "I can't say this outside the privacy of my office, but there have been complaints about the food and the costs. You have a real gift, and we need you. Laura's not very happy about the dinner plans for her reception. She told me she wished you were back."

Mom laughed. "I guess she's changed her tune, and I'm not surprised, but I think it'll work out fine. I've talked with LeAnn at our cancer support group, and she's getting some extra help from a couple of new members."

"Your support group? Are you going to Al-Anon?"

"I go now and then. It's not that. I need to tell you that my cancer is back, and this time with a vengeance."

"I'm so sorry. What happened?"

"Well, I had another CAT scan, and Ida and I have made the rounds of labs and specialists. My oncologist says the mass in my abdomen is inoperable. It seems to be growing fast."

"What about radiation and chemo?"

"They say radiation would make me incontinent within a week, and with my colostomy, that's plain unacceptable. He said chemo might slow things down, but I'd have four or five bad days for every good one. June, the truth is I'm dying. There's nothing I can do about it. I'm afraid I'm not going to have the time to bring this family together the way I need to."

June hugged Mom close as they cried together. Then she stood up and got tissues for both of them. "Who else knows?"

"Ida knows, and we'll tell Pop and Jeff and Junior on Sunday."

"How much time?"

"A month, maybe two. They have a full body scan scheduled for tomorrow. I've been confused and disoriented the past few days. Ida and I are worried I might have some lesions in my brain."

June held Mom's hands and prayed for her comfort and for her relationship with Christ. They sat quietly for a moment.

"I just keep wondering: Why me? Why now? Just as my family is doing better, now I have to go and die on them. I won't get to see them be happy, if they ever are."

"Are you afraid?"

"No, I don't think so. I probably deserve some of this. I'm angry at God, though. He knows this isn't the right time."

"What do you mean you 'probably deserve some of this'?"

"Did I say that? Oh, never mind, I've got to get back home."

"Do you really think you deserve this?"

"Maybe sometimes."

"What's going on with that? What are you worried about?"

"This is not a good time. Maybe later. Thank you for your prayers."

They walked out together. Mom drove home, filled the cooler, and drove her golf cart to the construction trailer for break time. "Hey, I brought drinks for everyone. Dinner will be set out about 7 pm. I know you guys will work late."

"Thanks," Junior said as Mom drove away.

Junior and Pop stood together with a Coke and a diet Pepsi. Pop put his hand on Junior's shoulder. "I've been worried about Mom. She's tired. It's like before."

"Sorry. I don't remember much about last time."

"I know. Trust me. She was really sick. Almost died. Didn't you know that?"

"I hate to sound selfish, but all I know right now is that I didn't drink today, and there's a higher power out there somewhere taking care of me."

On Sunday, right after a dessert of apple cobbler, Mom took Ida's hand and prepared herself to drop the news.

"I need to tell everyone something," Mom said.

The room became quiet except for the whirling ceiling fan.

"Ida took me to my oncologist and we found out my cancer is back. It's bad. They found some lesions in my brain."

Pop dropped his head into his hands and rubbed his face.

"What about chemo?" he mumbled.

"Can they start radiation?" Jeff asked.

Junior gently took her hand and put it up to his lips. His eyes filled with tears.

"Forget about treatment," Mom said.

"Chemo and radiation would destroy her quality of life," Ida said.

Pop folded his arms in front of him and bit his lip. "How much time?" he asked.

Mom held his face in her hands. "About a month or two, but it will be a good time."

Pop got up from his chair, kissed Mom's forehead, and then stepped out the door into the night. He held his fists up to the full moon. "Sonofabitch," he whispered. "God damn sonofabitch."

Mom turned to Junior. "When will the park be done?"

"Three more weeks. We want to have the dedication on the first Friday in May and then be open for business all weekend."

"Okay, then. I get to sell the first tickets."

"You've got it," Jeff said.

Junior hugged Mom and went to his trailer. He sat in the dark, and Popeye jumped up in his lap and licked his face.

"Hey little buddy," he said. "This is a tough day." He wiped his mouth with his palm and took a couple of deep breaths. "God grant me the serenity to accept the fucking things I can't change, the courage to change the things I can, and the wisdom to know the difference."

Mom began the march toward death with the same resolve she used to march through her recovery from surgery. She fixed her gaze on what she perceived was God's will for her. Pop and her children couldn't match her step or its cadence. It was a private march, and it would end when her death absolved her soul from the life she had taken so many years ago. There was a strange comfort about that, as though she would arise to a softer place without pain and find rest from all of her relentless activities. She would find release from her deep concerns about her fragile family. Would God receive and welcome her? Likely, especially the face of the countless meals she had prepared for the Kingdom. Yet God's welcome hid behind a filmy veil of doubt. It seemed both that it was her time and that it was too soon. The fervent desire of her life song, the hunger to bring her family into a state of respect and peace, would be unfinished, a tattered edge hanging from her journey. The thought of it wrinkled her nose, like the coffee grounds, fish, and orange peels left in the trash overnight in the church kitchen.

"Why don't you just ask him?" June asked again.

Mom came out of her reverie.

"I don't think he understands," she said.

"What can it hurt to ask? He does love you."

"Maybe I will, but I don't think he's up to it. It's not his nature."

After dinner that evening, Mom sat propped up in bed with a heating pad as Pop came in and lay down beside her with his clothes and shoes on. His hand quivered as he reached to take her hand. "I don't know what to do. I can't remember being without you. Do you hurt?"

"Ida brought me some stronger pain pills. I'm fine."

"What can I do?" he asked as he squeezed her hand.

Mom was quiet for a moment.

"There is something, if you're up for it."

"What?"

"For years I've been disappointed about our family. They're a mess and I want them to be normal. You know, respect each other, and talk about things. I want you to help with that."

"What do you think I can do? I can barely talk with them myself."

"You seem to be getting along okay with Junior."

"As long as he's not drinking, we do okay."

"Can you take over and tell him what I want? He doesn't listen to me."

"We'll see. Ida sees me as old and stubborn. Jeff thinks I'm an ignorant dirt mover, and that's about it."

"Don't be ridiculous. They both care about you."

"Maybe, but it's from a distance. They don't talk with me about much."

"Please give it a try. Take over. Make it happen. I'd like to die knowing someday I'll have a normal family. Can you do it for me?"

Pop put a pillow over his face and sobbed quietly. Mom stroked his shoulder until he fell asleep.

Junior and Pop started work just after sunrise each morning and worked until dark. They had a silent pact to finish the park quickly. Both had their eye on the image of Mom selling tickets from the concession stand. Ida and Jeff came in the late afternoons to do the painting, and they helped with other details until late in the evening.

The grand opening happened on schedule. The once-quiet Corley property now featured an array of noisy dignitaries. The City Councilors jostled for photo opportunities, and Donald brought all of the Forest

Guardian board members. June brought the trustees from the church, and the Martha Circle women were there with their families in tow. Ida brought a number of friends from work, and Jeff had given his staff a day off to attend.

Fernando Vigil led the festivities and arranged the speakers and the main photo, with twenty people holding a huge green pennant with photos of prairie dogs. Laura and the Forest Guardians provided free prairie dog hats. Somewhat reluctantly, all of the Councilors, Bob Epstein, Pop, Jeff, Ida, and Junior adorned themselves with pink caps. Mom wore her silk scarf and stood between Ida and Jeff. After the photos, they led her to the concession stand. Fernando Vigil and Donald stood waiting to buy tickets. Jeff and Ida helped Mom to her seat behind the ticket stand.

"Welcome to the Corley Prairie Dog Park," Mom said. "You are the proud owners of the first tickets."

"Thank you, this is a proud day indeed," Donald said.

Donald, Fernando, and the other Councilors led the way along the interpretive trail, as though they were the anointed scouts for an undisclosed adventure. They together discovered the Corleys' detailed handiwork. The trail wound by viewing areas near the main holes of the five prairie dog coteries. The coin operated telescopes provided close up views, and the photos of Big Al, Topper, Skipper, Little Ed, and Hopalong were enlarged and mounted on the waterproof plaques near each of the telescopes, along with short narratives about their characteristics and their females. A multicolor brochure explained, for an extra two dollars, visitors would receive earphones that plugged into a box near each of the telescopes. The earphones picked up actual sounds from microphones buried in the burrows. Each plaque had a list of words, and a "full experience" involved listening with earphones and watching through the telescope as Topper or any of the others spoke their words.

"This is remarkable," said Councilor Chavez, taking off his earphones. "I just heard that one called Topper say *yaap, yaap, yaap*. That sign says *yaap* means 'good person.' I think that little critter just said I'm a good person."

"You are," said Donald. "Look at the humane compromise you've helped create. I'm convinced that somehow these little creatures know you've helped to spare their lives."

Earlier Mom had magnanimously invited Laura to sell hats, shirts, plates, and cups at the concession stand. Laura offered plates with photos, and individualized cups with photos of Big Al, Topper, Skipper, Little Ed, and Hopalong. The full set of five was twenty-five dollars, and hats were ten dollars. Mom leased Laura the photo rights and the concession space for thirty percent of the gross sales ("it should have been forty percent," she told Pop). Ida and Jeff stood outside the ticket booth and greeted people. During a lull, Mom turned to Jeff. "Well, that's two-hundred tickets at six dollars each. Not bad for the first day."

"Who would have thought," Jeff said. "That doesn't count the quarters in the telescopes or the income from Laura's concession booth."

"Are you tired?" asked Ida.

"A little. I'll go to the house now." They helped Mom into her golf cart, and she drove down the path with her flags waving in the breeze as she beamed and waved to visitors.

"I think she's enjoying this," Jeff said.

"I can tell she's having fun," Ida said, "but I can also tell she needs another pain pill. She's up to two every four hours now."

"Are you still convinced radiation wouldn't help? She might gain some time."

"Maybe, but she's afraid of incontinence and being helpless. She can't stand the thought."

"She's always been in charge, so I guess she should be in charge of her dying."

"I guess so. We can make sure she's free of pain, and hospice can take care of her last couple of weeks."

"I don't know what to do without her," Jeff said softly. "I'm worried I'll lose some of my drive."

"Actually, that probably wouldn't hurt," Ida said. "You're headed for a burn-out."

"Could be."

"You know, Jeff, I've always resented Mom's judging me, but I think I'm going to miss it."

"Do you think this will be a problem for Junior?" Jeff asked. "Do you think he'll start drinking again?"

"He might. Danny's been good about hanging out with him."

"Danny seems like a really decent guy, but not your type. Are you two, you know, an item?"

"Maybe. I can't believe I'm starting to like puppies. They more or less come with the package: Danny and puppies."

"Is he good to you?"

"He's gentle, and humble. He knows what he likes. He makes me laugh with his silliness, and he seems grounded. He doesn't have much money, and he doesn't seem to care. He prays. Can you believe that? I'm with a man who likes puppies and prays. Yikes."

"Ida, I've always hoped you'd find someone normal, not like the egomaniac residents you work with."

"Well, Danny is decent, but he wouldn't like being called normal. Have you had any dates lately? Is there anyone on the horizon?"

"No, all I do is work, and now this park. Pretty much it." He waved his hand over the full landscape. "Topper and his females are my current friends. And there's you. I like talking with you. I think we can help each other with Mom's death, and Pop and Junior too." Jeff sighed. "Yes, we should help. This is hard. I hate it. She's our anchor, and she'll be dead before the summer is over. Why now, Ida? Why does she have to die now?"

21

On Friday evening, after the Serenity Group AA meeting, Junior and Danny walked out of Grace church and moved to a quiet spot on the grass, under a locust tree.

"Good meeting, don't you think?" Danny asked.

"There's a lot of sobriety in that meeting. I'm impressed. I don't like being here though," Junior said.

"Why not?

"That room makes my skin crawl. It's the old scout room."

"You looked squirrely—is it hard to focus?"

"Yeah, the room even smells the same, like a pile of old tennis shoes."

"Hey, I know it's hard, but you're going to have to deal with that old stuff, Junior," Danny said gently. "If you don't, you'll pick up again. I can promise you that."

"I could almost see his face in there, all shiny. I remember he wore a whistle on a red plastic lanyard. His gut hung over his belt and he looked like a toad in a scout uniform." Junior shuddered, almost involuntarily. "Creepy."

"That was twenty years ago, Junior. You carry him around like a backpack. It's time you put that guy Cunningham down. I mean, come on, did he really hurt you?"

"He scared the shit out of me. He controlled me. I felt, you know, trapped—I couldn't breathe."

"It was in a tent on a camping trip, right?"

"Yeah, me and two other boys. Like I told you, it was a three-day weekend up in the Jemez Mountains."

"What do you remember?"

"He fooled around with me, you know, with his hands and his mouth, but Danny, I let him. I didn't do anything. I didn't even tell anyone. None of us guys did. That bastard said he kill me if I told anyone."

"What an asshole. Whatever happened to him?"

"I heard he moved to California at the end of the summer. The other boys were from different churches. I haven't seen them since. I can't even remember their names."

"Not surprising. Cunningham, the church scout pedophile. Pitiful men like that prey on twelve-year olds. But you have to accept it, Junior, or you'll never be able to move on. It happened, and you've got to deal with this."

"Well, maybe if I could find him, I'd shoot him. I've had fantasies about blowing his head off with my 12-guage. That asshole needs to die."

"Hey, I'd feel like killing him too. Your feelings are normal, Junior."

"He needs to die. I swear I could kill him." Junior's face contorted around his clenched teeth and his hands began to shake.

"You've got a fire-breathing dragon in there, Junior. Hear me. You used alcohol to put out the fire, and alcohol is flammable. The problem is you keep feeding the dragon. They live on hate, you know."

"So what am I supposed to do?"

"You're on the right track. Go to meetings, work your program. And, I hate to say it, but you've got to find a way to forgive Cunningham. That's the only way the dragon will leave."

"Forgive Cunningham? No way. He fucked up my whole life."

"Well, okay for now. What about the folks on your amends list? How are you doing with that?"

"I talked with my boss. He has a brother with a drinking problem. He accepted my apology, and he said as long as I can stay sober, I've got a job with him."

"That's cool. How about Pop? Have you talked with him, or Mom?"

"No, not since rehab, but I talked with Ida. She understands. She said I didn't do anything that hurt her except the way I talked to her, and she usually knew it was alcohol talking. I don't know how she knew about Cunningham, but she did. She said she told Mom. I don't know if Mom told Pop. I'll bet she hasn't. Mom's good at keeping secrets."

"Did you get specific with Ida?"

"I did what you said. I told her I was sorry for calling her a slut, and I said I was sorry for being so mean. Is that specific enough?"

"Yes. General apologies don't mean much. People look for you to remember what you did that hurt them."

"So, what's next?"

"I think you should make amends with Mom. She's getting sicker every day, and you seem to be avoiding it. You're running out of time."

"I don't know why it seems so hard. I just—I just don't want to."

"Sure, I wouldn't want to, either. You've got a big knot to untie, but you know how horrible you've been, and you know she blames herself. You've got to make amends, Junior."

"Maybe I'll talk to Pop first. We've been getting along okay with the park project."

"Well, whatever, but my job is to keep you moving. Maybe this next week, huh?"

"Yeah, maybe next week."

"Okay, I'll pick you up for the Sunday night meeting in Bernalillo."

"See you then. Danny, I don't want to come back here. Let's find a different Friday night meeting, okay?"

"Fine. I'll be by at 6:30 pm on Sunday."

"Danny, thanks. Thanks for being my sponsor."

"Hey, it keeps me sober. No thanks necessary."

Late on Wednesday, Junior and Pop sat in the shade of the Corley Education Building, drinking Cokes. Junior took a deep breath and looked at the seat between his knees.

"Hey Pop, thanks for not calling me dum-dum anymore."

Pop offered a small, sheepish smile. "I'm sure that name got old after a while. No problem."

"I want to talk about something else," Junior said. "I need to apologize."

"For what? Are you drinking again?"

"No, it's not that. I need to apologize for all the times I cursed you out."

"Oh, that. It's okay. I figure alcohol does bad things to people. Forget about it."

"Pop, there were times I broke stuff to get even and so you'd need me to fix things."

"Like what?"

"One time I drove a 16-penny nail into a tire on the motor grader. Then I spent the next morning fixing it. I'm sorry for that."

"I'll be damned."

"I was angry at you. I was pissed off at you a lot."

"For calling you dum-dum?"

"You didn't think I could do anything right. You'd say, 'Get it right, dum-dum.'"

"That's my way of teaching you things. I figure it'd stick better."

"Yeah, it sticks and it hurts. I'm not stupid, you know."

Pop took off his hat, cupped it in his hands, and stared into it. "Junior, you're the smartest of all the kids. You've soaked up more than Jeff and Ida combined. Don't you know that?"

"No, Pop. In your eyes I've always felt stupid."

"Well, you're not. Get over it."

"I'm sorry for all the grief I've caused you."

"I like working with you when you're sober. It's almost like I'm working with another me."

Junior smiled, but he thought, *Oh shit. Maybe I'm turning into my old man.*

On Friday, Junior finally had the courage to approach Mom. He told Pop he was taking a break, and then followed Mom back to the house after she had brought lunch. Mom collapsed into her chair by the window just as Junior came in.

"Mom, are you all right?"

"No, I'm not. I'm dying."

"I mean, are you hurting?"

She sat up straight in her chair. "I took another pain pill, so it's tolerable."

"Can I talk to you? I have something to say."

Mom turned to face him and folded her hands in her lap.

"I don't know where to begin, but I want to apologize for all the misery I've brought you."

Mom pulled a tissue from her pocket and began to cry. The tears increased until she sobbed and her body heaved with convulsions. Junior kneeled beside her and hugged her. He began crying. He felt like a frightened child trying to shelter his mother from a growling wolf that had just entered the room.

"Why have you been so mean to me?" Mom said through her sobs. "Nothing I do for you makes any difference. Food, cleaning, laundry, money—nothing counts."

"I've felt smothered. I drank. I wanted you to leave me alone."

"I just wanted to help you, Junior, to be your mother, to help you get along with Pop and your brother and sister. Don't you see? I know I let you down. I know I've made mistakes. Being a mother is hard."

"You haven't let me down. Mom, I haven't been able to grow up. You've made all my decisions. You've covered for me. You hide my drinking from people. In your eyes, I feel like a little boy."

"Oh, Junior, what do you want from me? What can I do?"

"Mom, I'm sorry for the times I've shouted at you. I'm sorry for the times I've been mean to you."

"Sometimes I felt like you truly hated me. I could never do enough to overcome that."

"You were right, Mom. Sometimes I did hate you, but not deep down. Not really. It was about feeling trapped and smothered. Mom, you can't let your happiness depend on what I do. We're different people. Can't we just be separate and still care about each other?"

"Well, I am your mother, and I do have responsibilities." She looked toward the embroidery of Proverbs 31 in a frame on her desk—Her children arise and call her blessed; her husband also, and he praises her.

"Mom, I'm a grown man, and I have to take responsibility for myself or I'll die from this disease. It's not about you. I am an alcoholic. I have to deal with it."

"What do you want me to do, just shut you out? I don't have much time, you know."

"Right now, just accept my apology. I am sorry for being so mean and disrespectful to you."

"Junior, I know you're looking for forgiveness here, but I'm not the one who gives it."

"Look, Mom, I'm just trying to clean up my side of the street. I apologize for hurting you. What you do with that is up to you."

"Okay, Junior, I accept your apology. Now please go away and let me be for a while. I'm so tired."

Junior got up and walked to the door.

"Junior," she called after him. "If you are truly sorry, then you can show me you've changed."

"I am showing you. I'm sober, I'm working on the park, I'm going to meetings. It may be slow, Mom, but I'm changing."

"Well, you could show me by going back to church."

Junior looked at his shoes. "I wish I was strong enough, Mom, but I'm not. I'm sorry."

He walked out the door, back to his work at the park. He paused by the concession stand and took some deep breaths. He felt like his blood had just thickened and wouldn't move through his veins. He wiped his mouth and felt his throat burning. That worked out well, he thought. A big nothing. He dug out his cell phone and called Danny.

"I feel like I need a drink," he said.

"Where are you?"

"I'm at the park."

"Meet me in the parking lot in fifteen minutes and we'll go for coffee," Danny said. "Have you been with your mother?"

"Yeah, my amends did not go well. I'm having trouble breathing."

"I'm on the way. Get a Pepsi and walk on the trail. Say your serenity prayer, and talk to Big Al if you feel like it. Just don't drink. Do you have anything stashed?"

"No, there's nothing around. I'll be okay. Can we talk while you drive?"

"Sure. Get a Pepsi and eat a Hershey bar."

Junior let himself in the door of the concession stand, pulled a cold Pepsi out of the cooler, and opened a Hershey with almonds. He stuffed half the candy bar in his mouth and washed it down with Pepsi.

"Okay, I'm sugared up. I'm breathing again."

"Hey, I'm almost there. We'll go for coffee and then find a meeting. You can do it, Junior."

Junior walked up the interpretive trail, put a quarter in the telescope, and searched for Big Al. Then he sat down on the bench and prayed. "Oh

God, help me with this craving." He finished his candy, downed the rest of the Pepsi, and walked to the parking lot. Pop drove up in his pickup at the same time as Danny arrived.

"Hey Pop, Danny and I have something important to do. I'll be back soon."

"Don't hurry, Junior; I'm finished for the day. I'm going to sit with Mom for a while and see if I can help with dinner."

"See you in the morning, then. It'll be better if we stop for pizza somewhere."

"Okay," Pop said as he got out of the truck. "I'll tell Mom." He put his hand on Junior's shoulder.

"Junior, I'm proud of you. You're a good man. You can whip this thing."

"Thanks Pop. See you in the morning." As he walked around Danny's car to get in, Junior noticed something in the shade of the cedar bush.

"Just a minute," he said to Danny, and bent down. It was a dead prairie dog pup. He held it up to the light by its tail, but didn't see any visible wounds. He looked around, but no one was there except him and Danny. Junior tossed the pup in the nearby Dumpster and got in the car.

"Let's go. I can use some coffee."

22

Mom's hairdresser created a summery swept-back look that gave her a healthy glow as she sat straight in the driver's seat of her golf cart. Pop sat next to her with his chin up and his hands folded in his lap. His chiseled features provided an air of support, and he felt a strong sense of duty. The park-entrance monuments and overhead sign framed the golf cart, in a balanced composition lit by the early morning sun. Karen Thomas from KOB-TV and her cameraman appeared at 8 am sharp for the interview. Junior stood in the background drinking coffee from his thermos, and a crowd of onlookers gathered in the parking lot. Donald hurried to a place beside the golf cart.

"I hope I'm not late," he said as he smiled at Karen and shook her hand with both of his. "It's great to see you again."

Karen blushed slightly. "You're right on time," she said. "Let's get started."

The cameraman moved into position and framed the scene. Karen ran a brush through her hair and began.

"I'm Karen Thomas with a live report from the Corley Prairie Dog Park. I'm with Mom and Pop Corley, as they like to be called, and Donald Pressman with the Forest Guardians, the environmental group whose Albuquerque office is here at the Park.

"Mrs. Corley, may I call you Mom?"

"Sure. Everyone calls me Mom."

"Mom, this is remarkable. You opened the Corley Prairie Dog Park a few weeks ago, and you're already overrun with visitors. How do you feel about that?"

"We are most excited by all the children," Mom said with an easy smile. "We've provided a substantial discount for school children and church youth groups. It is a real learning experience for them."

Karen turned to Donald Pressman.

"Mr. Pressman, how does the Forest Guardian organization view all of this?"

"It is a testimonial to the best in human nature," he said. "All the people involved have come together in a sense of community to protect these little creatures and to preserve their habitat. I am proud of the Corleys and happy to be a part of all this."

"Mr. Corley, or Pop, you've come a long way from your days of exterminating prairie dogs with your, ah, Rodenator, I think you called it. How do you feel about that?"

Pop pulled at his cap and shifted in his seat. He felt his cheeks flush as the camera pointed at him.

"Okay," he said.

"Just okay? Anything else? Are you happy about having the Park?"

"Yes."

"Thank you. Mom, may we now walk along the interpretive trail?"

"Of course," Mom said. "I'll lead the way."

The camera stopped and Karen explained what her producer hoped to get on film. He wanted interview scenes by the viewing areas and an overview of life at the Park, particularly how the prairie dogs thrive in their natural habitat.

"I hope we can see Mother Nature come into this interview," she said. "We have telephoto lenses and special equipment. This is going to be a great feature story."

Mom steered her cart up the trail, and Junior shut the gate and put up a "CLOSED" sign to keep the crowd from following. Jeff arrived and staffed the ticket booth. He told people they would open after the TV station finished the segment. He instructed everyone in the crowd to keep their ticket stubs, because there would be drawings for free hats and cups.

They stopped first at the viewing station by Topper's coterie. Mom drove the cart up to the large plaque filled with information. Karen motioned to the cameraman.

"Tell us about this plaque," said Karen.

Mom pointed to the photo that towered behind her. "This prairie dog photo is Topper," she said. "If you watch him in the field, you see that he likes to be up as high as he can on top of mounds. He has a white tuft on his head. Dr. Pentoff, a prairie dog expert, said Topper is a natural born leader and he is probably the leader of the entire habitat."

"Pop, tell us about that list of words on the plaque."

Pop took a breath and pulled at his collar.

"Well, people say these prairie dogs talk and these are some of the words. *Aaach, aaach* means danger, and *thaa, thaa, thaa* means peaceful. The other words mean what they say up there on the sign." He pointed to the list.

"It says *yaap, yaap* means good person, and *yuuk, yuuk* means bad person. Do you really think these prairie dogs can judge people?" Karen asked Pop.

"I really don't know," he said.

"I do," Donald interrupted. "Dr. Pentoff studied these words for a month and has validated their meaning with repeated trials and recordings. He isolated eight words and may have discovered a couple more. These prairie dogs have been here for over a hundred and fifty years."

"Oh, look," Karen said. "That's really cute." She motioned to the cameraman. He quickly changed lenses.

"Are they kissing?" she asked Don.

"Yes, they are very affectionate," he said. Topper was rubbing noses with a female and then jumping up and down. "Dr. Pentoff thinks their affectionate behavior conveys happiness. Their kissing behavior seems to increase every day, as though they are more relaxed in their protected environment."

Pop bit his lip and shook his head. He felt like choking Donald with his bare hands. Junior walked up closer to Pop, and leaned against the golf cart. He whispered in Pop's ear. "Just let Mr. Hollywood be a star. It's okay." Pop put his hand on Mom's hand and dropped his shoulders.

"I guess prairie dogs are more affectionate when they are comfortable," Karen said. She smiled at Don. "Let's move on." The camera paused as Mom drove her cart and the crew followed to the next viewing station, which featured Big Al.

"Tell me about Big Al," she said to Pop.

Pop pointed to the picture. "Well, he's brown, and he has big flanks and a big chest. Pentoff said he reminded him of a football player. He likes to eat because he says *uha, uha, uha* a lot."

"Does that mean 'eat'"? Karen asked.

"It probably means 'food.'"

"Look how he is standing," Donald said.

Karen turned to Donald. "What do you mean?"

"He's standing tall and proud. He seems to feel as though he is part of things."

Pop rolled his eyes and Junior touched his shoulder.

"Could you elaborate, Mr. Pressman?"

"The Forest Guardians believe that all life is connected, and I think Big Al may be aware that his very being is part of this web of life. Look at him. He is proud, and he feels safe, as though Mother Nature surrounds him."

"I'm not sure I see what you do, Mr. Pressman, but he does stand tall."

Mom handed her some tokens and Karen put one in the telescope. She turned to the camera.

"I'm looking in the telescope now, and one of our cameras will go in close to see what I am seeing."

She put the telescope to her eye and the camera went in close on Big Al.

"His eyes are sparkling," she said. "This is incredible. Are you getting that on camera?"

"I'm telling you," Donald said, "he is proud and happy. His sparkling eyes mean he's spiritually connected. Don't you see? This park is a microcosm of the web of life."

"Let's move along," Karen said.

Mom glanced at Pop, smiled, and pointed the golf cart up the trail to the next station. Junior walked along with the cart and talked quietly with Pop.

"Hey, this is going well. Just have fun. The feature story will be great for business."

"I feel like I'm on display in a zoo," Pop mumbled.

"Yeah, me too. What do you think about what Donald's saying, Pop?"

"I think it's a crock of shit," Pop said.

"You've got that right," Junior said.

"My horoscope said I could see some flim-flam in my life today, and that I should be wary. Don't be fooled, it said."

"That guy Donald—he's smooth," Junior said.

"Well, look at Mom. She finds a lot of joy in all this, and that's enough for me."

The crew arrived at the viewing station of Hopalong. Karen told everyone this would be the last stop except for saying goodbye at the gate, and added that she had a lot of footage to edit. They set up the camera, and Pop got out of the cart and stood by the sign with his hands in his pockets.

"Could you tell us about Hopalong?"

"You can see in the picture that he has a thick neck. If you watch him, you can see that he's kind of crippled, like maybe he broke his leg, and it didn't heal right. He just hops along."

"Is that him?"

Pop watched for a moment. "Yup, see how he limps."

Karen put a token into the telescope. "Oh, look. I see five other prairie dogs. They are all scurrying around. What are they doing?" The cameraman had headphones plugged into the camera, and everyone heard the distinct sound of *eeek, eeek, eeek* as Hopalong scurried after one of the other prairie dogs.

"What's that sound?" Karen asked. "It sounds almost primal, almost like a scream."

"That's their word for sex." Pop assumed an innocent countenance, and suppressed a smile. Junior put his hand up to his mouth to cover a grin.

"Oh, my," Karen said. "So are they, you know, doing it?"

"He's trying to," Pop said. "Actually, he's quite a ladies' man. He has five or six females that he, ah, services."

"Oh, I see." Hopalong had mounted one of the females and supported himself mainly on one foot, thrusting vigorously. His mouth opened and his eyes sparkled.

"I guess Mother Nature is here," Pop said.

"Yes," Karen replied. "Like all animals, they add to the cycle of life."

Hopalong flopped down under a little bush and the word *thaa, thaa, thaa* came over the microphone to the camera.

"Isn't that the word for 'peaceful'?" Karen asked.

Donald spoke up. "I've been watching from the camera," he said. "What we have here is a remarkable sense of calm, something unusual in nature."

"What do you mean?" Karen asked.

"In a calm state, the personality traits of these individuals can emerge. I suspect the fierce evolutionary push for survival wanes in the comfort of a protected habitat. This is remarkable. Hopalong can relax and be peaceful."

Karen rolled her eyes. "Interesting."

"Think of it this way. As a sense of safety comes over the prairie dogs, they manifest the spiritual connection among all living things. Hopalong is likely in a state of mindfulness, you know, truly peaceful."

"He looks tired to me," Pop whispered to Junior. "I'll bet he's been screwing all morning."

"That's all we have time for now," Karen said into the camera. "We'll make our way to the concession stand to say good-bye and to help give out the awards. I understand there are some exciting prizes."

The camera crew gathered things up and made their way back to the Park entrance area. Mom drove her golf cart, and Pop and Junior said they would catch up in a few minutes.

"When do they show the program?" Pop asked.

"Tomorrow night," Junior said. "We better get some extra help for the weekend. I'll bet we'll be crowded."

"Not in a million years. I would never have guessed we'd be running a park," Pop said. "Never in a million years. I'll give you this. Those prairie dogs have a pretty good life."

"Who would have thought they'd be our meal ticket?"

"Just between us, I sort of envy that little Hopalong. All he does is breed and eat, breed and eat. He's got five females all to himself, and they're all hot to trot."

Junior grinned. "You're too old to talk like that."

"I know. I'll say you're a liar if you tell anyone I said it."

"You're right, though Pop. That Hopalong is a real party animal."

"Party down dudes," Pop said, smiling sheepishly.

"Where in the world did you hear that?" Junior asked.

"Oh, I don't know, on TV I guess."

"I haven't told you this, Pop, but it is good to see you laughing every now and then."

"I'm all tore up inside about Mom dying. The laughing just comes out. Do you think there's something wrong with me?"

"We're all sad. Laughing probably helps."

Pop paused. "What are we going to do?"

"My sponsor would say we should do the next right thing."

"What is that?"

"I don't know. Maybe we should just go say good-bye to the TV people."

"Yeah, we can do that. Then we can clean up trash and mop out the bathrooms."

"Sounds like a plan."

The crowd was moving all over the place, and people were shouting and pointing when Pop and Junior came around the concession stand. Mom's golf cart lay on its side, and Mom struggled on the gravel. Blood dripped from a deep cut on her knee. Her white thighs and panties seemed huge in the sunlight. Pop ran up and pulled down her dress. He and Junior sat her up.

"Are you okay? What happened?"

"She came down the hill and just flipped over," said Karen. "I called 911. The ambulance is on the way."

Mom held Pop's hand. Her eyes glazed over and she fainted.

"She's breathing okay," Junior said. Jeff came running through the commotion and turned to the crowd. "Out of the way, please. Get back. Give her some air."

Junior ran and got a water bottle from the concession stand, and put a wet compress on her face. Mom's eyes fluttered, but she didn't regain consciousness until the paramedic from the ambulance put an oxygen mask on her face.

Within a few minutes, she opened her eyes. "I don't know what happened," she said. "I just turned over."

They moved her into the ambulance.

"We'll take her to Presbyterian downtown," the paramedic said. "She needs to have X-rays. Do you know if she's on any medication?"

"I'm on a lot of medication," Mom said. "I have cancer."

The paramedic started a saline IV and adjusted her airway as Jeff, Pop, and Junior hovered over her. The paramedic turned to Pop. "Can you hurry and bring a medication list?"

"I'll be right along." He turned to Mom, whispering, "Just take it easy. I'll be there soon."

"Easy as I can," Mom said. "Easy as I can... Make sure Karen Thomas doesn't show any pictures of me tipping over." She smoothed her dress with one hand. Her eyes fluttered and closed.

23

The next morning in the hospital room, Jeff's nose wrinkled from the smell of rubbing alcohol and orange floor cleaner. He paced around the room, unable to stand still. Pop hovered over Mom and held her hand. Ida picked up a water bottle, distractedly, and then set it back down. Mom's doctor required a one-week hospital stay for tests, and confined her to three weeks of bed rest for the sprained knee and the gash that required twenty stitches. Jeff waved his hand as if to chase away an unsettling feeling that made it hard to breathe. Bags formed shadows under his eyes, shadows that hid an unceasing turmoil. It seemed months had passed since Mom confronted him, but it had only been two weeks. Her Al-anon group or her illness must have brought on her new behavior. After giving him a two-thousand dollar check, she had frowned and told him she wouldn't give him another dime except for the fees required to hire an accounting firm. Her withering face was pitiful but strong. She gave him no choice.

"No more, Jeff. I'm sorry, but now that I'm managing money for the park, I'm accountable to everyone," Mom said. "Our little secret is over—it's high time you grew up."

Jeff hung his head. "I don't think I can get by. I owe too many people." He felt abandoned, as though she had disowned him.

"Well, you'll just have to," she said. "Work with Emilio Vasquez. He's a CPA, an experienced tax accountant who works with all sorts of businesses. I'll cover his bill. He's helping with the park too."

Jeff's first meeting was the next Monday. Jeff felt ashamed when he met with Emilio that day, as though he had been put on a stool in the corner of the room. Emilio had found that Jeff had over one-hundred thousand dollars in debt spread over six credit cards. The average interest rate was twenty-one percent, and often Jeff paid late fees. Sometimes, Jeff got a cash advance on one credit card to pay his payments on the others. He opened a line of credit at one bank to make payments on his Mercedes, which he'd financed at another bank.

"Your finances are a royal mess. I've been through your credit cards over the last year," said Emilio. "Last November, there's over thirty-thousand dollars in cash advances from three casinos. Did you spend every weekend gambling?"

"Honestly, I got into trouble, but I have control of it now—it's more of a hobby. Sometimes when I'm bored I go to Santa Ana or Camelback, but not that often."

"The pattern shows you go to a casino at least three times a month, but you're right. The past few months have been better, under five-hundred a month. It appears you've spent all the cash advances, and you've paid over twelve-hundred in cash advance fees. No wonder you don't have any money."

"Now I usually stop after a couple of hundred. I mostly go for the atmosphere, to visit with people, play some bingo, things like that."

"You're a hard case," he said. "How you live your life is your business, but how you manage your money is mine. First, we're going to tear up all your credit cards. I'm putting you on a budget, and I'm countersigning all your checks over five-hundred. You get two-hundred dollars a week for pocket money and my job is to hold you accountable. Your job is to practice dentistry and make money. That's the deal. If you're not willing, I'm moving on."

"No, no, I need the help. Believe me, I want things to get better."

"Your mother is paying me, so I need to keep her informed."

"Can you just tell her we're making progress? She worries a lot, and with her cancer, I don't want her upset about the casinos."

"For now, I can tell her we're making progress. As long as you follow the rules, we'll stay with that."

Jeff felt relieved that Mom would hear of his progress, but worried that Emilio would share all the facts. Since that day with Emilio, Jeff had a hard time getting out of bed when he awoke, and he wore his pockets thin reaching for his credit cards. His nervous energy became productive during the day, but he roamed his apartment at night moving from one task to the next, and watching late-night movies. Jeff's anxiety overpowered him, and he tossed and turned until the sleeping pills kicked in.

The shiny hospital floor shimmered with annoying flashes of light. He hunched his shoulders, fearing his agitation would push him out of his skin. An attendant was mopping the hall again with orange cleaner. He wiped his eyes and turned to Mom as she took his hand gently.

"Are you okay?"

"I'm fine, just nervous."

She squeezed his hand. "Good. I need for you to handle the money at the park." She sipped some water through a straw. "I can show you."

"Mom, I'm not sure I can do it."

"You need to. I'm stuck in here, and the doctor said I can't walk on my knee for two weeks after I get home. He said the Park is off limits."

"It's up to you," Pop interjected. "Junior and I don't know how to run that accounting system."

Ida spoke up. "My shifts are usually evening, so I'm not out of here until after 11:30 pm. Sorry."

"I'll give it my best. I'm just worried. I don't want to screw it up."

Mom sighed. "Go see Emilio. He'll go over things. It's simple. You just need to pick up the money, make a deposit slip, figure the inventory on the concessions, and go by the bank. It only takes about forty-five minutes."

"Okay, so all I do is go to the concession stand, count the money, and take it to the bank, right?"

"Yeah, but you need to take it *all* to the bank," Pop said.

Mom's eyes widened.

"Sure, I know. Take it all."

"When you fill out a deposit slip, you decide what you need from the food and drink vendor," Mom said. "There's a form. Just fill it out and leave it on the clipboard. They come by three times a week. The list should match the cash register tape. Just push the total key, and it'll print out what the deposit should be except for the two-hundred dollars we keep for change. Oh, and you have to check the time cards. Payday is Friday, and Emilio has his office do it. Have Emilio meet you. He'll show you about the time cards."

"I'm off for the next two days," said Ida. "I'll meet you there and we'll do it together. It's not hard."

"Okay," Jeff said. "It's just that money and I don't get along."

"It's about time you learned how to handle it," Mom said.

Ida helped her take another pain pill.

Her gray face strained as she swallowed.

"Now, everyone go on and let me get some rest. My knee hurts."

That night, Jeff met Ida at the park. A moveable partition separated the two sales areas of the concession stand. Laura sold hats, tee shirts, and cups on one side, and student employees sold snow cones, candy, popcorn, hot dogs, burritos, and an array of drinks on the other. Mom hired four teenagers from the church to work in food sales and the ticket booth, and she handled special events from home. Junior kept an eye on the ticket sales in case there were difficult people, and he took the moneybag from the ticket sales to the concession stand for the bank deposit. There was a huge pile of cash in the evening, mostly small bills. Jeff and Junior closed the doors and Ida totaled the register and began counting the cash. "Mom's getting worse every day. This accident really set her back, and she's going to have a tough time. She's lost all her strength."

"What can we do?" Junior asked.

Jeff dug out a deposit book. "Not much. She knows what she wants."

"At least we can take care of the park," said Ida, "and I've hired a cleaning person to come in and a home health-care worker to help her with her personal care. The woman will come every morning." Ida handed Jeff a stack of money.

"My gosh, look at all this cash. It's amazing how much tickets and snow cones bring in."

They counted the money twice, made the deposit slip, figured the inventory for the food supplier and the drink vendor, checked over the time cards, and locked the door. "Take the moneybag to the night depository at Wells Fargo on Montgomery," Ida said.

Jeff put the bag under his jacket. "I'm on the way. I think I can do this."

Jeff's resistance faded, and he focused, perhaps excessively. His agitation turned to compulsion, clearly a more comfortable state of mind, and he watched the money at the park like a hawk, often with his teeth gritted. He worked hard at his office all day, and then he came by the park and counted food and money. He cleaned up the concession stand and added racks of peanuts, M & M's, energy bars, and other impulse items. Food sales increased by twenty percent. He and Mom talked almost every evening, and she slowly regained some trust in his judgment.

"I let that girl Lucy go today," Jeff said. "She's been snippy with customers for a week, and I've warned her twice. This afternoon I heard her call a little boy a 'stupid little shit,' so I told her she was fired."

"That was a good decision. I know Lucy's family from church, and they're kind of crude."

"Laura wants to start selling prairie dog tote bags and jackets, and I told her it would be the same deal, thirty percent. That's okay with you, right?"

"That's fine. She tried to chisel me down to twenty percent last week, and I told her no. We're still paying Dr. Pentoff royalties on the photos."

"I looked at that. We only owe him another thousand dollars for photos and we'll be done."

"That's good. We almost have the initial expenses paid."

"The way I see it, the rent from the Forest Guardians pays the mortgage, the hazard and liability insurance, and the taxes. After we pay Pentoff, the ticket sales, special events, and food income should leave us with about three-thousand a week in positive cash flow after our variable expenses. Of course, the balance sheet still shows the mortgage debt of three-hundred thousand, but Emilio figures the improvements are worth six-hundred thousand, since Pop and Junior built things way under budget. We've worked out a way to give you and Pop a lease payment for the land, so that will be a plus for your retirement, and its deductible."

"Where did you learn to talk like that?" Mom asked. "You don't know anything about money."

"I've been meeting with Emilio. He's making me behave and I'm learning a lot, but I still don't have any money." Jeff grinned at Mom and took her hand. "I don't want you to worry. I'm paying off my debts. Things are tight but I'm okay."

As the month of May passed, Jeff still had fits of loneliness, and his agitation plagued him. Sleeping pills helped at night, and occasional little orange pills kept him hopping during the day. His dental business picked up. His involvement in the park sometimes made him feel happy. Jeff played bingo a couple of times a week with ten-dollar cards. When he won, he would leave the room of elderly folks, and sit down at the blackjack table until his money was gone. Then he'd stop. He had kept one credit card that Emilio didn't know about for emergencies. Using it would bring a deep abyss of embarrassment and disappointment.

On Wednesday night in the first week of June, Jeff discovered the cash was exactly one-hundred dollars short. He counted again, separated the ticket sales, but still came up short. The same thing happened on Friday night. On Saturday, he was short two-hundred. Jeff came early Sunday and watched the staff, but everything seemed normal. In the evening, he told Junior and Pop. They decided not to tell Mom, for fear that the added worry would sap her already-fading strength.

More than one-thousand dollars disappeared the next week, and Jeff and Junior were fed up.

"We've got to figure it out," Jeff said. "It's not me. I'm worried Pop thinks it's me."

"He doesn't think that," Junior said. "I've got an idea. Let's put up a camera."

Late in the evening, Jeff helped Junior install a security camera eye in one of the recessed lights in the ceiling over the cash register. They mounted a CD recorder in a utility box outside. It was set to take a photo every ten seconds during work hours. Two nights later, they changed CDs and watched the first one.

"Well I'll be damned, would you look at that," Junior said. Nobody else has boobs that big."

The pictures showed Laura stuffing twenty-dollar bills into her bra and then closing the drawer. The camera angle was awkward. You could see the top of her hat, her nose, and her hand pushing the bills into her bra. Her cap hid her face, but her puffy cleavage gave her away. She had taken over twenty-five hundred dollars altogether. He wrote up a report of the missing cash, copied the pictures, and filed a police report with the district attorney. That weekend, he and Junior told Pop. He looked down and shook his head.

"I'll be damned. That Laura's got a mean streak, but I never figured her as a thief," Pop said. "This is bad, LeAnn's daughter."

"I'm glad you filed charges," Junior said. "We'd better tell Mom because all hell's going to break loose. Laura and Fred are supposed to get married in two weeks. They put down a deposit on the Gazebo and the chairs."

"I'll tell her," Pop said. "You guys stay out of it for now."

In the morning, Pop sat with Mom over coffee. They looked out the window and watched the hummingbirds zoom around the feeders.

"Is something on your mind?" Mom asked. "You're too quiet."

"I've got some bad news."

"Out with it. Time is precious these days."

"Jeff and Junior caught Laura stealing from the cash register. They've got pictures. She took over twenty-five hundred dollars. Jeff turned it over to the DA and pressed charges."

"Damnation," Mom said. "That little sneak, and after all we've done."

"It's going to hit the fan," Pop said. "The papers will pick it up."

"It'll be all over church. We better call June so she's not surprised. And there's the wedding. Oh God, what a mess." Mom began crying.

"Are you upset with Jeff?" Pop asked.

"No, she deserves it. I'm sick and tired of being nice. Tell Jeff it's okay."

Later that very morning, two detectives appeared and arrested Laura amidst her piercing protests.

"Leave me alone. You can't do this," she shouted as they took her to the car in handcuffs. They read Laura her rights from a printed card, eased her into the back seat, and drove away as a small crowd of employees and visitors watched. Laura still wore her pink prairie dog hat. She bowed her head low to hide her face as they drove away.

At 8:30 in the morning, June and LeAnn let themselves in Mom and Pop's house.

"Mom, are you here?" Pastor June said.

"I'm in the kitchen. You're right on time. The coffee's ready." Mom sat on the seat in a rolling walker dressed in her robe. "I heated up some coffee cake. Sorry, it's from the store. Pop bought it last night."

June and LeAnn sat down at the kitchen table, and Mom rolled over and took her place at Pop's place at the head of the table.

"How are you doing?" June asked.

"You both know how I'm doing. I'm dying."

"Are you in any pain today?" LeAnn asked.

"Some, but I have a patch now. Mostly my knee bothers me. It's hard to get around, and I hate being helpless."

"I'm sorry to add this problem to your life," LeAnn said. "I know you already have too much to deal with."

"Let's stop the chitchat and get to it," Mom said.

"This is a tough situation," June said. "Let's start with a prayer. Lord, we pray that you may bring the spirit of God to be among us as we discern your will for this difficult situation. May your love and presence prevail. In the name of Christ, amen."

"I'm so sorry, it's very embarrassing," LeAnn said. "Laura was scared to death in the holding cell. We bailed her out late last night. She's at home sleeping."

"Yes, it is unfortunate," Mom said. "We have to face the facts. Laura stole twenty five hundred dollars. That's a lot of money."

"She says she was just borrowing it," said LeAnn. "She intended on paying it back, every penny. She said Fred doesn't have any money for their honeymoon, and she wants to go to Hawaii. She was going to pay it back, really."

"If you borrow, you ask. If you stuff money in your bra and sneak away, it is flat-out stealing. You know that," Mom said. "A lot of people go to Santa Fe for their honeymoon. How much would that cost?"

LeAnn looked down at her hands. "I know it looks like stealing, but it's Laura. She's not a thief."

"Is there anything we can do?" June asked. "Maybe if Laura apologized and paid you back?"

"It's not just me. The park belongs to the whole family."

"What if she apologized to the whole family?" June asked.

"We would have to get the money back," Mom said. "Maybe I could arrange a meeting."

"Please drop the charges," LeAnn said. "Laura could go to jail. She couldn't handle that. Please give her a chance. Could you do it for our friendship?"

Mom invited everyone for dinner Sunday night. After dinner, June, LeAnn, and Laura arrived. Pop got extra chairs and made room for everyone around the table.

"I appreciate everyone coming together in the spirit of forgiveness," June said. "Laura has some things she wants to say."

Laura folded her hands on the table and looked at the cheesecake. "I am sorry for borrowing your money without asking," she said. "I'm going to pay it all back, and I ask for your forgiveness."

Jeff stood up and paced trying to hide his agitation. "Why did you take it?" He hated conflict, and he didn't like Laura. Brassy women bothered him.

"For my honeymoon. We wanted to go to Hawaii." She handed Jeff an envelope. "Here's what I can pay back now."

Jeff counted out the bills. "There's only eleven hundred here. Where's the rest?"

Laura started to cry, and wiped her eyes with a tissue. "I bought some clothes and shoes, and the travel company said they could only refund half of the two thousand I gave them. I'll pay you twenty dollars a day from my sales until the rest is paid."

Jeff looked at Junior, Pop, and Ida. Then he glanced over at Mom. His face flushed.

"You decide," said Mom. "You've been handling the money."

"How do we know we can trust you?" Jeff asked.

Laura blew her nose. "I promise. Please give me another chance. I am sorry."

"If you drop the charges tomorrow, Laura can save the cost of an attorney," LeAnn said. "I can vouch for her, and I'll make sure she pays you."

Jeff folded his arms and stared at Laura. "Okay," he said. "I'll ask our CPA to draw up a note for you to sign tomorrow. If there's ever any more money missing, that'll be the end. No more chances. The camera stays on."

Laura leaned on LeAnn's shoulder and sobbed. "Thank you."

June thanked everyone and she, Laura, and LeAnn left.

"I don't know what else we could do," Jeff said. "It would take months for this to come before a judge, and at least this way we get the money back."

"Sounds okay to me," Junior said. "Pop, Ida, are you okay with it?"

"Let's see how it goes," Pop said.

On Monday morning, Donald stood waiting for Laura when she arrived at the concession stand. He handed her the newspaper with a short article about Laura's arrest. "Laura, I need for you to take some time off. This incident could be tough on our fundraising. I've arranged for Crystal to take care of concession sales, and perhaps at the end of the summer we can find you something in the office."

Laura's mouth opened to say something, but she just turned and walked away. After a few steps, she turned back and put her hands on her hips.

"You son of a bitch," Laura said. She raised her voice to a near-scream. "After all I've done for you and these prairie dogs. It's my art. You can't sell my art. I'll sue you."

"You are in no position to get upset," Donald said. "I'm sorry for what has happened, but we paid you for your graphic skills, and these designs belong to the Forest Guardians. Please, just calm down and we can talk later."

Laura turned and walked away fast. She stopped, turned back, and threw her pink prairie dog hat at Donald. "Take it," she said. "I don't care anyway."

The hat landed in the dust under a chamisa bush near a dead prairie dog pup. Donald picked it up in his handkerchief and carried it to the dumpster. "Poor little fellah," he said. "I wonder what happened to you?"

24

The month of June brought events that no one expected. Laura postponed her wedding. Fred moved back to Farmington, the Martha Circle helped LeAnn organize a garage sale to raise money for Laura's debt to the Corleys, and Laura ceremoniously forfeited her fifty-dollar deposit on the Gazebo.

"I'm through living like this," she had said. "I can't depend on other people for me to be happy."

On the last Saturday of June, Pop and Ida walked in to the concession stand, where Jeff stood counting the money. Junior arrived with the cash from the ticket booth.

"Take a look at this," Jeff told Pop. "I figured we would have about three thousand clear this week, and it's almost five grand. This is a good business." He chuckled. "I might have to give up dentistry."

Pop put his hands in his pockets. "I'm proud of all of you. I want you to know I'm proud." Pop reached out, put his arm around Ida's shoulder, and pulled her to him. He wiped his eyes with his sleeve.

"Ida says it's time, so I need to tell you," Jeff said. "We talked with Mom's oncologist today, and he told Mom it's time for hospice. The doctor says Mom's got about a month, maybe less."

Pop looked up at the ceiling and took a breath. His shoulders sunk, and Ida pulled him close.

"The hospice nurse will come tomorrow," Ida said. "I told her to come in the afternoon. She wants to talk with Mom, and then to all of us."

Junior pulled down the brim of his hat. "I'll be there. Danny's here to pick me up. I'll see you tomorrow." He walked to the parking lot and got in Danny's car.

"We've known this was coming," Jeff said. He shook his head, wiping his eyes with his sleeve. He busied himself with counting and filling out the deposit slip.

Pop raised his eyes to the sky. "We've got to stick together. I used to know how to handle things like this by myself, but I don't anymore."

The next afternoon, the nurse came out of Mom's room and sat down with everyone.

"Hello, I'm Sandra, a palliative care hospice nurse. My job is to keep Mom as comfortable as possible as she dies. Please understand, I am deeply sorry for your sadness and the tough weeks that lie ahead. For the moment, however, I just want to share information so you'll be ready for all the changes."

Pop, Jeff, Ida, and Junior sat attentively, like children on the first day of school.

"First, you'll soon notice that she'll have episodes of fading away. That's part of the process, an inner preparation for detaching from this world and gathering her strength for the next. She'll want to be alone sometimes, and she'll want to talk with you at other times. It's best if you let her decide when.

"Second, she'll lose interest in food, but, please, we need to keep some simple foods in her stomach to help process her medications, like yogurt or soda crackers. Encourage her to drink water. She'll be more comfortable if she's hydrated. She's made it clear she wants to die at home in her own bed, surrounded by her family. When we get close to that time, I'll be here often and make all the arrangements. You can make this a good experience for her just by being present and letting her know you care. Be prepared: she may say things that are hurtful, but usually that's just fear talking. There will be a time when she gets very peaceful, and you can reassure her it's okay for her to die because you can take care of yourselves. Do you have any questions?" Silence covered the room, like darkness. Sandra handed out cards. "Here's my phone number. You can call me any time."

"She asked me to move her bed out here by her chair and the window," Pop said. "Do you see any problem with that?"

"That's fine. She should be where she wants. I'll bring a portable toilet that we can put by the bed. You already have a walker. Maybe you could build a screen or hang up a sheet or something for privacy."

"I'll do that," Junior said.

Sandra continued. "Normally the pain medications cause constipation, but this is one time when Mom's colostomy will be an advantage. Keep her hydrated. I'm going to put her medications on the table, and these forms are for charting. I'll rely on the family to make sure she gets her morning meds. Is everyone okay with that?"

"I'll be here most mornings," Ida said.

"So will I," said Pop. "We'll take care of it. I'll get her toast and orange juice. She likes blueberry yogurt."

"This month will be hard," said Sandra. "You need to talk with her about funeral arrangements and what she would like. Do you have a pastor?"

"Mom does," Jeff said. "Pastor June from Grace church. She comes by often."

"Well, let her know that we have a chaplain if she wants to talk with someone else. Would any of you like to visit with the chaplain?"

Pop looked around at Jeff, Ida, and Junior for a response. They all looked away.

"No, I guess not. We'll be fine." Pop stood up, walked to the door, and stopped.

"I'll be out in the shop. Come on, let's build the screen. Thank you." He talked over his shoulder so no one would see his tears. Junior got up and followed, and Jeff and Ida looked over the blue charting forms with Sandra.

Pop turned on the lights and flipped on the radio to a country station. "I've got a roll of green landscaping canvas. We could use that."

"There's some two-inch black PVC water pipe left," Junior said. "We can make a free-standing frame and put the canvas on it. Ida can pin up some pictures or something." He grabbed a pencil and sketched out a rough plan on the drafting table.

"That looks good." He started gathering pipe and elbows from outside.

Junior added dimensions to the drawing.

They worked quietly and efficiently together. Pop cut slowly and sanded the ends gently. He knew this could be the last thing he made for Mom. Junior matched his pace.

"Do you believe in an afterlife?" Junior asked. "Like heaven and hell?"

Pop paused. "I really don't know. There's got to be something, but I don't really believe all that stuff about the pearly gates and streets of gold."

"Neither do I," Junior said. "I don't believe all that fire and brimstone stuff either. I think people make their own hell when they're here on earth. Then they pack it up and take it with them when they die."

"Mom doesn't have to worry about that. She's one of the best people I know. If there's a good place after this life, then that's where she'll go."

"That's for sure," said Junior. "Has she said where she wants to be buried?"

"When she first got sick she told me she wants to be cremated and put in the flower bed. She said her ashes ought to be useful for something. I guess I'd better ask her again."

"That's what I would want, to be cremated and spread up there in the mountains." Junior pointed up to the Sandias. "What about you?"

"Sounds good to me. I'd like to end up close to Mom, though, in the flower bed."

"Do you think you would be with her in an afterlife?" Junior asked.

"I think our spirits exist forever, so whatever brought us together in the first place could keep us that way."

"Do you think that's God?"

"I don't know what God is like, but I think He's out there, and I think He's what makes love happen. My mother used to tell me that God is love. Fate controls a lot of things."

"What do you mean by that?"

"You know, fate. How things are everyday."

"Like gravity."

"The Rio Grande runs fast every spring, forest fires burn things up, people get sick. That's fate. It's a big world out there, and things come at us."

"Do you think it's a force? I can't believe fate rules us."

"This whole universe is already set out. That's what I believe. Nature runs by laws. We have to figure out how to live in it. I guess if you stand in a hailstorm, then it's a force."

"Why do you think Mom got sick?"

"She just did. There's no reason. There's cancer out there and Mom got some."

"They say it runs in families."

"I guess that's how those genes are. What the hell, we all have to die from something. I just hate that she has to die now."

"I know I'm grateful to be alive. I've come to believe it's the grace of God, and God takes care of me if I let Him."

"Maybe so, Junior, I just don't know. I've seen some pretty bad stuff, and God didn't do anything about it."

"I used to believe God hated me and made bad things happen," Junior said, "but I changed my mind. When I finally surrendered and ask for His help, my desire to get drunk just faded away. I can't stand churches, but God cares about each of us, and His grace covers us all. Now I feel like I'm okay just as I am. I think that's good what you said. God is who makes love happen."

"It's too bad God can't keep other stuff from happening," Pop said. "People do whatever they damn please."

"You got that right."

"Accidents happen, people get sick. Not much God can do about that. Mom's dying, and that's all there is to it. We've just got to accept it." Pop slammed his fist on the workbench.

Junior wiped his eye with his sleeve. "We all die. Some just die sooner than others do. I'm going to miss Mom."

Pop turned to Junior. Tears ran down his wrinkled face and dripped onto the dirt floor.

"It's good we've got the park. I don't want to go back to building roads."

"Me either."

"Do you still feel like drinking?" Pop asked. "I'd really be pissed if you started again. I need you now." He put his hand on Junior's shoulder.

"Sure, sometimes, but the craving is gone. As long as I keep up with my AA work and talk with my sponsor, I do okay. If I pray in the morning and write in my journal, I usually have a good day. Don't worry."

"That guy Danny, he's your sponsor, right?"

"Yes. I met him in the hospital."

"He seems to be sweet on Ida."

"They spend a lot of time together. Ida likes him."

"He sure is different from those doctors she used to bring by," Pop said.

"He's a gentle soul, and a good man. I think he's good for Ida."

"That's good. I'd like to see her settle down."

Pop and Junior carried the dark green screen into the house and set it up by the wall next to the window. Mom rolled out of her room with her walker, stopped, and sat down on the seat. "Now what in the world is that?"

"Sandra's going to bring a portable toilet. The screen makes a nice bathroom," Pop said. "It'll be right next to your bed."

Mom put her hand up to her chin.

"Could you turn it around? I want the head of my bed by the window and the foot of my bed by the wall. Then when I get out of bed, I can roll this walker behind the screen."

Junior grinned. "Sure Mom, we'll move it. I guess she's still in charge."

"Yup, still in charge. Anything else?" Pop asked.

"Could you please put those photo albums on my desk? I want to pick out some pictures to put up on that tacky canvas. It looks like a job site."

Junior took several albums from the bookshelf and opened them on the table. As Mom rolled over in her bed, she blocked the light from the window, and a dark shadow fell over a photo of Junior with a BB gun when he was eight years old.

"Remember when Pop got you your first gun?" Mom asked.

He looked at the photo. "Sort of. I think it was a Red Ryder. You're not going to put that one up, are you?"

"No, I'll find something more cheerful. Now go on. I want to be alone."

"I'm going to the shed. Got some work to do," Junior said.

"Hold on, I'll go with you," Pop said. He kissed Mom's cheek.

As they stepped outside, Junior turned to Pop.

"When things are going to come at you, do you sometimes get a warning?" he asked.

"Yeah, my horoscope, feelings, things like that. Why?"

"I'm nervous, Pop. It feels like there's something bad out there."

25

Pop closed the gate, and he and Junior waved goodnight to Jeff. Pop limped toward the house as Junior walked beside him. As he pulled himself along, he knew that Mom's gray pallor, sunken eyes, and nearly weightless body awaited him. He felt drained and heavy. He wanted so desperately to hug her, but he was afraid he would break her fragile bones. Twilight covered the park, and the fireworks show at the soccer field on Paseo began with a loud report and a red, white, and blue starburst. They both turned and listened. *Aaach, aaach, aaach* came from the habitat.

"I guess those little guys sense danger," Junior said. "I'm glad the fireworks are a mile away. That sounded like Topper, and maybe Big Al."

"Could be. I'm tired. I'm going to eat some Hamburger Helper and go to bed."

"I'll come in and check on Mom," Junior said. "Sandra left about an hour ago."

Pop ate, Junior put glycerin on Mom's dry lips, and they said goodnight. Pop threw a sheet on the couch in the living room and lay down with his clothes still on. He fell asleep to the sound of Mom's labored breathing.

The shot that woke him up sounded like a muffled 12-gauge shotgun. Pop sat up quickly, and then heard it again. He pulled on his shoes, grabbed his shotgun out of the closet, and filled his pocket with shells. He loaded the gun as he stomped out the back door, then he crossed the drive and pounded on Junior's trailer.

"Somebody's shooting out here," Pop shouted. "Come on out."

Junior came out in his jeans, slipping on his tennis shoes. He put his cell phone in his pocket and started loading his rifle. "Where? Where's the shooting? Maybe it's fireworks."

Pop and Junior rounded the machine shed and looked out over the park. Roman candles shot skyward followed by explosions. The roman candles were twelve-bangers, and six or seven of them were going off at the same time, lighting up the habitat with red and white light. Other fireworks exploded randomly.

"Those are cherry bombs or M-80's, I don't think anyone is shooting."

As they approached the habitat in the moonlight, a dozen or so kids scurried around putting roman candles in prairie dog holes and lighting them. Others were tossing lighted explosives down into other holes. Pop and Junior stopped beside a clump of cedar.

"Those kids are scaring the shit out of the prairie dogs. What do you want to do?"

"Call 911 and tell them there's vandals at the Corley Prairie Dog Park and there's about to be a shooting, and then hang up. That should get 'em here fast."

Junior called, and Pop started walking down the path to the habitat. He and Junior climbed the fence, and stood by the last station on the interpretive trail.

"I figure Hopalong and the rest of them are deep in their burrows," Pop said. "Now let's scare the shit out of those kids."

Pop pumped his shotgun. He gritted his teeth and planted his feet next to a hole.

"You kids want trouble? Here's trouble." He shot two rounds in the air.

Junior leveled his rifle and put a couple of well-placed shots at the feet of two boys lighting cherry bombs. "Get your asses outta here."

One by one, the teenagers looked up and then at each other. "Somebody's shooting at us. Run, you guys." The little kids started crying.

Pop moved quickly and got in front of the group. He fired a shot over their heads. "You guys stop right there."

Junior ran up and fired shots over their heads to their left, then to their right. "You better do as he says. He'll shoot your asses."

"Everyone down on their knees," Pop yelled.

"Hands over your heads," Junior shouted.

Then Pop walked slowly up to the kids, stood about twenty yards in front of them, and listened to their sobs. He looked toward Eubank and saw two sheriffs' cars coming with sirens and red lights. Another siren screamed from deep inside his mind. He squeezed his eyes shut and swallowed hard. He felt the urge to vomit, and for a moment, he couldn't hear. He shook his head and opened his eyes just as four deputies ran up the trail with flashlights, guns drawn.

"Over here," Junior said. "Pop and I caught 'em."

"Roy, Junior, is that you?" asked the sheriff.

"We got them," Pop said. "Looks like seven teenagers and five little kids."

"For Crissake, put those guns down. We don't need any problems here. Junior, are you drunk?"

"Nope, not a drop for four months. These kids set off a bunch of fireworks and vandalized the habitat. We just stopped them—scared hell out of 'em too."

Pop cocked his head and grinned at the sheriff. "They should be arrested. Take them to jail."

"We'll take care of this." The sheriff motioned to the kids, and they slowly filed over toward him. Two deputies started taking names and checking IDs.

"Now why don't you and Junior go on back to the house and leave this to us," the Sheriff said. "You can come down to the station in the morning and press charges if you want. In the meantime, we'll hold them on malicious mischief. By the way, how's Mrs. Corley doing?"

"Not well. It won't be long now. I'm sure all this racket woke her up. Thanks for asking."

"Go on now. You boys go back to the house. Unload those guns."

Pop and Junior unloaded their guns, put them over their shoulders, and walked slowly back toward the house. Feeling dizzy, Pop stopped by a prairie dog mound, and looked up at the blinking red lights on top of the antennas on the mountain. To keep himself from falling, he sat down on the ground.

"Are you okay?"

"Yeah, you go on. I think I'll just sit here and think for a while."

"You sure?"

"Yeah. I'll be along soon."

Pop watched Junior walk away with his gun on his shoulder. His sweaty back shone in the low light, a soldier headed home after a mission.

Pop eased his crippled foot to the side and leaned on his elbow.

It began slowly. First tears came into his eyes. Then he started to shiver, as though a cold wind had caught him on a prairie. Wiping his eyes with his calloused palm, he felt waves of nausea surge up into his mouth. Then he began to shake violently, turned over, and crawled up onto the mound of earth. Carefully placing his hands on either side of the hole, he looked down into the darkness, and began to sob and moan as dead and bleeding children flashed before his eyes, reaching out their hands and screaming for help. Tears dripped onto the prairie dog mound—some fell into the hole. Bright light streaked though his mind as the children disappeared into vapor and the school bus faded from view. His sobs abated as he laid his head onto the damp dirt and whispered through his teeth, *Lord help me.* He lay quietly like that for a while and listened to the night sounds. Muffled chirps came up from the hole. Footsteps crunched nearby.

Junior called. "Are you okay? You've been out here a long time."

Pop stood up and wiped his face with his sleeve. "I'm on my way back to the house now to check on Mom."

"The light's on."

"She needs us with her."

"I know." They walked along in silence.

"Do you think those prairie dogs are all freaked out?" Junior asked.

"Yeah, but they're quiet now. I think they've calmed down."

"That's good. I was worried we'd have to close the park tomorrow."

"No, the females and the little ones will probably lie low for a while, but the males will be around. You can hand out free telescope tokens and give all the kids a snow cone. They can still walk around and use the trails."

"We'll make it happen."

In the morning, Pop and Junior wandered through the habitat and picked up fireworks trash. As they approached Hopalong's coterie, Pop found a couple of dead prairie dogs.

"It looks like a couple of females died from the concussions," Pop said. "They don't have any wounds on them."

"Here's a couple more," Junior said.

Within a half hour, they found about a dozen dead prairie dogs.

Pop paced around at the Sheriff's station later that day. The teenagers had spent a few hours in jail, and their parents had bailed them all out about 2 am.

"Are you sure you want to file charges for vandalism? All these kids and their parents will pay a fine for malicious mischief. I think they've learned their lesson. Most of them peed their pants from being shot at. You guys scared them to death."

"There's a lot going on," Pop said. "I'm not sure what to do."

"Maybe they could do some community service, help you clean up the park."

"That would be okay. We have a lot of trash."

"Here's what I'll do. I'll have each one call you and apologize. Then you can schedule them to work."

"Let's have them call Junior. I don't really want to see them," Pop said.

"Give me Junior's cell phone number and I'll set it up. Give my best to Mrs. Corley. I'm sorry."

"Thanks." Pop got up and started toward the door.

"One more thing. I forgot to tell you, someone from the neighborhood saw you and Junior last night in the park with your guns. They called the office and said they thought you were shooting prairie dogs again. You might be on the lookout for rumors."

"Thanks, but there's no chance we'd shoot any of them, not now."

"I just wanted to warn you."

"Thanks, see you around."

26

Ida changed Mom's colostomy bag, washed her face, brushed her hair, and helped her slip on a fresh gown.

Mom took a sip of water. "I think I could eat some yogurt."

Ida got a small cup from the refrigerator and helped Mom take a couple of bites.

"Do you need another patch?" Ida asked.

"No, I'm fine. I don't want to just sleep all the time."

"Sleeping is normal. Your body needs it."

"Is June coming over?"

"She'll be here after lunch. LeAnn might come with her."

"Have you heard anything about Laura? Do you know if she's paid us back?"

"Jeff said LeAnn's garage sale brought in about eight-hundred dollars, so she still owes us six hundred. Laura wants Jeff to apply the fifty-dollar deposit from the Gazebo reservation to the debt."

"What did he do?"

"He told her she forfeited the deposit because she cancelled the Gazebo, and that had nothing to do with the money she stole."

Mom chuckled. "That Jeff, I think we've turned him into a penny pincher. What did Laura say?"

"She told Jeff he was an asshole."

Mom laughed aloud, and then coughed. Ida held a tissue up to her mouth.

"Laura has never been a diplomat," Mom said. "I guess they'll work it out. Tell Jeff I don't really care. Laura is deeply troubled. Her father's abandonment was traumatic. After I die, tell Laura I've prayed God will forgive her."

"Sure Mom," I'll tell her.

"Do you really like your new friend Danny?"

"I surprised myself. I like him a lot. He doesn't have any money, and he's not flashy, but there's something very genuine about him."

"Is he good in bed?"

"What kind of question is that?" Ida laughed.

"Good sex is important. Most relationships don't last without it. Is he?"

"He's gentle and a very good lover. No problems in that department."

"That's good. You ought to marry him. Junior has told me a lot about him. I think he would be good for you."

"He has to ask me, don't you think?"

"Now come on, you know very well how to encourage men to ask you things. That shouldn't be hard. You're quite a catch."

"What in the world has gotten into you?"

"I just don't want you to waste time. Your biological clock is going to kick in here soon. I wish I could live to see your children. I know they'll be beautiful."

"I'm going to get a master's degree. It will be a while before I'll want any children. They can be a nuisance."

"I guess you're right, but sometimes I wonder."

"Wonder what?"

"Can I tell you something? I think it's time, and you can keep a secret."

"Sure."

Mom reached for Ida's hand and pulled her close. "When I was seventeen, before I met your father, I had an abortion."

"Oh, I didn't know. Did your parents know?"

"My mother did, but afterwards, we never spoke of it again. I sometimes wonder how my life might have turned out if I'd had the baby."

"Wow. I never imagined," Ida said.

"I want you to find the right man and get married so you won't ever have to go through that."

Ida folded Mom's hand gently up to her face, and held it. Then Ida put her head down on the pillow next to Mom's face. "We'll be okay, we'll be okay." Mom's tears dripped into the space between their hands, as if to create a seal of generational pain, an eternal secret between mother and child.

Mom's panoramic view from her window captured the mountains to the east and north. When she rolled her walker out on the porch, she could see to the horizon on the west. Sitting outside, she noticed her filmy roof, her protective veil, fluttering up and away from Saint Peter's Anglican Catholic church and the roof of the million-dollar house. The tethers came loose and disappeared into the sky, leaving a gaping space on the west and north. Fluffy white clouds drifted through the gap, and for a moment, she imagined the faces of her mother and father filling the space. Just then, her face flushed, and her heart fluttered as her pain lifted for a while. She thanked God for the comfort that comes in when pain disappears, if even for a minute. Her mind was blurry. The muffled sounds of the birds distracted her. She could either look or listen, but both at the same time seemed too much. It helped the pain to keep her head still.

Slowly, the filmy protective veil tied to the police substation fluttered skyward and disappeared. The space filled with a gray smoky cloud that pushed and strained against the tether attached to the peak of the Sandia Mountains. The cloud gathered force, broke the ether loose, and seemed alive at it expanded to fill the space. A part of her wove a pattern through the cloud as she waved her hand. "Pop, take me in, I'm tired."

June and LeAnn arrived after Mom's nap with some fresh flowers. LeAnn arranged them in a vase and put them by Mom's bed.

"We pray for you every day," June said.

"Thank you. I always need prayers." Mom propped herself up with a pillow, and smoothed her gown. "I'm afraid I look a mess."

June leaned closer. "Have you been crying? Your eyes are red. Would you like some drops?" June reached in her purse.

Mom nodded, and June put drops in each eye and handed her a tissue. "This air is so dry I have to use these drops all the time."

"Thank you. That feels nice." Mom dabbed her eyes.

"We're making plans for the Fall Membership Roundup," LeAnn said.

"We're going to have a big dinner. We were wondering if you could help us with the menu."

"How many people?" Mom asked.

"We hope to feed two-hundred and fifty," LeAnn said.

LeAnn got a pad and pencil, and they visited for nearly a half hour about the dinner menu and the table decorations. June shared about the program.

"Have we worn you out?" Pastor June asked.

"I'm tired, but I'd like some water," Mom said.

LeAnn held the glass as Mom sipped water through a straw.

"Laura is having a hard time," LeAnn said as she brought the yogurt. "I'm sorry she's so difficult. I know it's been a strain on our friendship. I've decided I can't do much about it. I'm sorry I haven't been a good friend lately."

"Oh, you've been fine. We've had our support group."

"I know, but Laura has been between us, and I'm sorry. She's supposed to be a grown up, but it's not happening. She went to a grief support group two nights ago. I'm hopeful."

"Let's put it behind us. Laura's working out so many things. She's going to be all right, I just know it. She has a good heart, and God will take care of her."

"Yes, let's give all these conflicts up to God," June said. She offered a quiet prayer before they stood up to leave.

"Get some rest. We'll see you tomorrow."

Their quiet voices sounded as though they were under water as they said goodbye and walked out the door. Silence came over her like a cool down comforter.

Junior stood at the drafting table sketching when Pop came into the shop.

"Take a look at this." Pop looked over his shoulder at a layout of spaces in the Corley Education Building.

"I met a guy who's a climber, and he wants to start a business. His brother-in-law is a bigwig with REI, and he's going to back him. He said if we'll build a climbing wall and design the space, he'll sign a three year lease."

"What kind of business?" Pop asked.

"He teaches climbing, rents time on the climbing wall, and sells all kinds of climbing equipment. I guess it would be a satellite of the main REI store."

"Can you make money doing that?"

"There are hundreds of climbers around, and they hang out with hikers. We're only fifteen minutes from the trailhead of the La Luz trail. There are some good climbing areas in the Sandias. He thinks it'll catch on."

"Can we afford it?"

"I told him he'd have to share in the costs of the climbing wall, but we could do all the tenant improvements for his sales area and classrooms."

"Let's talk with Jeff and get Epstein to look at a lease," Pop said.

"Sure. I'll get these drawings finished so we can get hard costs, and then we can attach it to the lease. Pop, I need something else to do. My job is only about four days a week now. I can't afford to stand around. I worry about Mom and get jumpy."

"If you want something else, one of my contractor friends wants to retire and run a miniature golf course. I can't imagine why. I guess he likes to tinker with all the water wheels and stuff. Want to build a golf course?"

"We've got the room east of the Education Building," Junior said. "Why not. Once we build it, the tenant can take over all the maintenance. We could keep the concession stand open later and make some extra money."

The following week, Pop, Jeff, Ida, and Junior met with Epstein. Junior talked about the climbing gym, and Pop confirmed that his friend would be willing to invest in a miniature golf course if he could be the manager. The sadness that covered the Corley family lifted for an evening as they discussed plans for expansion. Ida said Danny had met some artist-types at a pet adoption festival, and they were all looking for studio space. Jeff suggested they add some shared studio space with some private storage areas at a reasonable rent. Artists seemed compatible with Forest Guardians, and could easily share the building.

Epstein listened, commented that the mortgage covenants did not prohibit any "associated park businesses or amenities," and recommended leases with the tenants paying for part of the improvements. Within a week, construction began on the golf course, and Junior submitted permit applications for tenant improvements in the Corley Education Building. Donald Pressman couldn't imagine any conflicts, and agreed to support the expansion. The climbing gym permit required a variance for the forty-six foot tower. Permits for everything else appeared within a week, a clear reflection of the importance of the Corley Prairie Dog Park, the idea whose time had come.

Later in the day, Jeff and Junior sat with Mom. Jeff put a cool compress on her forehead. "Things are going well, Mom, and we've decided to expand. Jeff ran everything by Emilio, and he says it looks like a good return on investment. Bob Epstein drafted all the leases and agreements, and the Forest Guardians approve."

"That's nice. You guys will have fun building everything." Mom's heavy-lidded eyes didn't open.

"We got the permits right away," Junior said. "They like us down there at the City. We have to wait for a zoning meeting on a height variance, but they said it would be approved."

"Could I have a little water please?" Mom asked.

Junior held the water and guided the straw into Mom's mouth. Her pasty lips closed around the straw as she sipped for a moment. "I would like to sleep now."

In the morning, Jeff walked in, followed by Junior and Sandra. Ida came in with Danny. Pop shook Danny's hand.

"I brought Danny along," Ida said. "We were out to breakfast."

"Sure," Pop said. He looked over at Junior. "He's a good friend of the family."

"Thanks, Pop," Danny said. "I guess I'm involved anyway. I'd be honored to be part of this."

Sandra sat down at the head of the table and rustled through her charts. "We've reached the point where Mom's changes come more rapidly," she said. "Imagine a downhill trajectory. As Mom moves down, the changes come faster. I want you to be ready. At any time now, she could go to sleep and not wake up."

Pop's head dropped into his hands. He rubbed his eyes and then sat up straight.

"So it could be anytime?"

"Anytime. Mom might last another week or two, but no longer. Have you discussed the funeral?"

"We've been over all that," Jeff said. June came by and she and Mom wrote out the program and chose all the music. Mom helped figure out the food for after the ceremony."

"Wow," Danny said. "She's in charge of her own funeral."

"That's Mom," Junior said. He smiled at Pop and then at Jeff.

"We're going to cremate her and put her ashes in the rose garden," Pop said. "She said she wants her ashes to be good for something." He shook his head. "Imagine that. Good for something."

"Is that okay with you, Pop?" Danny asked.

"Yeah, that's fine. It's what she wants. You should do the same with me. Put my ashes beside her."

"That's sweet," Ida said. "If that day ever comes, we'll put you next to her."

"Anything else on the funeral?" Pop asked. Everyone was quiet.

"As long as we're all here," Jeff spoke up, "I want you to know I heard from the zoning commission. They're planning to approve the height variance for the climbing gym on Tuesday night. There's no opposition."

"That's good," Junior said. "I've got to get busy."

"There's something else," Jeff said. "Mom made an agreement with Emilio Vasquez about my dental practice, and we need to make some changes before she, you know, passes away."

"He works for Mom *and* me," Pop says. "I've been paying him the last two weeks."

"You have? You never do stuff like that."

"I do now. Ida helps some. She's learning QuickBooks."

"What about Emilio?" Jeff asked. "He's got me tied down pretty tight."

"I promised Mom we'd stay with the plan until you pay your debts.

You're always free to get someone else, but if I pay him, he has to do what Mom wanted. Everyone worries about your gambling."

Jeff flushed and looked at Sandra. "Don't worry. All kinds of discussions happen around hospice. It's all confidential."

"I really like my work at the park," Jeff said, "but sometimes I get real anxious, like right now." Jeff paced around the room rubbing his hands together.

"That's normal," said Sandra. "When a loved one dies, people often move into their old behaviors."

"Speaking of old behaviors, Junior, it's almost noon. Let's make that meeting at the Foothills," Danny said.

He and Danny left quietly.

"Well, does anyone have any questions?" Sandra asked. "We are entering the final stages. You'll begin noticing daily changes. She may stop eating soon."

When Mom awoke, Ida and Sandra bathed her and dried her gently. Ida got a fresh gown from the dryer, and Sandra brushed Mom's hair.

"You girls are good to me," Mom said.

"June is coming over," Ida said. "We want you to look your best."

"Is anyone else here?"

"Junior's in the kitchen. He's making sandwiches. Pop's running the Bobcat today and getting the site ready for the addition," Ida said. "I think they're planning to pour footings on Monday."

"What's today?" Mom asked.

"Friday."

"They work well together, don't you think?"

"They're a good team. I guess you trained them well." Ida smiled at Mom.

"I feel pretty good today," Mom said. "No pain at all."

"I changed your patch. You might get a little sleepy."

June let herself in and came over to the bed.

"My, don't you look good. I like your hair that way."

"Sandra brushed it. It feels good." June's glance moved quickly to Mom's feet and then back to her face. "I don't have my slippers on. My feet turned dark. Cover my feet please."

"Have you been talking with God at all?" June asked.

"Some. I still can't figure out why I have to go now. I've asked Him to tell me when I get there."

"It's a mystery to me too."

Junior came over to the bed with a cup of water and a straw. "Would you like a drink?"

Mom sipped and swallowed.

"Would you like some yogurt or broth?"

"I'm not hungry. Food is too much trouble."

"Okay. I'm going to take some sandwiches to Pop."

"Wait. Why didn't you tell me about Mr. Cunningham?"

Junior looked down at his feet, and then took Mom's hand.

"Who told you about that?"

"Ida told me. I would've called the police."

"I was afraid, Mom. He said he would kill us if we told."

June sat quietly, a confused look on her face.

"I'm so sorry. I wish I could've helped."

"I know. I felt trapped and I got angry with everyone. I still want to kill him, but I'm working through it. Danny helps me pray for him."

"Pray for him?" Mom asked. "You mean pray for Cunningham?"

"I think the only way I can get to where I can forgive him is to keep praying for him. I've been praying that somehow God can straighten out his soul."

"You can't forgive him. Only God can do that."

"God has already forgiven him. I won't be free from him until I do too. Danny says I still have Cunningham chained to me."

"You think God has forgiven him?"

"Like me. You know, God forgave me for everything long ago, but until I surrendered, He couldn't really come into me. He forgave me and just waited until I was ready."

Mom's mouth opened. Her eyes filled with tears and she clutched the neck of her gown with both hands.

"I believe God forgives me whenever I do anything I shouldn't, right then. So long as I maintain our spiritual connection, I get to know He loves me and forgives me. Actually, for me, it's simple. I have a daily reprieve from alcohol so long as I maintain a fit spiritual condition."

June folded her hands and watched Mom pull at her gown.

"You think God forgives you right after you do bad things?" Mom asked.

"Yes. I think God is love and He forgives us all—all the time. That's why He's God and I'm not. I just have to get my self-centeredness out of the way."

Mom felt as though water washed through her, as though she was utterly transparent and lying in the surf with waves everywhere. Her skin was warm and cold all at once and she began to shiver. "Do you think I'm forgiven?"

"Well, of course Mom. You were born forgiven and you'll—ah—die forgiven. Who knows, you might even be a saint." Junior kissed her forehead. "I've got to go. I'll bet Pop is starving."

"Did something just happen?" June asked.

"I think I can die now," Mom said.

In the morning, Pop moved Mom's chair out on the patio and sat in a chair beside her.

"Is there anything I can get you?" he asked a second time.

"No, just sit here."

Mom felt very tired and she could barely hear the birds. She sat quietly for a half hour or so listening for what she could not hear. She gazed at Grace church in the distance as the rising sun lit the roof and the cross. She squinted. Suddenly, the tether of the remaining veil untied itself from the roof of the church and soared upward. The light changed, and a gray darkness undulated across the sky. Mom saw memories. Pop and her children paraded across the sky displaying themselves at all ages and times, from newborns to yesterday. Pop grinned as he changed from young to old, and Mom saw herself whirl by in her wedding dress. The veil disappeared completely above the church, and she felt strong and huge as the horizons could hold. Gray clouds billowed and opened as she rose and followed the light from the sun across the sky.

"Mom, do you want to go back in?" Pop asked.

Her chin slumped against her chest. She didn't answer. He touched her hand and knew at once. He went in the house, sat down at the dining room table, and sobbed.

Within two hours, Sandra appeared at the house with the funeral home people, pronounced Mom's death, and helped straighten up as they wheeled the gurney to the vehicle. Jeff, Ida and Danny, and Junior arrived just before they drove away. They gathered around the gurney for a while, holding each other and crying. Ida pulled Pop into the group.

"She's gone," Pop said. "She's gone."

After a while, the driver said, "Please come by the funeral home whenever you can, and we'll make the final arrangements."

"Sure. This afternoon."

June carefully followed the Order of Worship she and Mom had designed for the funeral. Any change might have brought displeasure to Mom's orderly passing. Mom's admirers filled the church, and many of Pop's working friends attended. Junior's AA friends from his home group came, and Ida invited several other nurses from work. Jeff closed his practice for the day, and his staff attended. The Corleys sat upright in the first pew, breathed slowly, pulled at their tight clothes, and together displayed the air of a mismatched group seeking an appropriate countenance in a foreign country.

They listened attentively to June's eulogy of Mom's life and her influence on Grace church. A glass box on the altar displayed a simple brown urn containing Mom's ashes, and Ida brought photos that LeAnn arranged on an easel with Mom and Pop's wedding photo at the center. After the service, the family dutifully stood in a receiving line as people filed by with expressions of sympathy, and then into the Fellowship Hall for food. The Corleys left quickly and drove straight home. Pop jerked his tie loose and headed for the refrigerator.

"God, I'm glad that's over," he said to Jeff, Ida, and Junior. "I feel like I'm trapped in a maze in that church. Besides, I want some real food."

Ida touched Pop's shoulder. "We're home now. " Pastor June did a nice job on the service."

Junior shook his head. "Mom sure had a lot of friends. I had no idea."

"She touched many lives," Jeff said. "One woman there said Mom's kindness saved her life."

Ida fixed lunch, and then everyone pitched in and cleaned up the house. They moved the bed back into the bedroom, and put everything away. The house returned to normal except for the glaring absence of Mom and the presence of her ashes.

Junior carried the urn out to the rose garden to where Pop stood by the hole. Ida and Jeff stood nearby. Junior handed the urn to Pop.

"Here you go." He opened the urn and poured Mom's ashes into the hole. Then he took a handful of dirt and sprinkled it into the hole. Jeff, Ida, and Junior followed, and then Pop filled it up.

"Make those roses bloom," Ida said. She reached out and hugged Pop.

"I'll be out in the shed," Pop said. "Come on, there's work to do."

"See you tomorrow," Ida said. "I'm working an evening shift tonight."

Jeff followed them out and gazed back at the house. "I can't believe she's gone. Hey, Pop, are you okay with sleeping here tonight?"

"I'm fine. We've got a low tire on the backhoe and the Bobcat needs hydraulic fluid. You guys go on. Junior and I have stuff to do."

The month of August came and went, days blending into nights. As long as they stayed active, Mom's absence brought pain less frequently, usually only at night before restless sleep. Pop and Junior worked every day and on into the evenings on the remodel, and by the end of the month, several artists and a photographer had moved into studio space. The climbing gym scheduled a grand opening for mid-September, and the miniature golf course subcontractor hoped to be finished by then as well. The Corley Prairie Dog Park even hosted a "music in the park" evening for the neighborhood.

Jeff took on extra patients and Ida worked some double shifts. Jeff continued to come by in the evenings, and he and Pop checked over the deposits before they went to the bank. Pop set up an office in the machine shed and kept the deposit slips and receipts for Ida, who made entries and paid bills on Saturdays.

Ida walked toward the shed one Saturday evening just as the breeze shifted and came from the north. She stopped and sniffed the air. She wrinkled her nose and her eyes watered as she recognized the acrid stench of decomposition, the odor that came from the biological waste container behind the hospital.

Ida came in the door. ""Something died out on the trails. You should check it out."

"I smelled it earlier. Junior and I will walk out there in the morning. It's probably a dead rabbit or something."

"The smell's bad. It'll chase off customers," Ida said. "You guys should check before we open on Monday."

Just after daylight and two cups of coffee, Pop and Junior walked out to Big Al's territory. As they approached his main entrance to the burrows, the stench floated around them like heat waves. It rose from the holes. There were dead prairie dogs everywhere.

"Look at this." Junior pointed to a hole where a female died trying to crawl out. "This is bad. I'll go back to the house for a garbage bag."

He and Pop put two dozen prairie dogs in a bag, and carried it back to the shed.

"What do you think?"

"I don't know. We'd better get Ida over here."

Ida and Jeff came by later and looked in the bag. Jeff put on gloves and examined one of the females. Fleas jumped off her dead carcass.

"They've got fleas. Are you thinking what I'm thinking?"

"We'd better get a vet out here right away."

The vet came early on Monday, walked around with Pop and Junior, and then double bagged a couple of carcasses and put them in his truck.

"I'm headed to the Center for Disease Control," Dr. Hamel said. "This looks bad. You should shut things down until we find out what's going on."

The State of New Mexico Center for Disease Control confirmed the presence of tularemia, bacteria deadly to prairie dogs and transferable to humans. They required immediate closing of the park. Officials gathered, and, talking through surgical masks, they recommended depopulation of the park—extermination of all the remaining prairie dogs.

On Friday morning, Pop and Junior put up "Closed—Danger" signs at the entrances. Pop felt as though someone pulled the world out from under him. This time, fate came at him like a runaway train. Later, he and Junior put on gloves and masks. They rummaged through aboveground carcasses and found who they thought was Big Al. They buried his little body in a shoebox near Mom in the rose garden. The next day, two trucks appeared with fumigation hoses, and workers systematically pumped cyanide gas into all the burrows, a quick method of depopulation. Karen Thomas from KOB-TV, dressed in a hazmat suit and a hospital mask, filmed a feature story. She focused on "tularemia," interviewed protestors, warned people to stay away, and gave out the Disease Control 800 number. Swollen carcasses littered the landscape. State employees in hazmat suits filled gunnysacks with dead prairie dogs, loaded them in pickup trucks, and took them to a landfill for incineration. The stench continued for days as scores of prairie dogs decomposed deep in the burrows. All the businesses in the Corley Education Building announced they would close for at least the month of September. The climbing gym and the miniature golf course postponed their openings.

The Corleys sat around the kitchen table with Bob Epstein, the Disease Control Veterinarian, and Donald Pressman. Danny sat next to Ida, and Popeye curled up in Junior's lap, dusty from recent flea powder.

Jeff got up and paced in the kitchen. He stopped behind Dr. Hamel. "What do we really know?"

"We know tularemia is vicious and it runs through prairie dog coteries like a forest fire," Dr. Hamel said. "The Center for Disease Control did the right thing. It can be transmitted to humans. In fact, it probably came from a human, or a dead rabbit. I'm sorry."

"What happened here?" Pop asked. "It's so fast."

"Normally," Dr. Hamel continued, "wild prairie dogs can withstand minor disease exposure, although tularemia and plague can still get them. I think the built-up pressure from relocation, poisons, park construction, and steady human observation contributed. Their natural immunological systems weaken when they are hyper-vigilant day after day. Human pressure often can be the tipping point. I read a recent article from a research vet at Washington State University in Pullman. They've reported unexpected diseases and fungus that killer whales can get from the human pressures of whale watching. Day after day, all those boats and people wear them down."

"So once it started, that was it?" Jeff asked.

"Yes. From what I understand, this civilization of prairie dogs has been self-contained here for generations and was likely never exposed. Given the construction noise, poisons, hoards of people and the density of the prairie dog population, a minor exposure to tularemia set off the devastation. No telling where the virus came from, maybe a puppy, a rabbit, or even a sick child."

Pop took a deep breath. "I'm glad Mom's not here to see this. I couldn't stand to see her in more pain. Do you think we have any liability, I mean, what about the people that rent from us and the mortgage?"

"I don't think you have any liability. The law sees this disaster as an act of God."

Junior glanced at Danny. "An act of God?"

"Well, I didn't mean it that way," Epstein said. "Legally, the phrase 'act of God' describes a disaster that is beyond human agency, like a flood or a hurricane."

Donald stood up. "Tularemia is a natural occurrence, part of how nature works. Sometimes, unfortunately, humans invite disasters."

"That may be," Epstein said. "But it's clear that the Corleys are not at fault. Their liability insurance policy has an exception for 'Acts of God'. Legally, this devastation is just like an earthquake."

"Do you think any park visitors got sick?" Jeff asked.

"Probably not," Dr. Hamel replied. "If they did, we have a range of treatments. Just to be safe, the Disease Control people will put ads in the paper and notify everyone we can find. They can come in for tests, and we can advertise the symptoms."

"What about the businesses?" Pop asked.

"If they have their own business interruption insurance, they can file a claim. Otherwise, they absorb their own loss," Epstein said. "As for you, the lessor is not liable to the lessee for acts of God. You're in the clear."

"What about our mortgage payments?" Jeff asked.

"I looked at the mortgage covenants, and nothing contemplated a disaster having any influence on the debt. You have to make the payments as agreed."

"What are we going to do?" Ida asked.

Everyone looked at Pop. He shifted in his chair and rubbed his head. He slammed his hands on the table, and took a breath. "Hell, I don't know. This whole place stinks."

"We can always go back to work," Junior said. "People still need water lines and roads."

"There's not much time. We need money now," Jeff said.

28

Pop and Junior submitted bids on a couple of jobs, and spent a couple of weeks fixing up equipment. Jeff worked Saturdays, and Ida put in extra shifts. Pop couldn't shake an unsettled feeling—he felt lost, adrift. On Sunday night, after fussing in the kitchen, he moved a chair out to the rose garden and flopped down rubbing his face. Tears came into his eyes. He took deep breaths for a few minutes, and then whispered, "Janice Corley, I don't know what to do. I feel like something is over, and I don't know what's next. What should I do?" He looked down to where Mom's ashes were buried as though he expected a reply, but all he heard was the deep quiet of the night punctuated by distant sounds of traffic and kids playing soccer over at Griener Field. "Do you think I should find that guy Whitman? Maybe he's still interested." Pop sat quietly for a while longer, and then took his pocketknife, cut a half-dozen roses, took them in the kitchen and put them in a glass of water. He rustled through the drawer until he found Henry Whitman's card and put it in his shirt pocket.

Restless all night, Pop was in the shop by daybreak drinking coffee and working on a bid for a water main extension. Junior came in.

"I'm almost through with this bid," Pop said. "I need you to check over the numbers. I haven't had much sleep."

"I heard about a new subdivision that was approved this past week, out on Tramway Boulevard. They need water, sewer, curbs and gutters, and a long cul-de-sac, about a quarter mile. I figure we could handle it. Think I should get the plans and bid forms?"

"I don't know. It sounds like a lot of work. Maybe we should do something else."

"What do you mean something else? We've got to make a living."

"Maybe we should sell the land."

"Are you serious?"

"That's what Mom would have done. That Whitman fellah said he wouldn't give up, remember? I've got his card right here."

"I don't know. That doesn't feel right. You should probably talk with Jeff and Ida. I shouldn't make any big decisions for a while. My mind's not dependable."

"Would you call them? We can meet at the house for coffee on Sunday."

"Sounds like a plan."

On Sunday morning, everyone gathered for coffee and donuts.

Jeff said, "Where did you get these donuts?"

"I went to Dunkin'."

Ida laughed. "You went shopping? Good choice Pop." She sat down at the table, wiped powdered sugar from her lips. "What's up? Why are we here?"

"I've been thinking," said Pop.

"Look out," Jeff said, "Pop's operating his mind."

Pop grinned, pointing to his head. "It's not that bad. I'm getting old, but my head still works. Anyway, maybe we should sell the land. That guy Whitman may still want to buy it. What do you think?"

Jeff warmed everyone's coffee and put the pot down. "I guess Mom would like that. It was her dream."

"That's what I've been thinking," Pop said.

"Doesn't feel right to me," Junior chimed in.

Ida stood up and crossed her arms. "I don't know," she said. "Maybe we should wait for a while, you know, until we get over things. We're all grieving. There's been a lot of death around here. I knew I would miss Mom, but my God, I've been crying about Topper and Hopalong. Can you imagine? I'm sad about some silly prairie dogs."

"I'm okay with how things are," Junior said. "I don't feel like moving away."

"You wouldn't have to move," Jeff said. "We would keep the house and everything. Just sell the land we were going to sell in the first place."

"I don't know," Ida said. "It's too confusing. Anyway, I've got to get going. I work today."

"Someone needs to call Whitman and see where he stands," Pop said.

"I'll make the call," Jeff said.

Henry Whitman responded right away. He suggested they meet at the Corley home the following weekend. Everyone gathered around the dining room table. Jeff asked Epstein to be there. Whitman brought Francisco. Ida brought Danny.

"I still want the fifteen acres," Henry said. "Same price. Unfortunately, I'll have to tear down the education building. It won't work with my master plan.

"Three-million, right?" Pop asked.

"Yes, and I need some time and permission to survey."

"What for?" Pop asked.

"I need a contour map and a boundary survey for my negotiations with the City," Henry said. "We're designing a Village, and the City wants a Master plan of the whole area. I offered to hire Donald Pressman to help design the preserve areas and the walking trails. He's thinking about it. He needs the survey too."

"He's not going to fight you?"

"He said the death of all the prairie dogs broke his heart. I told him it was inevitable. You can't let a few hundred prairie dogs stop progress. I think he'll help with a Village design that blends human life with natural surroundings—that way he can have an impact on the environment."

"We need to count all the free labor that went into the building," Junior said. "Plus we have to pay off the mortgage."

"Well, that'll have to be your problem," Whitman said. "The building has no value to me. In fact, it'll cost me to tear it down."

"Pop and I built that building," Junior said. "It is way valuable." He stood up, wiped his mouth with one hand, and then put both hands in his pockets, looking at Pop.

"Should Francisco and I work out a purchase agreement?" Epstein asked.

"Here's the deal," Pop said. "You tell me when you have the three-million, and we'll be there. I'm not signing anything."

"I don't know," Jeff said. "These lawyers are professionals, and they'll make sure everyone is protected."

"I've been protected before," Pop said. "I got burned. Remember?"

Danny held Ida's hand, glanced at Junior, and smiled.

"You can come onto the property, survey whatever you want, do soil tests, and lay out roads. I've got no problem with that. When you're ready, show me the money and we'll go from there."

"Pop, in all due respect, I think you need an agreement," Jeff said. "Three-million is a lot of money."

"Bring the money, Mr. Whitman. That's all the agreement I need."

Francisco raised his eyebrows and opened his hands. Epstein folded his arms.

Danny stood up, clapped Junior on the back, smiled at Ida and said, "It looks like Pop is in charge of this one."

"Meeting's over," Pop said. "Come on, we've got to make some money to pay the mortgage. We're bidding on three miles of water line for Guadalupe County."

Over the next few weeks, Pop and Junior closed the entrances to the park. They notified the businesses in the Corley Education Building that the property might be sold. A "CLOSED UNTIL FURTHER NOTICE" sign hung on Donald's office door. They pursued several bids, hired two employees, and leased a new International loader. Bleak inevitability settled over the land, as though all the energy gathered for preservation and life-rights had dissipated, and all the factions had simply gotten tired.

LeAnn and others suggested that the tularemia and the stench of death on the land had somehow sullied the property, and that Mother Nature may have abandoned the area in favor of greener pastures. "It's as though the Spirit had just moved on when Mom did," she'd said. "Mom made that place a home."

Ida insisted that people naturally turned away from death, and they preferred to busy themselves with lighter concerns. People who knew Mom were reluctant to come around at all. In the eyes of others, it was as though Mom lived separately, and the remaining family members seemed unattached. Pop, Jeff, Junior, Ida, and Danny had together become one big stranger, an interloper inhabiting property previously defined by Mom's life and dreams.

Junior and Pop worked together, saved money for the mortgage payments, and waited for Whitman to work through his Master plan for what he called "Foothills Village, a Mixed Use Community." The Village would reuse water from cisterns, collect electricity with photovoltaic panels on roofs for parking areas, provide lofts for living over commercial shops and offices, and create central courtyards for community activities— all together a noble vision. The Forest Guardians recommended plans for walking trails, open spaces, and a soccer field. They also provided a plan for natural landscaping and energy conservation. Donald designed a "Prairie Dog Memorial" for a dedicated open space.

Word spread, and despite a few protests from the neighbors, the City Council unanimously passed the Master plan during the meeting after the Balloon Fiesta in October. There were only a handful of protestors at the meeting, and their remarks were essentially ignored. The former passion associated with life-rights and Mother Nature vaporized in the excitement of economic development. No one wanted to talk about the dead prairie dogs or the past issues, as if all the bickering and acrimony may have caused the tularemia, and they were therefore somehow complicit. The Martha Circle had moved on to other concerns, and the emptiness at church left by Mom's death filled in quickly with new volunteers.

During the approval process, and without objection, Francisco Romero insisted on an amendment to the Planning Commission's approval. Based upon the presumption that all the prairie dogs were all dead and gone, the City Council ruled that both the new prairie dog ordinance and the new endangered species ordinance would not apply to any of The Village property, a remarkable concession no doubt powered by the desire to forget.

Just before Thanksgiving, Henry Whitman called Pop, told him he was ready, and Pop gathered the family at the Title Company. Pop took his place at the head of the table, and the others sat in their birth order, Jeff, Ida, and Junior. Ida invited Danny, and he settled in beside her with Lucky. Popeye sat on Junior's lap. The room seemed alive, and the vents breathed an air of peace as everyone talked about a new life opening to them just outside the door, a future filled with possibilities, yet sadly without Mom. Pop frowned, chewed on his lip, and squirmed in his seat.

Francisco handed the deed to Epstein. "Here's the deed we drafted before. It's in order."

Epstein looked it over.

"It looks good. I have the mortgage payoff calculated through tomorrow and the release prepared. The title insurance lists no exceptions, and the survey is complete."

Henry Whitman turned to Pop. "I've got the three-million plus the closing costs, just like I said."

Pop flushed, stood up, took a deep breath, and adjusted his belt with both hands. Junior stepped toward him, and put his hand on his shoulder.

"Are you okay? Your face turned red."

"I'm okay." He lowered his head. "I've been thinking."

Jeff grinned at Pop. "Now we're in trouble."

"Whoa, you'll strip a gear." Ida leaned her head back on Danny's shoulder.

"Are you thinking what I'm thinking?" Junior asked.

"I think so," Pop said.

"I hate to see that building torn down, don't you?"

"Yeah, and they'll just bulldoze the rest of it."

"Now, hold on," Henry said. "I brought the money, and we've got a deal." He frowned and clenched his fists on the table. "Don't even think about backing out."

"We'll file a suit for damages," Francisco said. "We've got a fortune tied up in this project."

"I didn't sign anything." Pop glanced at Epstein.

"Sorry," Epstein said. "There's no written contract, so he can do what he wants."

"We have a firm verbal agreement. I can sue on that basis."

Pop turned to the title company officer. "Oh, by the way, have you sent out your inspector?"

"It wasn't required. We just updated the survey."

Pop said, "I saw a couple of prairie dogs scurrying around."

"I saw some too," Junior said. "They were digging new burrows over by the Education building."

The title officer was stunned. "Oh, my gosh, you did?"

"I think Danny saw some too, right Danny?"

Danny furrowed his brow. "I thought I saw a couple of females by the parking lot headed for the field."

The title officer looked through her folder and shuffled her papers. "We presumed all the prairie dogs were dead. Mr. Whitman's zoning approval is contingent upon that. Are you absolutely sure you saw prairie dogs?"

"I'm sure. There's at least a half dozen."

"We're going to have to postpone things, at least until the inspector can get out there. We have to issue the title insurance to the bank. After everything that's happened, no one can afford another fiasco."

"The City has approved everything, and so has the bank. Just go ahead," Whitman said. "Francisco, tell them it's okay. You need to sign that deed."

"I'm sorry Henry," Francisco said. The zoning approval of the Village is contingent upon the absence of prairie dogs. If they've come back, we've got a new problem. It could hold up your grading permit."

Pop stood up. "Well, give us a call after the inspection, but I know I saw prairie dogs. As far as I'm concerned, this deal is dead." He turned to his family. "Hey, you guys want to get some more prairie dogs?"

Ida jumped up. "We need a couple a males and new harems of females." She smiled, turned, and gave Danny a high five.

Jeff shook his head, threw up his hands, and laughed. "I think I can find that guy Eddie the Relocator. I'll bet he's got some prairie dogs from Santa Fe."

"I'm sure we could all adjust to Santa Fe prairie dogs," Pop said. "This could be fun."

Junior, Jeff, Ida and Danny stood up, and the Corleys walked out together. They all seemed light on their feet, snickering and pushing at each other. Danny put Lucky on his shoulder and touched Ida's back lightly with his palm as the door shut behind them.

www.ingramcontent.com/pod-product-compliance
Lightning Source LLC
Chambersburg PA
CBHW031947010726
47493CB00007B/2116